M000094341

LIGHT OF DISTANT SUNS

LIGHT OF DISTANT SUNS

By Lauren C. Sergeant

INtense Publications
www.intensepublications.com

INtense Publications
Light of Distant Suns
Copyright 2019 Lauren C. Sergeant

Paperback ISBN-13: 978-1-947796-20-1

All rights reserved. Except for use in any review, the reproduction or utilization of this work in whole or in part in any form by any electronic, mechanical or other means, now known or hereafter invented is forbidden without the written permission of the publisher, INtense Publications LLC, Contact@INtensePublications.com.

This is a work of fiction. Names, characters, places and incidents are either the product of the author's imagination or are used fictitiously and any resemblance to actual persons, living or dead, business establishments, events or locales is entirely coincidental.

This edition published by arrangement with INtense Publications LLC. The opinions expressed by the author are not necessarily those of INtense Publications LLC.

www.INtensePublications.com

To those North Carolina friends
with whom I first spread my creative wings,
who showed me the power of narrative.

PROLOGUE

"SHALL WE?" A dark, hooded figure crept forward, forcing Theophilus's back to the bedpost.

The flame of a single candle flickered beside them, struggling to light the room, but inky shadows swallowed its weak rays. The tall, oak bed frame trapped Theophilus before the approaching figure. He glanced at the heavy curtains, drawn together as though to obstruct the night from entering, but now they seemed to imprison him with an even more disturbing darkness. He turned his eyes back to the dark being before him.

It gave a mirthless, throaty chuckle. Theophilus's muscular arms tensed as he squared his broad shoulders and straightened his back, firming his feet on the ground. His normally soft brown eyes grew piercing and cold, and he lifted his chin to shift a wavy copper lock out of his face. His mouth twisted in a resentful grimace.

"Follow me," he said, his voice quivering. He tried to harden his expression in a show of resolve, but the pain of internal conflict continued to contort his face. He maneuvered around the hooded figure and led it out of the room into the hallway.

He made quick steps, and his eyes darted to and fro, watching. His gaze passed over the paintings on the walls of countryside scenes and of mountains and dragons and castles, searching instead for anyone who might interfere. No one else was about at this hour, though. The horrid being glided along beside him, never touching the slatted floor beneath. They arrived at a set of doors, where an intricate carving of a stylized sun with rich inlays adorned the wood. Theophilus brushed his fingers over one of the handles, hesitant, tentative, then bolstered himself with determination and gripped it tight. In a quick but soundless motion, he swung the door open.

The room was dark, but the light from the hallway filtered into illuminate Theophilus's way. He drew in a slow breath, trying not to let it rattle in his constricting throat, then grabbed a torch from a sconce beside the doorway and stepped inside.

In the room, everything was still and quiet. The neatly made bed centered itself on the near wall, its linens dark and colors unidentifiable in the low light, though Theophilus was familiar with the forest greens of the duvet covering. It was Theresa's favorite color. No, it had been her favorite color, he reminded himself. A shudder ran through him, though of grief or horror, he was not certain.

His eyes shifted to the two inanimate forms wrapped with linen strips lying on the bed. One was thin and measured about the span of a forearm. The other was longer, measuring about five and a half feet. Theophilus froze, unable to tear his eyes away.

"Take him," the dark figure commanded.

Theophilus drew in a slow breath and took a slow step forward, then another, then another. He stopped at the edge of the bed, his knees trembling. Putting out a hand toward the small bundle, he felt an almost magnetic tug toward the other wrapped form.

"Forgive me, Theresa," he breathed.

His mouth twisted again as he gathered himself, then he picked up the small bundle. It was stiff and felt somehow colder than the air around.

"Unwrap him." The figure's voice was flat and emotionless.

Theophilus unwound the linen and uncovered an infant. Jet black hair like a layer of down covered its head, and its skin was pale blue. Its body was rigid and chilled as stone.

"Now, Theophilus, see him Raised."

The shrouded being stepped back, and a ball of violet light appeared before it. Theophilus inhaled a sharp breath. Tendrils extended from the purple sphere to the babe's body, and Theophilus found he could not look across at the figure if he was to keep himself steady. As it was, fixing his eyes on the child, he had to fight the urge to draw back out of reach of the light. The beams encompassed the small frame, grasping at it and enveloping it for a moment. Just as Theophilus's resolve began to waver, the violet winked out.

The child's tiny body stirred in his arms. He glanced down, and its eyes opened. They were as dark as the night around and as full as Theresa's had ever been. Theophilus's own gaze became blurry, though anger took the place of sorrow in an instant as the figure's voice sounded again.

"Now, her fee."

Theophilus looked up at the cloaked being. Where its face should have been, a cavernous darkness lingered. The figure started forward toward Theophilus and the babe, but Theophilus backed away.

"She may have it. Only, allow me to provide a proper place for it to rest," he said, his words hurried.

He searched the room, and his eyes landed on a large jewelry box on the vanity. The dreadful, dark form stood still in front of the door as Theophilus walked over to the chest. He laid the child on the polished wood table before the mirror, careful to place it far from the edge, and opened the box. Gold and pearl necklaces, diamond bracelets, earrings set with all sorts of gems, and a brooch in the shape of the sun filled the box, things that meant little to Theophilus as Theresa had rarely worn them. He pulled them out and placed them on the table, his movements slow, trying to buy time. What would time do, though, except delay the inevitable? He pulled out the final necklace, then took the babe back in his arms and gave a single dip of his chin as he looked back at the hooded figure.

The figure snickered. "Very well. Hell's Mistress will have it all the same."

Theophilus lowered his eyes but said nothing.

The purple sphere of light re-appeared above the child, tugging at it. It whimpered, then cried out. Theophilus squeezed his eyes shut as a cavity appeared in its chest and its heart wrenched from its body. The babe started wailing, its tiny voice rising to a squall, and it struck Theophilus with bitter, almost physical force that he would be the child's comforter in place of its mother. He opened his eyes just as the purple light disappeared, leaving the heart hovering in the air. It contracted in quick, rhythmic beats.

Theophilus set the infant onto the table once again and reached for the tiny heart with a jerking motion. His breath caught as his fingers curled around it. It was soft, but not as soft as flesh, and it slipped a little in his hand, slick with a layer of something wet. Theophilus's mouth twisted, and his eyes shone with grudging tears. He took the heart and placed it inside the jewelry box, then lowered the lid. His eyes shut again as he spoke quick words under his breath, inaudible beneath the child's crying.

"Oer forgive me, Oer forgive me, Oer do not betray me now, do not betray your Chosen Son. Oer forgive me."

Not a second later, a brilliant, white light flashed surrounding the small box. The babe's wailing cut off, and Theophilus's eyelids flew open. The dark figure cowered against the wall. A voice resounded in the chamber as the brightness faded.

For one whose heart he holds
Shall be this living token,
Shall the curse be broken.

For the one whose heart is pure
Shall it be to face the fire
Between death and his desire.

A moment passed as the words echo in the chamber. Theophilus stood, stunned, then bony hands snaked toward him. He looked up and found the dark figure had come nearer, only a couple paces away. Theophilus reacted in an instant, dropped the box, and grabbed the child into his arms to hug him to his chest. The box did not open but remained sealed, leaving Theophilus baffled. What had Oer done? For surely that and the voice and the light had been Oer's doing, he told himself. He cowered beneath the sacrilege of the thought.

The hands moved past Theophilus and snatched the tightly shut box, then a burst of violet filled his vision. The next thing he knew, the hooded figure and the box had disappeared.

Blinking still, Theophilus backed up to brace himself against the table as he stared at the empty space where the dreadful being had been. His muscles were still tense as though he expected the thing to return any second, but a few moments passed with no change. He looked down at the infant in his arms. The child's chest had sealed itself as though nothing had happened, and a corded necklace with an unworked piece of red stone lay on its bare skin. Theophilus clutched the babe to himself. Shameful tears gathered in his eyes as he watched the door for any sign of intruders, then he sank to the floor.

"My son," he whispered.

CHAPTER 1

IHVA WAS WANDERING UP THE CITY STREET beside Kronk when she saw him, Gregorio. The street was emptied of most of its people as the sun was low on the horizon and it was almost dinnertime, but there were still a few passersby between Ihva and Gregorio, and he hadn't seen her yet. Her heart stopped as she froze, though only for a second. A moment later, she pulled Kronk behind some barrels at the edge of the pathway. Kronk yelped and struggled a little against Ihva's tugging.

"Hush, Kronk! Gregorio's heading this way!" Ihva warned, dragging the other woman out of sight.

It wasn't easy hauling Kronk along. She was a head taller than Ihva and powerfully built. Her gray skin and bulging features marked her an orc-blood to anyone who saw her, and her delicate gown drew a double-take from those who hadn't encountered her before and even from many who had. Ihva was used to the attention Kronk's appearance brought them, but the last thing she wanted right now was for Gregorio to spot them.

"Hide. Quickly. He'll see us if you're not quiet!"

Kronk's protruding nose and lumpy facial features screwed themselves up in a look of confusion. As Ihva pulled on her, the orc-blood woman tripped on the hem of her rose-colored gown and stopped, still in view of the street. Frantic, Ihva tugged the woman's sleeve, and she yielded, letting Ihva lead her behind the barrel barrier.

"But Ihva like rich pretty boy…"

Kronk's broken Common was nothing new to Ihva, either. Fathered by an orc, the woman had returned to his tribe for the latter part of her childhood and teen years, and that she remembered anything of Common spoke of her intelligence. Still, she wasn't the wisest creature, and it took some explaining to get her to understand many concepts, but Ihva didn't have time to clarify anything now.

"Exactly!" was all Ihva said.

She raised her emerald eyes just above the height of the barrels and brushed back a blond strand that had fallen from her bun. Her figure was slim, her lean muscles tensed with nervous anticipation. With one hand, she was still holding the folds of her sage green skirt. As soon as she realized, she let go and surveyed the scene before her.

The sun shone bright and heavy, and the late afternoon shadows lengthened. The dark gray stone that paved the street looked almost polished from frequent traffic, and the path wound its way up to the palace. Ihva just had one errand to run, then she would return home, but this was a welcome interruption to her day, sort of. It also made her nervous.

Her eyes landed on Gregorio, and she drew in a sharp breath. His shoulders swayed with confidence as he strode down the city lane, and his platinum hair cascaded down to his shoulders like white crests of the waves that she so dearly loved to watch. And those lovely eyes, blue as the deepest sea and just as full. Not to mention his voice, so kind and melodious, or at least Ihva imagined so. She'd never actually heard his voice, come to think of it.

Ihva stretched forward, pressing into the barrel to catch the last glimpse of Gregorio as he disappeared. As she did so, the barrel tipped over. She froze again as it tipped in slow motion, bounced off the ground, then started rolling down the incline after him.

Ihva looked at Kronk, who was busy scratching her enormous, lumpy ear, oblivious. Realizing it was all up to her, Ihva leapt up and sprinted down the lane toward the accelerating barrel. She had almost reached it when Gregorio turned around to catch sight of her and...

WHAM! She cringed as she heard the cask crash into the boy with a thud. It knocked him flat, then propelled itself farther down the walkway.

Ihva stopped at Gregorio, though, and crept up to him. He was lying on the ground, still, his eyes shut. As she peered down at his unconscious body, her heart jolted, and her breath shortened in panic. She motioned Kronk over, and the woman lumbered toward the scene. Ihva caught herself gazing back at the boy longingly. He was the son of the king's trade advisor and she the daughter of one of the wealthiest merchants in Agda, in all Oerid. She'd imagined of late how she and Gregorio might journey through foreign lands together, seeking business and adventure.

Kronk arrived next to Ihva and looked down at the boy. The woman furrowed her brow and seemed to be calculating the next steps. She gave Gregorio a gentle push with her slippered foot, but he didn't awaken. She shoved him sideways with the same foot. He still lay unconscious on the ground.

"Ihva, Kronk think rich pretty boy not wake up," Kronk said.

"But Kronk, he has to! There must be something we can do!" Ihva's voice was high-pitched with fright.

Kronk tilted her head for a moment, and Ihva saw the moment an idea unveiled itself in the woman's mind. Her eyes widened, and she spoke in an excited whisper.

"Prince breathe in princess's mouth, wake her up. It in stories. Ihva must breathe in rich pretty boy's mouth, bring back air."

"You mean kiss him?!" Ihva's voice squeaked. "I cannot do that, Kronk!"

"Rich pretty boy need air. Rich pretty boy not breathe enough."

"But Kronk!"

Ihva looked at Gregorio's face. His lips were perfectly colored and smooth, but she drew back at the thought of meeting them with her own. This was not how she'd planned her day and definitely contrasted with how she'd pictured her first real meeting with young Lord Rinaldo. She knelt down, hesitated, then laid her head against his chest.

She wasn't whether it was because the pounding in her ears was too loud, but she couldn't hear a heartbeat.

"Well, if it will save his life…"

She hesitated. She was sure her eyes revealed her fears, so she closed them and leaned down. Her lips tingled as they reached for his. She forgot to breathe and gulped in a bit of air. Then something scraped against the ground, and Gregorio gasped. Ihva's eyelids shot open with surprise, and she found herself face-to-face with the boy, his eyes wide and his mouth slightly ajar.

"What in the name of Oer?" he demanded; his voice hard. His blue eyes had grown cold, and he wore an indignant frown.

Struggling a moment, avoiding touching Ihva, he managed to get to his knees. His gaze was still on her, his eyes flashing, as she scrambled to scoot back. He rose to his feet and scowled down at her.

Ihva stood, too, and found that Gregorio towered above her menacingly. She took a quick step back but tripped on her skirts and fell backward into Kronk. Ihva felt the woman's muscles rigid and ready to act, so she spoke quickly.

"You were unconscious. We were saving your life…"

"Well I don't need saving now, do I?" Gregorio said.

He shook his head, and Ihva felt humiliation flush her face. Then he turned and stalked back up toward the noble's district, opposite his original direction.

"Can't even run a simple errand among these peasants without getting attacked by one," he muttered to himself as he disappeared up the road.

Ihva could feel the red on her face intensify as she looked after him. She turned back to Kronk, whose eyes were sympathetic. Ihva tried to sound offhanded.

"I guess that's that, then."

"Foolish rich pretty boy."

"Foolish Ihva," Ihva replied under her breath, thinking Gregorio's voice sounded much harsher than she'd imagined.

She turned to follow the path that Gregorio took toward the palace, heading toward the temple of Oer. She kept her pace slow to avoid catching up with him and tried to ignore Kronk's concerned looks.

"Foolish Ihva," Ihva repeated to herself.

She should have expected Gregorio's rejection. It was something she'd experienced half a dozen times before with other noble boys, and she shouldn't have presumed anything would be different with young Lord Rinaldo. Once again, though, she wondered why the wall between her and her desires seemed so very tall and wide, so insurmountable. Noble boys would never have anything to do with a girl of self-made wealth, she should know by now. She did know, only she hoped one of them might prove her wrong. Holding out hope just led to hurt, though. She hardened her gaze at the path ahead, determined that from now on she would dream realistically. She would find a way to live within her confines and receive joy from that. She would take what was given to her, whatever scraps they might be, and mold herself into someone contented by those things. She would find a way to do it, she told herself, and busied herself trying to believe it.

———◆◆◆———

"Ihva okay?" Kronk asked.

They had walked for a couple of minutes up the city street in uncomfortable silence. Ihva tried to keep her eyes on the road, but they kept drifting to the storefronts and individuals milling about. She had the creeping feeling that people were watching her, and not just that, that their gazes were graceless and disparaging toward her.

"Yeah," was all she replied to Kronk.

She knew her tone wasn't convincing, her voice small, and out of the corner of her eye, she spotted Kronk looking at her with concern. Kronk always had been motherly, perhaps more so than Ihva's own mother, Isabella Danielle Marchand, who wanted more than anything to protect Ihva but often ended up crushing her in the process. She quashed whatever dreams Ihva had of a life beyond what she was born into-dreams of love and noble boys and adventure-but then again, maybe she was right to, Ihva thought to herself. Still, Isabella wasn't one to console Ihva when things went awry. Rather, Kronk was the comforting one.

"I don't know, Kronk. I feel like everything I want is what everyone else doesn't want. It's like I'm always swimming upstream."

Not that Kronk would understand the idiom, but it helped Ihva make sense of what she was feeling. Her hopes and aspirations, everything she stood for, seemed at odds with society's expectations, with her parents' expectations, with everyone's expectations, everyone's except Kronk's. Kronk always supported her, but Kronk's support wouldn't get her very far. People might respect an orc-blood as a bodyguard or soldier even, but they would never listen to an orc-blood's thoughts and perspective, certainly not like Ihva did. Yet another thing that set Ihva at the edge of social circles.

"Ihva brave. Ihva make her own way," Kronk replied.

A nice sentiment, but Ihva didn't feel very brave. She'd grown up free-spirited only to be tethered down to learn history and religion and the arts as she grew older. Not that she minded studying, but she'd rather have studied bladework than just read about royal lines and famous battles in wars long ago. Her parents had kept her inside the city walls for so many years, more so as time went on, seeming afraid for her. She'd learned to stand down in arguments with them and to follow the path laid out for her. Now her parents wanted her to make her Exchange and settle down, get married, and take over her father's business when he grew too old to manage it. He'd already tried to start teaching her, pointing out important members of the merchants guild when they were out. She'd had to bite her tongue from stopping him as he rambled on about trade politics and price inflation. All she wanted was to return to Calilla by the sea and be free to roam and explore and find love as she pleased. Her father had reprimanded her too many times for her to mention it again, though.

"Ihva?"

Ihva shook her head, trying to come back to the present. Kronk had stopped and was standing, turned to face her. Ihva tried to remember what the woman had last said. Something about how Ihva would be brave, that she'd make her own way.

"Yeah, I guess," Ihva replied.

Kronk was still looking at her.

"Rich pretty boy not nice. Not good boy to love."

That was true. If he treated her with such disdain, he probably wasn't worth trying to get to know. A part of Ihva was unwilling to admit defeat, but the more rational side of her conceded that he wasn't what she was searching for anyway.

"You're right, Kronk."

Kronk gave a pleased, decisive nod, then looked around.

"Where we going?" the woman asked.

Ihva's gaze shifted from Kronk to a large, marble building near the palace gates - the Temple of Oer.

"The temple, remember?"

Kronk's eyes followed Ihva's gaze.

"Oh."

A short silence as Kronk looked back at Ihva.

"Why? It late?"

"I just need to."

The thought of visiting the temple set Ihva on edge again. The Exchange, the ceremony of sacrifice and receiving of Oer's Power. She had to decide soon what she'd bring. Time was running short with only a couple months left before her eighteenth birthday, and she still had no idea what her sacrifice would be. Oer only gave much to those who sacrificed much. Maybe, if she could gain a strong Power, her parents would finally see she was capable of taking care of herself and let go of some of their control. She'd heard some people had received Powers to create fire, others to shape and control water, and others could turn invisible. Some received Healing and others the ability to move with increased speed. Some were only able to create light, and others could mend clothes and other broken things. Ihva didn't want those Powers. She wanted something stronger, something that would let her wield a sword or bow with great adeptness or the ability to speak and comprehend other languages. Maybe then she'd finally be able to venture beyond the city walls on her own and explore Oerid, maybe even some of Eshad or M'rawa. The world of Gant would be hers, she dreamed. Maybe, if she gained potent magic, people would respect her. It just might be that life would be better if she could gain the right Power. Before she could ask anything, though, she had to give something.

They were approaching the temple, now just a block away. Desperate, Ihva hoped Oer would guide her, give her an idea, and help her find her way.

CHAPTER 2

IHVA STOPPED AT THE TEMPLE DOOR to brush a few loose strands back into her bun, then smoothed her skirt. Taking a deep breath, she stepped inside. She took a few tentative steps and looked around. The space was nearly empty except for a couple parishioners at the altar. Ihva drew in another breath, this one a little easier, and hurried forward.

She heard Kronk's pattering steps behind her. She really shouldn't have let Kronk wear her slippers outdoors, but the woman had been adamant and was always more at ease in slippers than in the boots she was supposed to wear around the city. Ihva held back a sigh. She could hardly make a good impression on anyone, much less on noble boys, with Kronk hanging around. Kronk, with her menacing stature and feminine attire, but the woman was a part of Ihva's family, and Ihva wouldn't give her up for anything. With a small sigh, Ihva turned her attention to her surroundings.

The cool of the shade felt refreshing after being out in the afternoon heat. Ihva looked around the temple as she proceeded further in. Gold flourishes embellished the majestic white columns that towered above her. The ceiling looked like an embroidered masterpiece with a scene of creatures of every kind worshiping at an altar beneath the sun, lions and bears and birds and fish, men and elves and dwarves, and even a dragon or two that Ihva could make out in the glinting afternoon light.

She marveled over the scene once again. It never failed to bring her to a loftier place, a more peaceful place, a place where people were kind in thoughts and deeds. The temple banished her fears and gave her courage to speak her mind, as least to herself. Ever since the first time she'd been to the place with her parents seven years ago, she'd felt like she belonged. It was a place of hope, a place where dreams found acceptance.

She eased her pace. With a slow spin, she continued to look at the scene on the ceiling. A smile played on her lips, and she didn't try to hide it, just shifted her gaze to her favorite part of the temple - the globe of a sun above the altar, a sphere made of precious metals, of evadium, gold, and silver. It brilliantly reflected the rays of light that came streaming through the wide, paneless windows, and the air shimmered where the beams bounced out to the rest of the temple, almost as if the metal orb were giving its own light.

As Ihva stepped forward, she stubbed her toe on some uneven tiling in the floor. She bit back a yelp and bent in a quick motion to clasp it between her fingers. There was still something about this place that didn't add up and made her feel like she was missing something important, like she was being somehow disrespectful with her simple presence. That wasn't entirely it though. She felt profound peace as she beheld Oer's holy place, a different sort of reverence than the kind she heard others speak of but veneration, nonetheless. She did belong, she knew, and her thoughts were nothing if not dutiful. Maybe she just had a different relationship with Oer than other people. She shivered. Different was not a characteristic to be strived for when it came to Oeridian religion.

Perhaps it just had to do with the Exchange. Her parents had suggested she give the expensive, intricately carved fan she received for last year's birthday, but she didn't value the niceties they often bestowed on her. She didn't have the heart to tell them how insignificant the fan was to her and how little she would likely receive in return if she offered it. If she was honest, she'd already given up what she most deeply desired, or those things was taken from her, as it were. Travel, adventure, romance-these were what she valued, yet her parents didn't seem to understand any of it.

Her mother was a charming woman and kind enough, but she spent most of her time on fashion and social standing and had little time for a daughter who cared more for the blade and tales of princes than for the plaiting of hair. Her interactions with Ihva were pleasant, to be sure, but they lacked depth. Isabella couldn't understand her daughter, and in her seventeen years, Ihva had never been able to understand her mother.

Ihva's father, Charles Henri Marchand, was only a little better. He seemed bent on keeping Ihva inside the city gates the rest of her life, "keeping her safe." She missed hearing his stories of pirates and bandits and far-off places. He didn't tell them anymore, not since he'd lost a ship captained by his good friend, a man whom Ihva only knew as Uncle Olier. Father hadn't spoken of the man since the day Ihva had overheard him and Mother discussing the storm that took him, but something changed that day. Now, if Ihva asked for a story, Father just told her she was too old for such dangerous nonsense, so she'd learned to stop asking.

She sighed. She knew one day these things would no longer plague her. She'd find and marry a man who would love her and take her on adventures and share a life with her unlike any she'd known thus far. She'd be able to speak her thoughts to him, and he'd understand. Until she found him, though, she'd just have to keep waiting. She couldn't give up yet. Her shoulders sunk in despondency.

She'd reached the altar. Her gaze eased upward as she beheld the golden sun up close. She noticed the carved words that marked the face of the globe. They were in the Old Tongue, which many thought to be the language of dragons. No one could actually read the words, but relics such as this helped people remember what the language looked like. If the tongue were indeed draconic in nature, only the dragons could bring back knowledge of what the carvings truly meant, the dragons and Oer's Blessing, but no one had seen dragons for thousands of years, and no one wanted to acknowledge that Oer's Blessing could appear at any time. It was one of the Blessings who had driven away the dragons, those blessed creatures, in the first place, and no one wanted to think about a new one appearing.

Shaking her head, Ihva set her gaze on the shining metallic mass above her and marvelled. Then she knelt beside the other worshippers, lowered her head, and closed her eyes. She'd come to the temple trying to figure out what she'd give in the Exchange, but as she sat in her reverential pose, she realized once again that she had no idea where to start thinking on the subject. Everything she valued was so immaterial. It was strange that Oer would even want anything, in any case. What use was a sword, a locket, a piece of clothing, or a sack of gold to the deity who created everything? Oer certainly had no use for these things, yet he exchanged magic for sacrifices in the form of Powers.

Ihva opened her eyes, and watching the glimmering reflection of the sun's rays, she pondered the relationship between Oer and his people. Most everyone treated Oer as a being to appease. Those praying around her were likely praying penance for sins they'd committed, or perhaps they were praying for something to receive something they desperately desired, for something to come about in line with their wishes. Everyone knew that nothing was acquired without a price. Most Oeridians felt that Oer would only give if one's efforts to attain the thing pleased him, if one was worshipful enough or determined enough or persistent enough. Oer was a reluctant giver, a miserly father, in most people's minds. Ihva couldn't help but wonder if the balance shifted more in favor of his people, though. A god didn't just give away magic like Oer did without some sort of interest in its use and its users. He had to be more invested in his kingdom than as a mere critical bystander. He must have involved himself in his people's lives, or at least in the life of Gant, more than just to demand appeasement. Ihva was certain of this, but she didn't dare share her thoughts. It would have been insubordinate, not to mention foolish, dangerous even.

Dangerous because Ihva wasn't alone in her thinking. Mari Fabron had been a prophet before she'd called herself Oer's Blessing, and though she'd spoken in metaphor and parable, her message had been clear. Oer cared for His people and intended to rescue them from the Lady of Shadows. It just so happened, though, as soon as Mari had set off to seek that salvation, everything had gone wrong. Ihva recoiled to think of it. The world had nearly fallen apart at the seams, the dragons had fled never again to be seen, and the nation of Oerid had fallen into turmoil arguing over Mari's final words. It had taken nearly a century for Gant to recover. The entire thing had discredited Mari Fabron's prophetic sayings and her insistence that Oer intended good for His people. No, for Ihva to speak her thoughts aloud would have been unsafe at best. She was already an outcast in many ways. Best to let some things remain unsaid, she told herself.

She focused again on the shining globe before her. She still had no idea what she could bring for the Exchange. She could still back out (not everyone had to make the Exchange), but then, this was one thing she really wanted to do. Everything else she wanted was out of her reach, but this was something she and her parents could agree on, and she was determined to follow through. She would follow through.

With a sharp nod, she rose and looked around for Kronk. She found the woman wandering near the back of the building. She motioned for Kronk to follow her, and they exited the temple, heading home just as the colors of sunset were most brilliant.

CHAPTER 3

IHVA NEARED HER HOME, the Marchand estate, just as the few remaining rays in the sky began to fade to twilight. The front gate was shut, but the evening guard, Marrell, smiled at her and began to unlatch the metal bar behind it. She nodded at him and smiled back. A slim, elderly man, he was bald with a small, trim beard. He was also one of the servants Ihva got along best with. He let her and Kronk in through the gate, then shut and locked it behind them.

"I trust you had a good day, Miss Marchand?" he asked, still smiling.

"Yeah, I guess so," Ihva replied, trying too late to sound cheerful.

Marrell's face took on a slight frown, but he was not one to pry, just gave her an inquiring look to which she said nothing. He moved onto Kronk.

"And you, Miss Kronk?"

Ihva shot Kronk a warning glance. No one needed to know about what had happened with Gregorio.

"Kronk have good day! Kronk always have good day!"

Ihva breathed a sigh of relief.

"Very good," Marrell said.

"Thanks, Marrell," Ihva said, cutting in before the other two could say anything else. "Have a good night!" she added, her voice pitched high with false brightness.

Then she made her way up the winding path to the front door, pulling Kronk alongside her. The shadows the hedges cast were dark and ominous, and Ihva wished once again that her parents would place more torches along the path. Mother said they interfered with the look of the garden in the daytime. Ihva turned her eyes to the sky. The stars always made her feel better, but clouds obscured them tonight. She sighed and continued on her way. Finally, she and Kronk reached the front doors, made of heavy oak and carved with flourishes and whimsical designs. They weren't exactly Mother's style, but then, her family had bought the house, not built it themselves.

Ihva eased the door open and crossed the threshold, holding a finger to her lips to warn Kronk to keep quiet. She tiptoed as cautiously as she could past her mother's parlor, hoping to make her way up to her own bedroom to change for dinner without conversation. She had just grabbed hold of the banister and ascended a couple stairs when Kronk tripped and landed with a thud and squeal of pain. Ihva stopped to cradle her forehead in her hand as she heard her mother's voice echo.

"Ihva, is that you, dear?" the woman called from the sitting room near the front doors, her voice strained with the sound of forced patience.

Ihva turned around and started reluctantly down the stairs.

"Ihva, is that you?" her mother's voice cried again, her words clipped short with her irritated tone.

"Yes, it's me," Ihva replied quickly She shook her head and continued walking.

"Come here, Ihva," her mother said, her voice tense.

Ihva looked back at Kronk, who met her gaze. She felt a second's frustration with the orc-blood woman, but upon seeing the desperate apology in Kronk's eyes, Ihva simply waved her toward the stairs and turned toward the parlor. Ihva knew by her mother's tone that this next exchange was only for the two of them, not for Kronk. She watched Kronk steal away upstairs and envied her for a moment, wishing she too could just slip away. Instead, she wandered over to the room where her mother sat.

"Coming, Mother," Ihva managed through gritted teeth.

She rounded the corner with her gaze lowered and stopped when she could see her mother out of the upper end of her glances. She didn't meet Isabella's eyes.

"Ihva, I understand that you had a slight, er, run-in, with young Master Rinaldo today. Do you have anything to say about this?"

By politeness in her mother's tone, Ihva could tell they were not alone in the room together. She looked up past Isabella, and her gaze stopped abruptly at the sight of a royal messenger and, next to him, a royal guard. Fear prickled in her. What had Gregorio told his parents that they would send a royal envoy to her home? She gulped as her thoughts ran frantically through her mind, and she searched for what to say.

"Young lady, it was told to us that a woman of your description attempted to assault Gregorio Rinaldo just hours ago. One witness named you at his attacker. As you might be aware, assault on noble persons is considered an offense against the Crown," the messenger began. "Do you have anything to say to this charge?"

Shame heated Ihva's face, and inside she berated herself for her clumsiness. She had a sinking feeling in the pit of her stomach that left her wanting to melt into the ground. She couldn't meet the mens' gazes nor her mother's, for that matter.

"Well, Ihva, what do you have to say for yourself?" the woman asked, her voice raised half an octave above her normal pitch.

Ihva looked up for a brief second to meet her mother's eyes and found a pleading look in them.

"It was me, yes," she began, and as the words passed her lips, she saw the guard straighten and brandish his weapon slightly. At the same time, she watched her mother's expression turn from anxiety to fear. Ihva continued hurriedly, "It was me, but I didn't mean to. I was really just minding my own business when clumsy me, er, my clumsy guard, knocked over a barrel and it ran over Lord Rinaldo."

Oer in Heaven, why has she just lied to them? Ihva mentally rebuked herself. She could see in their faces that they wondered whether to believe her. She knew she was a terrible liar, but the truth sounded worse than anything she could fabricate.

"Are you saying it was Kronk, dear, who assaulted young Lord Rinaldo?" Ihva's mother suggested. Her eyes flitted from her daughter to the men, especially to the one carrying the scroll with the charges.

Ihva paused, frozen in a moment of indecision. She could imagine Kronk's fawn-brown eyes trying to understand her betrayal. The hurt was more than Ihva could bear.

"No, no, I did!" sshe said with greater force than she'd intended. "I just, I thought Gregorio, er, young Lord Rinaldo, you see, well, my father, he owns a lot of merchant vessels, and he trades a lot, and so you see, I love to learn about trade and foreign lands and all those kinds of things, and well, I figured Gregorio, er, Lord Rinaldo, would be interested in those things too, with his father being the Trade Advisor and all, and so I really just meant to say hello, maybe not today, but someday, and then I was trying to muster up the courage, but then I ended up knocking over a barrel, and I tried so hard to stop it in time, but by the time he turned around, it was too late. So then I tried to, you know, breathe air into him to bring him back, but he didn't need my help apparently, so then when he woke up, I was right there, and I know this looks really bad, but I didn't try to hurt Gregorio!" Ihva finished, breathless.

A look passed between the two men, and the messenger spoke. "If you speak the truth, your sentencing shall be light. As it is, we will appeal to the King to have your case placed under the jurisdiction of the City Court of Agda rather than under that of the Royal Court." His voice had a hint of kindness in it, though his tone remained grave.

Ihva nodded and looked down at the ground. She couldn't understand, or maybe it was that she couldn't believe, that one foolish moment had landed her in so much trouble. She had fumbled before, but never had it come to such humiliation, not to mention legal action. The turn of events bewildered her.

"You will remain in the city until the trial to occur at a date set by the judge. You will not go near the Rinaldo manor nor will you or any of your family approach any person of the Rinaldo household," continued the messenger.

At the last statement, Ihva's mother fidgeted and looked concerned.

"How long until the court date and this can be cleared up?" she asked. "My husband has business with Lord Rinaldo."

"We cannot know," the man with the scroll replied.

Isabella shook her head and aimed a cross look at Ihva while she wrung her hands. Ihva winced.

The man straightened and finished by stating, "You will be informed of the trial date as soon as it is set. Take care not to get into any more trouble, young lady."

With that, he turned heel and exited the room, giving a quick nod to Isabella on the way out. The guard followed in suit.

As the men passed out of earshot, Ihva cringed, waiting for her mother's inevitable reproval. It didn't come at first. Ihva looked up and saw her mother staring straight ahead with a blank expression. Her eyes seemed to be searching. Then her gaze landed on Ihva, and her admonishment poured forth.

"Why? Why, Ihva?" the woman began. Before Ihva could open her mouth to respond, her mother continued, "You foolish girl. All you think about is yourself. You are so caught up in your fantasies of adventure and romance, you have no idea the implications that this has for your father and me." Isabella pointed a finger toward her own chest, her voice cracking. "You think life is all about finding your own happy ending, and you have little idea how hard your father and I worked to get to where we are. You take all this for granted." She motioned to the show of wealth in the decorations of the room.

"No, Mother, I don't!" Ihva broke through the tirade, pleading.

"You do!" Her mother cut her off. "You don't know what it's like to have little anymore, and you think you're fit to marry a prince. You're not, Ihva! You're of common blood, like your father and me, and this is the most extravagant life you will see. Don't you get it? Your father and I have been building your happy ending, right here, in this house, with all that we have accumulated."

Ihva stood, silenced.

Her mother continued, "Forget your adventure. It's not what you think! It's full of danger and darkness and death! It's filled with the Shadow. Forget your romance. No man of nobility will ever marry you."

Ihva began to feel a crushing weight come over her.

"Ihva." Her mother's voice softened, and her gaze became tender. "Ihva, darling, we lived in Calilla with next to nothing for so long. You won't remember because you were too small at the time to understand, but your father made a few good investments, and we grew our prominence. Now we're here, in Agda, the wealthiest and most powerful city in Oerid, maybe in all of Gant, and all you can think about is grasping for more. This life is more than grasping for what you can't have. Stop reaching, Ihva. Stop. Just be happy. That's all your father and I want for you." She looked away with tears in her eyes.

As for Ihva, she felt an emotional turmoil she couldn't make sense of. Her mother loved her, she knew, but the woman insisted on crushing her hopes time and again. So, what if Ihva wanted to marry a prince and travel the world? Wouldn't it be better to try and fail than to never have tried at all? What if her definition of happiness was not wealth but living life?

Yet Isabella made sense. Ihva was being selfish. She strove for something that wasn't attainable, not for her. Her face grew hot with shame. She looked at her mother with tears in her own eyes, then turned and sprinted out of the room and up the stairs. Reaching her bedroom, she threw herself on her bed and wept.

"Um."

Kronk cleared her throat upon entering through the doorway that connected to her room to Ihva's. Ihva lay on the bed, crying. She heard Kronk but didn't look up, hoping the woman would believe she hadn't noticed her. Ihva wanted more than anything to be alone. Even Kronk couldn't comfort her in this.

Ihva's thoughts turned back inward as Kronk slowly shut the door on her way out. Ihva tried again to sort through the confusion of her mother's tirade. It would have been no use to argue with the woman. She had a forceful personality and was almost always certain she was right. She often seemed determined to convince Ihva of the same. The problem was Ihva had ideas of her own and dreams besides, and she wasn't willing to give up on them yet. The force of her mother's earlier rebuke overcame her, though. Maybe Mother was right. Ihva's adventures had brought ill to her father's trade partnership with Lord Rinaldo. Shame burned inside her when she thought of how her mother viewed her pursuits. Was it so wrong to want to journey the lands of Gant? Was it wrong to yearn for love?

Ihva sat up and looked at the book at her bedside table. The Unfinished Journals of Marcia Polenya. She brushed her fingers across the volume and then grasped it, pulling it toward her. Opening it, her eyes fell on the tale of Marcia as she was imprisoned by the natives of the land of Jinad.

DEAR READER,

YEA, PERHAPST THOU SHALT ONE DAY READ THIS. I CANNOT BE CERTAIN I SHALL ESCAPE UNASSAILED. THE TALES TELL NO FOREIGNER HAS SET FOOT IN THE CITIES OF JINAD FOR MANY YEARS PAST, AND CERTAINLY NONE HAVE FOUND THEIR WAY OUT. I HOPE, THOUGH YET IN VAIN, THAT I SHALL BE THE FIRST TO DO SO.

THEY HAVE ME IN CHAINS. JINI PRISONS ARE OF EXCEPTIONAL CONSTRUCTION, I MUST CONFESS. BY SOME MEANS THEY HAVE SHIELDED MY CELL AGAINST THE MAGES OF OER. ON MY CAPTORS I ATTEMPTED TO USE THE VOICE, TO NO AVAIL. 'TWAS AS THOUGH THE VOICE FELL UPON DEAF EARS.

AT FIRST LIGHT, I AM SENTENCED TO APPEAR BEFORE THE SULTAN. THE JINI FEAR THEIR SULTAN. THEY WASTE NO AFFECTION IN THEIR SPEAKING OF HIM BUT YEA AND TREMBLE AT HIS MERE MENTION.

Ihva knew the story well of how Marcia had escaped the Jinadian prison later that night, a tale that always left her breathless in wonderment. That wasn't the story that she wanted to read though.

She flipped to the very end of the book. There, Ihva found the story she was seeking. The unfinished tale of Marcia on her way to the Lost Isle of Hildur.

DEAR READER,

SOON AND VERY SOON SHALL I COMMENCE MY JOURNEY 'CROSS THE NORTHERN SEA. I DESTINE FOR THE LOST ISLE, WHENCE NONE HAS RETURNED. I AM AWARE OF THE DANGERS OF THIS VOYAGE, THAT IT MIGHT VERY WELL BE I SHAN'T RETURN FROM THIS PILGRIMAGE.

ALREADY, I REGRET THE LOSS OF MY HOMELAND, THE LAND OF MY PEOPLE. ALREADY I YEARN TO RETURN TO THE SEASIDE VILLAGE OF MY BIRTH, SMALL VILLAGE THOUGH IT WAS, CLIFTON ATOP THE ROCKY PRECIPICES OF THE WESTERLANDS.

OH, THAT I SHOULD NEVER FORGET THE PEOPLE OF MY HOMELAND! OF ALL THE PEOPLES I HAVE ENCOUNTERED, THE OERIDIANS ARE DEAREST TO ME, FOR OF THEM, I AM ONE. SHOULD I RETURN FROM THIS JOURNEY, IT IS TO OERID I SHALL ARRIVE HOME.

NEVERTHELESS, I JOURNEY TO THE LAND OF THE DRAGONS, TO THE ISLE ON WHICH I CAN ONLY PRESUME EVERY ILL-FATED CREATURE WHO HAS LANDED HAS MET HIS DESPAIRING END. I KNOW OF NO WOMAN WHO HAS MADE THE JOURNEY, WHEREFORE I PRAY BY OER'S LIGHT THAT I MIGHT ARRIVE SAFELY, AND FURTHERMORE, THAT I MIGHT RETURN SAFELY.

THE DRAGONS HAVE NOT APPEARED BEFORE MEN THESE THOUSAND LONG YEARS, YET IT IS SAID IN THE DAY WE AGAIN SEE THE FACE OF THE DRAGON, THE DAY THEY CALL THE DAY OF THE DRAGON, THE DARKNESS WILL FADE TO NAUGHT. I JOURNEY SEEKING THAT DAY.

WHOSOEVER MIGHT RECEIVE THIS MESSAGE, READ IT TO THY WOMEN AND THY MEN, TO THY BOY CHILDREN AND THY GIRL CHILDREN, TO THINE OLD MEN AND THINE OLD WOMEN, TO THINE INFANTS. THE DAY OF OUR SALVATION IS NIGH, AND SHOULD I NOT RETURN, READ THIS LETTER

THAT ANOTHER MIGHT SEEK THE DAY OF THE DRAGON IN
MY STEAD.

I GO IN PEACE AND ACCEPT MY FATE. I SEEK ALL THAT IS
GOOD AND PREPARE MYSELF TO FACE THE SHADOW'S
ENMITY. MOURN ME NOT SHOULD YOU NOT HEAR FROM ME
AGAIN. I GO FORTH UNDERTAKING THE ONLY TASK I SEE LEFT,
AND I AM SATISFIED.

Ihva's eyes paused on the final word. She let out a shallow sigh, afraid to breathe and break the magic of the moment. Satisfied. That was what her mother wanted for her. However, like Marcia, Ihva wouldn't be satisfied with a life of ease. She wouldn't be satisfied with wealth and a place in the capital nor with an arranged marriage she knew would be made for political purposes. She wouldn't feel fulfilled with such a life.

Ihva's eyes grew wide with wonder as she admitted that she wanted to pursue something more, but she could not put her finger on what her hope entailed. She wanted something more profound than prosperity, something higher than an heiress's life. With the amount of wealth her parents had accumulated, she could live like a noble until death took her. Yet it all seemed too empty compared to fighting the Shadow and pushing back the Darkness.

Something inside Ihva broke in that moment. In times like this before, she had ended up bending beneath the weight of the shame, thinking about all her parents had done for her and how she ought to be pleased. This time, though, something snapped, and she stood up abruptly. She knew what she needed to do.

"Kronk!" she almost shouted, forgetting Kronk was likely right behind the door.

Kronk opened the door slowly and peeked in. Ihva motioned her inside the room impatiently.

"Kronk, we're going to the temple," she said, straightening into an authoritative stance. She was commanding herself as much as she was Kronk.

Kronk hesitated. "It after dinner. It late. Kronk hungry." She rubbed her belly.

Compassion broke Ihva's intensity.

"Oh, Kronk," she said with affection. "No, tomorrow we'll go ask Oer's guidance."

"Ok, dinner dinner!" Kronk said with relief. "Tomorrow, Oer bless!"

"Now, you mustn't say anything about it, though!" Ihva exclaimed, nervousness surely evident in her voice.

"Oh, dinner secret?" Kronk was confused.

Ihva laughed, releasing the tension that remained inside her.

"No. No, not really, at least. We must say nothing about the second part. Seeking Oer. No one must suspect."

"Oh, ok, Kronk still get dinner. Just no blessing," Kronk said patting her stomach in a satisfied manner.

"Sure, Kronk," Ihva said, shaking her head and chuckling. With that, she tugged on Kronk's hand and the two exited the room and descended the stairs to the kitchens to find some scraps from the dinner they'd missed.

Chapter 4

THE NEXT MORNING, Ihva arose during the last hour of third watch. The cool air and the secrecy of her mission lent her a sense of boldness and adventure, so she picked out a blue silk riding skirt to cover her usual breeches. Split down the middle and made of less cumbersome fabric than most of Ihva's clothing, the skirt allowed freedom of motion. Ihva nodded to herself, pleased with her choice. This morning was about freedom.

As soon as she was dressed, Ihva slipped into the next room and woke Kronk with a finger to her lips. Fortunately, Kronk was too stunned to let out a cry and was just as quiet as she donned her favorite lavender gown. Fighting hunger, Ihva guided Kronk past the kitchen with a small grumble in her stomach. Breakfast could wait, as Ihva was determined to arrive at the temple before dawn before the rest of the city woke and others decided to offer their prayers at the altar.

Barely breathing, Ihva passed through the darkness with hardly a sound. Kronk, on the other hand, dragged her feet with a quiet scraping. Ihva halted and motioned for Kronk to stop, too.

"If you're coming with me, you must be quiet. Otherwise we might be seen and stopped," Ihva said. After last night, she had a feeling the palace guards would treat her as one under house arrest if they found her out this early.

"Quiet. Like this?" Kronk replied, stepping lightly on her tiptoes. She demonstrated noiselessly for Ihva, looking quite the spectacle while she awaited Ihva's response. Ihva stifled a giggle.

"That will do."

She made her way ahead of Kronk through the garden, where she was delighted to find the clouds had broken to allow the last of the night's stars to shine through. Ihva almost skipped down the rest of the pathway with contentment. At the last turn before the gate, she broke from the path and led Kronk to the secret entrance at the north edge of the garden. They made their way out without incident and continued on toward Oer's temple.

There were merchant shops and inns and some of the more expensive weapon smithies along the way, and with each one they passed, Ihva felt her exhilaration increase. The secrecy and daring of her journey thrilled her, and she shot Kronk a conspiratorial smile. Kronk just looked at her, confused, and made to speak, but Ihva quieted her with a wave of her hand and they made their way farther up the path.

They moved quickly, and ten minutes later, they arrived at the temple. Ihva cracked a side door just wide enough to allow Kronk and herself through, then eased the door shut behind them. It was heavy but fortunately well-oiled. She breathed a sigh of relief as it shifted back into place.

She turned to take a closer look at the scene inside the temple. It had rarely been this empty before. The pre-dawn light peeked through the windows, bringing slight illumination to the room. The golden orb in the center of the temple reflected the light, and it looked like heaven. Ihva glanced around one more time to be sure no one else was in the building but herself and Kronk.

Then she approached the altar before the suspended orb that represented Oer's presence. She thought of Marcia's words that she'd read the previous evening. Satisfied. Ihva wouldn't be satisfied until she was out in the world doing something courageous, until she did something worth being satisfied with. There was no way she could accomplish something so praiseworthy locked up behind the city gates of Agda, and she wasn't going to break free on her own. There was no way she could fulfill her desires without Oer's help, without a Power or a direction or something to prove to herself and to others that she was doing what was right. She approached the altar and knelt again, this time keeping her eyes open and fixed on the suspended metal globe.

The words of the Prophecy almost glowed in the morning haze. Ihva watched as the light glinted off them and admired the inlay of evadium into gold. It was a beautiful relic, which was probably why they'd chosen it to sit in the Agda Temple. Ihva was about to whisper a prayer in admiration of Oer's artifact when the writing begin to change. The letters silently shifted and morphed before her eyes until they radiated white light and formed words she could recognize. She read the words before she knew what she was doing.

The darkest hour shall come to pass
With One shall come the end, alas,
The breaking and his death shall be
The breaking of eternity.

Ihva shivered as comprehension dawned on her, then jumped back. She couldn't decipher the Old Tongue. Nonetheless, she read on.

War engaging every nation,
Blood runs thick as their libation:
A bitter taste, this darkest hour,
When all the righteous kneel and cower.

All ill and loss shall Gant befall.
The uncrowned king shall offer all
To keep the joyous hope that's dreamed.
What's lost shall be redeemed.

The end shall then be the beginning;
The righteous bury all the sinning,
All to Reality conform,
And then shall end the storm.

No. These couldn't be the actual words of the Prophecy. Yet, they sounded so familiar. Tongues was one of the signs of the Dread Prophet, of Oer's Blessing. This couldn't be happening. Ihva's stomach churned. Everyone who spoke of Oer's Blessing shrunk back from the terror of the title, and their gazes became wary. This couldn't be. Ihva was no prophet, certainly no Dread Prophet. She was nothing, a mere commoner, wealthy perhaps, but of no more significance than that. She began to tremble and stepped back from the altar, trying to unsee what she'd read. As she did, the words only glimmered all the more determinedly.

She backed into something solid, someone. She didn't turn, though. She was busy trying to breathe. As it was, she was having a hard time filling her lungs, and it felt like the world had started spinning. She staggered backward and felt Kronk catch her, only when she looked, she found it wasn't Kronk at all.

It was a dwarf. His dark brown eyes were watching her, and the streaks of gray in his long auburn beard completed the aged look of his weathered face. She backed away instinctively, her thoughts racing. Who was he? Why was he there? What could he want with her? She felt torn. She wanted to run, but then he'd know for sure that something was wrong. She stared back at him, frozen, waiting for him to speak.

He didn't say anything at first, though, and Ihva noticed he wore a tunic with royal blues and purples. Now she wished she'd run. He was staring back at her with a strange expression, like the look her father had given her when she'd expressed interest in wielding a dagger. Before she could discern it further, the dwarf spoke, his voice deep and full, his tone calm.

"Not many have heard the Words of the Ancients, child, much less pray them."

He sounded somehow approving, but he was peering at her with a question in his eyes. She stood silenced for a moment. Not only had she read the prophecy, she must have read it aloud! She didn't know what to say, so she just said the first thing that sprang to mind.

"Um, thanks." She tried to make her expression as innocent as she could.

The dwarf just kept looking at her, so she turned her eyes down and toyed with a loose pebble on the floor with her foot in her nervousness. Just then she remembered she was wearing her riding boots and withdrew her foot beneath the hem of her skirt.

"That differs a bit from what bits and pieces we retain," the dwarf went on.

"Oh, I mean, I've been studying them with my tutor. I like history, you see. I was trying to memorize the words, but it seems I have some of them mixed up."

Ihva tried to find Kronk without giving the appearance of looking around. She discovered the woman out of the corner of her eye a few paces away, standing and swaying, looking anxious.

"Well, your tutor is certainly wise to have you studying such things, young lady," the dwarf replied. "There exists nothing more beautiful that the words of the gods, unadulterated and pure. The sayings of Oer are some of the last things that have not been corrupted by the Shadow, whereas the hearts and the lands of mortals become more polluted day by day. The Father help us, may His Blessing quickly free us."

Ihva stood frightened in awkward silence. Everything she'd heard about the one called Oer's Blessing had led her to believe the Blessing was no blessing at all, but rather a harbinger of doom. Every five hundred years since Mari Fabron, an individual had emerged as the Blessing of Oer. Havoc and destruction lay in the wake of this "Blessing." Many came up with their own names that they used outside the Church of Oer for this individual - the Wrath of Oer, Doomspeaker, the Dread Prophet, and so on. Ihva watched as the dwarf looked into the distance and his expression turned sorrowful. He stared off for several moments while Ihva stewed in her thoughts. He couldn't be thinking she was Oer's Blessing. She wasn't. She couldn't be.

"I will need you to come with me, child."

39

The dwarf's voice was kind but left no room for argument. He reached out his hand to pull her from the ground, where she realized she'd fallen. She jerked back at the sound of his voice while her eyes locked on his. Her mind cleared a little as he drew closer.

"But…" she countered.

She grew fearful as she recognized the sun embroidered on his shoulder, his royal emblem.

"Child, I know with whom I am speaking. I do not fear you, and I can protect you. You do not need to run."

He drew her up, so she was standing and put a firm hand on her arm, pulling her forward. He was taking her toward the back of the temple, and Ihva saw Kronk lunge toward him out of the corner of her eye.

"Stop!" Ihva cried, not sure who she was speaking to.

The dwarf stopped, and Kronk halted a pace away from them.

"Where are you taking me?" Ihva asked, trying to sound calm. Even so, her voice wavered. Surely the dwarf would recognize the terror in it.

"I have someone who needs to meet you."

He gave so little information, but Ihva felt something trustworthy about his tone. He didn't fear her. He would protect her. How? How could he not fear her, or who he suspected her to be? He couldn't protect her. But if she ran, he'd surely tell others and she'd find herself on the execution block within a week. If she followed him, there was at least a chance what he was saying was true. Besides, she wasn't who he thought she was. It was a mistake, and as soon as she could make him realize that, he'd let her go free. Ihva turned to Kronk, who was tugging her toward the door.

"No, Kronk. I think I should go with him," Ihva said. She spoke with hesitation, which must have put Kronk on edge.

"But Kronk protect Ihva. Ihva not know hairy stubby man."

Ihva paused, then turned to the dwarf and tried to settle the shaking in her voice.

"What is your name?"

"I am Cor Gidfolk, advisor to the reigning King Theophilus. May I inquire after your name?" the dwarf replied, straightening his posture.

"I'm Ihva. Ihva Marie Marchand. And this is Kronk of Deepgrove," Ihva said with greater conviction. This was something of which she could be certain, if there was nothing else, and she clung tightly to her statement.

"Pleased to make your acquaintance, young ladies," Cor said, glancing at Kronk.

Ihva let the silence settle among them. She needed to know anything Master Gidfolk could tell her about the Dread Prophet. If that was really who she was, of course, which she wasn't. Still, she was desperate. She could sense all the responses within her pointing toward following the dwarf. She straightened, as Master Gidfolk had, before speaking.

"Well, I suppose that settles it. He's not a stranger anymore, Kronk."

She feigned confidence she didn't feel. Kronk appeared confused but let her stance relax while the dwarf watched Ihva with an unusual look, as though trying to decipher something. He shook his head slightly and turned toward the back of the temple. Ihva followed him as he walked behind the altar to the back wall, where he touched a few stones in succession. The wall slid away to reveal a staircase down to a tiled passage. Kronk followed beside Ihva as they entered through the doorway, and the wall slid back into place behind the three of them.

Things instantly went darker than a starless night. Then, just as suddenly, light filled the passage. Ihva looked for the source and saw a simple ball of pale-yellow light hovering above Master Gidfolk.

Striding forward, the dwarf began in a more comfortable tone than before. "Well, child, I do not know much about you. What can you tell me?"

"I, I don't know, Master Gidfolk. There's not much to know," Ihva stuttered.

"A young woman of mystery, it seems," the dwarf mused. "And please call me Cor. We shall see enough of each other, I expect."

"Oh," was all Ihva said at first.

Master Gidfolk, or Cor that was, expected to see a lot of her. At least that meant he wasn't planning to have her executed straightaway. Still, Ihva felt uneasy about his comment. What did he want with her? She remembered his question.

"I'm the only daughter of Charles and Isabella Marchand. I, um, I'm seventeen years old…"

She trailed off, searching for information.

"Ah, a merchant's daughter. And none other than the daughter of Charles Henri Marchand, the great merchant of Agda!"

"Yes."

"And this young lady, who might she be?"

"She's Kronk, my companion," Ihva said a bit more confidently.

"An orc-blood companion. It is a progressive family you have, is it not?"

"Well, not a companion. Just a guard, really," Ihva corrected. Noticing Kronk's fallen look, though, she added, "She's been my loyal protector for years, and the best friend I could imagine."

Kronk's shoulders lifted.

"The daughter of the great Charles Henri Marchand with an orc-blood woman for a guard. Interesting," Cor murmured. He appeared to be thinking, but a moment later, he brought himself back to the present and spoke. "And what were you doing in the temple this fine day?"

"I was praying. I am only two months from my Exchange. I sought Oer's aid," Ihva lied.

"Pious as well."

Ihva barely caught the remark Cor made under his breath. The three walked in silence for a few moments until Ihva mustered the courage to speak a question.

"Um, sir, may I ask where we are going?"

"To the palace, of course." Cor seemed somewhat jolted by the question. "I suppose we must see the Prince first," he added.

Ihva started. Memories of the incident with Gregorio seared her mind. And of the incident with James, when she couldn't even stutter out her name when he asked. And with Lucas and the shame when he'd found her wandering in the district of the nobles without an errand. And, well, the shame of every incident involving a boy since she could remember. She hadn't even met the Prince, but she'd seen him from a distance during festivals. He'd just turned twenty, she knew, as the Crown celebrated his birthday in the streets a month ago. Ihva was suddenly certain she was doomed to humiliate herself and her family. She fought to breathe normally.

Just then, her head smashed straight into something solid and unyielding. She stepped back and looked. A lever stuck out of the wall just above eye level.

"I was trying to warn you, child," Cor said with a sympathetic tone and a hand pulling at her shoulder. "Are you hurt?"

"I'm fine," Ihva replied quickly, though the world was spinning.

Cor kept his eyes on her for a moment. Then, he turned and grasped the level, his gaze still on her, and pulled it down. The tiles slid apart to reveal a small room with a simple desk and some soft chairs.

Shaking her head to rid herself of a probable concussion, Ihva followed Cor through the doorway. Kronk came after her.

"Back so soon, Cor?" came a dry voice from behind the desk.

Ihva looked up and found herself staring straight into dark, piercing eyes framed by mid-length, black hair. She felt the pain in her head overcoming her, and black overwhelmed her vision. She fell to the ground, unconscious.

Chapter 5

THE GIRL COLLAPSED before Jasper knew what was happening. She must have surprised Cor as well, as the dwarf hadn't moved to catch her. Before Jasper could wonder what was going on, someone moved from behind her, and Jasper's eyes darted to a figure looming over her. He jumped up from his chair. An orc!

His eyes wide, his hand rushed to the dagger at his side, but the creature didn't move to strike. He watched it warily. It-she-was a bizarre sight. She (it had to be female) wore a light purple dress, richly adorned with lace, but had a club hanging in her hand. Jasper brushed his fingers over his dagger's hilt. Looking at the creature's facial features, though, he realized she was not a full orc-her nose was large but not bulging, and her mouth, which hung open in concern, was smaller than the drawings he'd seen of the full-blooded creatures.

Stranger still, though, was her demeanor. She was acting concerned, genuinely concerned, about the girl on the floor. Orc-bloods were not common in Agda, but Jasper had seen a few on the streets outside the palace. The ones he'd seen had all had a domineering, even threatening, look about them. They'd hardly managed to look civil, certainly never warm-hearted. Yet, despite this orc-blood's weapon, which she'd let fall to the floor at this point, she appeared mild and harmless, even kind. As he watched her jerking motions, he could even have sworn she felt anxious. He let his hand fall from his belt knife. Confusion had taken the place of danger in his mind. The orc-blood's eyes were glued to the girl on the floor.

Jasper shifted his gaze down. The girl was motionless. Was she breathing? He came out from behind the desk to move closer.

She was alive, her chest rising and falling. He let out the breath he'd been holding. She was an intriguing sight as well, for different reasons. Her white silk blouse and brightly dyed blue skirt spoke of wealth, but he didn't remember ever meeting her. Perhaps a noble's daughter from an outlying province, her family visiting the capital? He didn't recall his father mentioning any lords come to meet with him, much less a lord and his family.

"Who is she, Cor?"

Cor's eyes flickered to the girl. She didn't make any sign of motion. The dwarf looked at the orc-blood, but she was distracted, kneeling beside the girl.

"She is the one we have sought," Cor said simply. His brow furrowed.

Great. Cor's "theories" again, and this time he'd caught a noble girl up in it. Jasper wanted to bury his face in his hands, but he restrained himself. Cor had always proven himself wise and discerning, apart from this idiosyncrasy. What made Cor think he'd found her, anyway? If Cor was right, the girl could be worse than dangerous.

"How do you know?" he asked, eyeing the dwarf.

"She has Tongues. She Read the Prophecy. You are aware of what that means." Cor trailed off.

Right. That was not a good sign. If Cor was not mistaken, that was. What if he was? Cor's sneaking into the Prince's office did not reassure Jasper that her parents knew where she was or why. Of course, Cor wouldn't tell them, though. Who was she?

"What's her name? Her house?" he asked Cor.

"Her name is Ihva Marchand. She has no house, but her father is Charles Henri Marchand, the merchant."

Miss Ihva Marchand of the Marchand merchant family. Jasper summoned to mind what he'd heard about this man, her father. Charles Marchand was wealthy, as wealthy as some of the minor lords of the kingdom of Oerid. The merchant's trade network was a major underpinning in Agda's peacefulness and its population's contentment.

45

Charles Marchand's business supplied the shops that employed nearly as many men and women as the palace itself. Father had a good opinion of Charles Marchand, if Jasper had been reading his tone right, though the man sounded a bit more progressive than King Theophilus usually preferred. Jasper looked at the female orc-blood that was the girl's companion. Indeed, her father must be rather progressive.

A soft rustle roused Jasper from his thoughts, and his gaze moved back to the girl's face. She was beginning to stir. Her features were soft-her nose was narrow and rounded at the tip and her mouth was somehow both small and full. Her hair spread around her, long and fair. Her eyes opened slowly. They were a deep, verdant green. She blinked.

"Miss Marchand," Cor began.

"Ihva! Ihva alive!"

The orc-blood's exclamation interrupted Cor.

"Kronk?"

The girl's tone had a far-off quality, like she was dreaming. Her eyes focused on the orc-blood.

"Kronk, where are we? I could have sworn…"

The girl caught sight of Jasper now. Of course, she did. He was standing right over her. He realized his mouth was agape. He'd been about to speak, after all, but now he clamped his lips together,smoothed his face into what he hoped was a reticent expression, and stepped back.

"Miss Marchand."

Cor addressed the girl again before the orc-blood (she'd called her Kronk?) could butt in. Miss Ihva Marchand, Jasper reminded himself. He prided himself on remembering names-he made a habit of repeating them a few times before the end of a conversation, at least in his head, and it worked more often than not.

The girl stood and looked down, fixing the wrinkles in her skirt.

"I would like to introduce you to Prince Jasper Aurdor, Miss Marchand."

The girl looked up at Jasper, her eyes wide. And green, very green. Jasper sighed inwardly but kept his face blank. Had Cor failed to mention where he was taking her?

The orc-blood tugged on the girl's sleeve, but the girl didn't seem to notice, else she did a very good job of ignoring it. Jasper studied this Miss Marchand. She didn't look capable of hiding much, but he couldn't discern what she was feeling either.

Cor cleared his throat. He expected Jasper to say something, didn't he? It would be rude to let her stand there without addressing her, Jasper reminded himself. It wasn't like she could tell him anything if he didn't ask her.

"Good morning, Miss Marchand," he started.

"Good morning, Your Highness," she replied quickly with a deep curtsy.

Her father had taught her courtly manners, from the looks of it. Her eyes were still on Jasper, and he sensed her nervousness. She looked like a child caught with her hand in a pie. How much had Cor told her? Could he be right?

Jasper was choosing his words when the door to his small office burst open, no knock. Jasper whirled around, ready to reprimand whoever had opened the door, but then he caught sight of the man's expression.

It was Chester Herron, a Captain of the Royal Guard, one of the more respected. A short man, Captain Herron was nonetheless powerfully built with a full face and piercing blue eyes. Right now, his face was flushed, his breathing heavy, and his eyes full of anxiety.

"Captain Herron."

Jasper greeted him succinctly. What could be so important that Captain Herron would burst through the door in such a state, so urgent that he came unannounced?

"Prince Jasper." Captain Herron bowed quickly. "I regret I bear distressing news."

Jasper nodded.

"It is Lady Cibelle, Your Highness. She has been taken captive. Dwarves, Your Highness. Shadow-sworn, we must presume."

Captain Herron paused to suck in a breath, and Jasper lost his.

"When?" was all Jasper could manage to get out.

The Captain explained with jarring pauses as he steadied his breathing. "They left last evening, Your Highness." He drew in a breath and hurried on. "I was on patrol, and just before sunset, a small band of dwarves left with several wagons. We found it strange that they would begin a journey so late in the day, and they had the look of smugglers, so Colonel Burk sent a small company to follow them." A slower breath. The Captain had regained some composure. "I led the company. We caught them around midnight. One of our number was scouting ahead and returned, saying the Shadow-sworn kept mentioning Lady Cibelle. Assuming the worst, we caught up and were met with their guards. It was a hard-fought battle, but they fled, leaving a few able fighters behind. Only I and one other survived, and we questioned their wounded. They confessed to having taken her. When we found out what we could, we rode straight here and discovered that, indeed, Lady Cibelle has gone missing. I came straight here to inform you."

Jasper was silent a moment and hoped the desperation of his distress did not come across to the Captain. Cor knew, of course, and Lydia and Father Xander, as well as a few other trusted servants, but no one else, and no one else could find out. No one.

Captain Herron faltered as though he'd remembered something and added, "One we captured mentioned something else, a curse. His final words were a message for you, Your Highness. He said, 'There shall be no escape.'"

Now Jasper really did forget to breathe. He didn't speak, terrified the Captain knew something, or if not, that he might give something away in his response. Questions raced through his mind. Who had escaped with the Captain back to Agda? How much did the two soldiers know? Where could he send them without rousing suspicion or risk them telling others?

"Did this Shadow-sworn explain any further?" Cor asked. Rational and astute, the dwarf hadn't missed a beat, and Jasper realized he'd jumped ahead of himself. Maybe Captain Herron knew nothing more than what he'd relayed.

"No, he did not, Master Gidfolk. He was mortally wounded and died. So did the others." The Captain dropped his eyes. "I apologize, Your Highness. We tried all within our power to find out more, but they refused to speak to us. We failed you."

Jasper exhaled slowly. Captain Herron's slumped shoulders spoke genuine remorse. Unless he was Shadow-sworn himself, the man knew nothing more than he was telling.

"You have done nothing of the sort, Captain." Jasper tried to sound reassuring, though his legs felt like jelly. They'd taken Jessica, and with her, his arrangements.

"Would you like the Colonel to send a regiment toward Eshad?"

"No!" Jasper replied too quickly. He gathered himself and went on in a calmer tone. "No. This requires certain discretion, Captain. Tell the stablehands to have Lanon readied. Lanon and Irtax."

He glanced over at Cor as he mentioned the dwarf's mount. Cor would come with him, right? Cor looked back at him, his face stern but lacking a certain reproach that Jasper had expected. The dwarf would join him. Jasper gave him a small nod and looked back at Captain Herron.

"You will inform my father tomorrow we are going after her but tell no one else."

Father wouldn't approve of this plan, but it had to be done this way. No one could find out. Oer, where were they taking her?

"I will do as you say, Your Highness," the Captain replied with only slight hesitation.

The Captain was aware enough to understand that King Theophilus might not be pleased with his son's plan, but the Captain also knew his own loyalties would be shifting to the Prince before too long. A pang of regret caught Jasper, and he promised himself they would return soon. He couldn't worry Father like that, not unless it was something dire. Which this was.

"If you have no further information, you may leave, Captain," Jasper said.

Captain Herron nodded at Cor and gave Jasper a deep bow, then exited the room. He looked back briefly as he shut the door, and his eyes grew wide, but a second later, the latch clicked shut and everything was silent.

Jasper focused on inhaling and exhaling for a moment before he turned to Cor. The dwarf must have understood his distress, but still. His breathing calmed, but a realization struck him that sent his anxious thoughts racing again. The girl was still in the room, the girl and her orc-blood companion. Oer! Why today of all days?

Jasper turned slowly to look at her. Miss Ihva Marchand. He wasn't so flustered that he'd forgotten. She was looking at him, still wide-eyed, but she broke his gaze as soon he saw her. Her agitation was appropriate. She must have understood she'd heard something that wasn't for her ears. What could he do with her?

"Will you consider taking some armed men with us, Your Highness?"

Cor's voice broke Jasper's concentration, and he felt exasperation crease his brow as he turned to face the dwarf.

"No, Cor. You know as well as I do the reason."

"I know." Cor said softly. He lowered his eyes. "But I cannot say I find this wise or reasonable."

Well, it wasn't, but it was necessary. Jasper eyed the girl, still wondering what to do about her. As if to answer his question, Cor spoke.

"If we are truly going, we must take her with us."

"No, we must not."

How could Cor want to take her with? She looked less than battle-worthy by far, and the road would be dangerous, especially if they were tracking Shadow-sworn. Besides, then the orc-blood would want to come too, and her pathetic glances at the girl beside her increasingly convinced Jasper she didn't know how to use the club at her side.

"Jasper."

Cor's voice was barely louder than a whisper, and he'd foregone his customary formality, which gained Jasper's rapt attention. When the Jasper met Cor's eyes, the dwarf went on.

50

"She is who I told you she is. She needs our protection."

Cor was convinced, then. This Ihva Marchand, Oer's Blessing? Jasper looked her over again. She didn't look at all intimidating. He doubted she could wield even a knife.

"It will be Gant that suffers if you do not heed me. She is the only way to break the cycle," Cor went on, impressing his words on Jasper.

She'd slow them down. They'd never reach Jessica in time... But if Cor was right, well, Cor's discoveries and reasoning had far from convinced Jasper that this Blessing would indeed rain favor on Oerid. Taking this girl away from Agda and out of the land Jasper was born to protect could be the best way to guard its people.

Jasper gave the girl an impatient look, masking the fear he actually felt. He shot a vexed glance at Cor as well, for good measure, then fueled as much disapproval as he could into the nod he gave the dwarf.

"Fine. She will join us."

"But..." Her voice was small, barely perceptible.

Jasper cut her off. "Your companion may join us as well," he conceded, not needing to feign the irritation in his voice.

Two tagalongs, and one of them might be fated to destroy the world. Joy. Thoughts of Jessica Cibelle trickled back into Jasper's mind, unbidden. He had to find her before anyone else, most especially before the Lady. He hated to admit it, but at this point, he was just as much a danger as this Ihva Marchand. He wouldn't be taken without a fight, however, and he knew how to fight.

CHAPTER 6

IHVA TRIED NOT TO STARE at her surroundings. The palace was full of finery and had servants bustling to and fro in nearly every hallway. She didn't meet anyone's gaze, not even the maids' or errand boys'. She was afraid they'd recognize she didn't belong there, especially accompanying the Prince.

It wasn't until they arrived at Cor's apartments for Cor to change Ihva realized he and the Prince were guarding her like a mother bear would guard her cub, a cub that might run, that was. The men shared a look before Cor closed the door behind him that set Ihva even further on edge. Something was wrong; very, very wrong.

Ihva turned her eyes down when the door clicked shut. She wasn't sure what to do around the Prince and certainly didn't want to meet his gaze, so she tried to look interested in the tiling on the floor. Kronk was beside her but must have sensed Ihva's discomfort and known not to speak. The Prince didn't say a word the entire time that Cor was changing, and by the end of their wait, Ihva was looking forward to the dwarf's return, no matter how peculiar he was.

Once both the men had changed into riding clothes, the Prince led the others outside. His garb must not have been his usual attire, as many servants didn't recognize him until after they glanced away. Ihva regarded him out of the corner of her eye. His clothing was all of dark hues except the white bit of his undershirt showing through. His vest was such a deep blue Ihva mistook it for black at first, and his coat was dark as the ink she used for writing. The color stood out well on parchment, likewise the Prince's jacket set off his figure starkly.

They arrived at a shed. Honestly, it was big enough to be a middle-class house and filled with weapons and armor, more than Ihva had ever imagined together in one place.

"Just in case," Cor told Ihva in a soothing tone as he chose a large hammer.

He motioned for Ihva to pick a weapon. Ihva took a nervous look through the options-an elaborately crafted longsword, another dwarven war hammer, a plethora of daggers, a turquoise studded rapier, and a far-reaching glave, to name a few. She'd always dreamed of using a two-handed sword, but she knew her small frame wouldn't support that choice. She picked up the rapier. The turquoise reminded her of younger days in Calilla where turquoise had been a major trading good. She carefully closed her grasp on the hilt and used her other hand to support the scabbard.

"A fine choice, child," Cor said. "That one has seen only a few wielders, but as few as have held the blade, they have found so great their victories."

Ihva drew the rapier from its resting place and found a blade that reflected sunlight in a brilliant display. She wondered if the sword had a name. Sometimes weapons did, she knew. She quietly asked Cor.

"Indeed. This one is named Sun Dancer," Cor replied.

Ihva looked back at the blade and repeated its name under her breath. Meanwhile, the Prince hurried back to the others. As he approached Ihva and glanced at her choice of weapon, he gave her a skeptical look. Silently, he looked over another selection of rapiers and chose a rather lackluster one. Then he disappeared into the other side of the armory for a moment and returned with some sort of wooden blade. Ihva watched in confusion. He picked up a dagger on the way back and brought it her.

"You're not trained with such a weapon," he said in an emotionless voice as Ihva sheathed Sun Dancer. "You'll need this."

He handed her the dagger he'd just picked up. Ihva felt her face redden, and she looked down at the dagger instead of meeting the Prince's gaze. She accepted it without a word and placed it in a belt

Cor had handed her, then tightened Sun Dancer's scabbard on the belt as well.

It took another minute to choose some armor from what hung on and along the walls. Ihva looked at the selection of plate armor but knew she wouldn't be able to stand under the weight of it. Plate was Marcia's armor of choice. Cor brought over a leather piece to cover the bodice of Ihva's blouse. She tried it on. It fit snugly, and Cor said it would do. Ihva refused the other pieces that Cor offered her, already feeling a bit restrained in her movements.

With hardly a chance to catch their breath, Cor and Ihva followed the Prince to the stables. Ihva noted four packs lying on the ground near the entrance. The Prince tossed one to Cor, one to Ihva, and one to Kronk, keeping one for himself. Ihva caught her pack and almost toppled beneath its weight. She found her balance and watched as a stablehand brought a stout, gray pony to Cor. Another servant brought out the most enormous horse Ihva had ever seen and led it to Kronk. It was brown with a white face and shaggy coat, and the hair on its legs was so long that it nearly hid the horse's hooves. As Ihva was ogling over Kronk's mount, the stablehand led a dappled gray-and-white horse to her. Seeing the animal approach, Ihva forced her attention to her own mount. She refused the servant's assistance getting into the saddle but kept him a moment longer as she inquired the horse's name.

"Her name is Mabel, my Lady," the stablehand replied with deference.

Ihva almost corrected him when he called her "Lady," but she realized in time it would only cause embarrassment for both of them.

In the time that elapsed between Ihva receiving her horse and talking to the stablehand, another servant had brought the Prince his own horse. He quickly mounted the tall, black, perfectly muscled stallion. The horse tossed his head wildly but was soon soothed by the Prince's whispers. It was strange that such a coldness as Ihva had encountered so far in the Prince could melt so quickly into the calm he spoke to his mount. As the thought passed through Ihva's mind, Mabel jerked her forward and broke into a trot behind the others. They were exiting the city.

The walls overhead drew Ihva's eyes as they passed by. She'd never been this way before, and the metal gates opening before the group looked like they must have cost a ship's worth of fine goods. Ihva wanted to look back into the palace into Agda but restrained herself. This had to be the adventure she'd hoped for just the evening before. The metal gates clanged shut behind her. Whether or not this was what she'd been seeking, it was too late to back out now. One simply didn't refuse the Prince, no matter how reluctant he'd seemed to have her and Kronk come along. Ihva fought the rising anxiety within her.

The tranquility of the countryside helped ease her nerves a little. The grass surrounding them rustled in the breeze, and there was a slight chill about as the morning sun hadn't had enough time to breathe heat into the air. It wasn't long before Ihva rode along in a daze again, though, with only a vague awareness of these things as she watched the Prince's back before her. He made riding look easy, even at a slow trot. She'd ridden before, but trotting had always jostled her about, and she could never seem to keep steady at that pace. The Prince made it look as smooth as gliding on ice.

A few miles outside Agda, she remembered her parents. It hadn't crossed her mind to inform them of her plans, and she figured it was too late now. She and the others had entered a shallow valley, and looking back, she saw they were out of sight of the city. It was too late to turn around, much too late. How would the court rule her hearing against Gregorio and his family in her absence? She cringed as she remembered. There was nothing she could do now, she hated to admit. She tried to put it out of her mind.

The Prince had increased their pace to a quick trot now that they were a league or so outside the city, and the rhythm began to relax Ihva's nervousness. The Prince led them on a road to the west, and the sun shone down on the late summer morning. Its rays were pleasant and warm. Smells of wildflowers danced in and out of the constant fragrance of the sweet grasses of the surrounding fields. Maybe the journey wouldn't be so bad. Maybe it was what Ihva had been seeking, what she'd prayed for the evening before. For the first time in a long time, perhaps since she had lived in Calilla with her parents, she felt free.

Early in the journey, the party began to see scattered clusters of trees among the grasses, but they were not nearly enough to call the place a forest. An hour after sundown, when the sky's light was no longer enough to travel by, the Prince consented to stop and make camp, but only at Cor's insistence.

Ihva dismounted and unsaddled Mabel without help. She knew a thing or two about horses. Her family's vacations were often in the countryside, and the activity of choice there was usually a leisurely trot through the fields. Cor gave her an approving smile as she walked past him to tether Mabel with the other mounts to a small tree. Ihva then went to help Kronk, who was looking almost as uncomfortable and out of place as when she had sat atop her gigantic mare, Betti. Ihva wasn't tall enough to physically help Kronk, but she provided instruction for how to remove the saddle.

In the meantime, Cor had kindled a small fire and was heating water in a pot. He tossed in various rations to make a vegetable soup to accompany the dried meats found in the packs. Ihva watched as the Prince sat down on a small boulder near the flames. He took the meat out of his pack and chewed it but seemed distracted. Ihva and Kronk joined the other two by the fire. It was silent except for the crackling of the few thin logs and sticks that Cor had gathered.

Ihva found the meat in her pack and pulled out both hers and Kronk's. Ihva ate hers as the party waited for the soup to finish cooking. Cor stirred the pot every now and then and finally announced it was done. He pulled a metal cup from his pack, and Ihva dug around in her pack to find a similar cup. She offered it to Cor for some of the soup.

The next several minutes were similarly quiet until Cor broke the silence.

"We are now three weeks or so from Irgdol. That means only about ten days to Eshad. It is a beautiful place. I possess some bias, of course, but truly, the mountains near Irgdol make for an impressive view."

The Prince's face tightened until he finally commented solemnly and with more patience than Ihva knew he possessed, "We are not going to Eshad for leisure, Cor."

"Yes, Your Highness. I apologize," Cor replied, frowning a little, too.

The silence returned. Ihva shivered but wasn't sure whether it was because of the chill in her company or the temperature. She was afraid to look at Kronk in case the woman decided to speak up. It was clear from the way the Prince was frowning into the fire that conversation was not welcome. Thankfully, Kronk remained silent.

Finally, the Prince stood and unpacked a bedroll. He placed it where he'd been sitting and laid down beneath a light blanket. Then he laid down and rolled over, his back to the others. Ihva was relieved to hear Cor speak a few moments later.

"Better get some sleep, child. His Highness and I will split watches for tonight."

Grateful but still trying not to trigger the Prince's chiding, Ihva replied with a nod and dropped her gaze.

Cor drew nearer to Ihva and whispered, "He is not always like this, child. Just forgive him for now. He has many responsibilities and hardly enough of himself to care for them. He will come around, I assure you."

He trailed off and motioned Ihva to unfurl her bedroll on the opposite side of the fire from the Prince. Ihva quietly obeyed and whispered for Kronk to follow. She curled up beneath her own thin blanket, and despite the whirling of thoughts in her head, she was soon fast asleep.

CHAPTER 7

A SLIGHT BREEZE BRUSHED IHVA'S FACE. It was still mostly dark, just a few rays of sunlight peeking up over the eastern horizon. She took stock of her surroundings. Kronk was sprawled out on her bedroll, a bit too large for it, still asleep and snoring.

Ihva looked toward Cor's bedroll and found it empty only to look up and find him tending to the horses. He looked up at the same time and gave her a friendly smile. Suddenly, Ihva realized that apart from Kronk, Cor was just about the only person she knew who treated her with true kindness. She felt like even her parents had their own agendas in their interactions with her, but it seemed like Cor was inviting her to stop her acting or striving and just be. She remembered how she'd met the dwarf, though, and doubt of his motives seeped in to color her thoughts. Cor might be nice, but he wasn't to be trusted. He seemed to know too much about her, though she'd shared barely anything at all. His interest stemmed from his concern about Doomspeaker, and she couldn't count on him to stand beside her should she prove to live up to the name.

Ihva brushed these thoughts aside as she looked over to Prince Jasper's spot on the other side of the fire's remains. She didn't see him near his blankets either, so she scanned the surrounding area. Some dirt crunched, and Ihva looked westward to find him practicing forms with his sword. He was clearly an expert, and she became entranced. He made it look so fluid and easy, as though the rapier were an extension of his arm. The blade sliced through the air as he brought it down, then around. Then, it zipped up as though he could split reality in two by his own graceful movements.

Ihva looked down and brushed her fingers over the hilt of the rapier she had chosen just one day earlier from the armory. "Sun Dancer," she whispered to herself. The hilt was cold to the touch. The pommel was smooth with small divets along the side of the turquoise encrusted handle for better grip. The silvered cross-guard was an image of the sun, and it extended into sweepings such that the sun guarded the entire hand. Ihva felt a sense of pride well inside her as she pulled it slowly from its scabbard, which was detailed with an orb and extending rays.

The Prince's voice interrupted her inspection. "You will need to learn to use that." He pointed to the rapier in her hand.

As was becoming routine around the Prince, Ihva's face reddened and she quickly re-sheathed Sun Dancer. The last thing she wanted was for him to see her clumsy attempts to wield the blade. He didn't move though.

"The more you know of sword work, the less a burden you will be. As it is, we must worry ourselves with guarding you in addition to caring for our own lives."

His voice was cold, and his figure towered over her. She stepped back and looked at him, then her eyes flickered back to the ground. He had come so close while she wasn't watching. Her mouth had gone dry, but she managed to get out a few words.

"How then should I learn?"

She glanced up to see the Prince's eyes narrow a bit.

"Your Highness," she added quickly.

Nothing changed about his expression.

"Tomorrow, you begin rising the last hour of third watch, and I will teach you."

He sounded none too pleased with the prospect. Ihva nodded her assent and quickly turned to busy herself with rolling up her bedroll. She could sense his gaze still on her back, but she didn't dare turn to meet it. Her stomach was knotted as she thought of him teaching her. It was sure to end in her humiliation. She wished she could melt into the ground. She remembered when the greatest obstacle in her life had been arguing with her parents over the times she'd stayed out past dark watching the stars.

It was too late to return to that time, though. Just one day lay between Ihva and her former concerns, and yet miles lay between her and simple living. Today, she traveled with a moody prince, who seemed bothered by her very existence; a dwarf who saw her as a fulfillment of a cursed prophecy; her bodyguard, who has little idea what trouble they were in; and herself, confused and frightened by all that had transpired since she visited the temple yesterday morning. Ihva looked at the waking Kronk, suddenly grateful. Kronk was treating her no differently than before. The woman encompassed everything familiar Ihva had left. At least there was Kronk.

Ihva's attempt at optimism worked until she was back in the saddle, trotting quickly and continuously away from normalcy. It was too late now, too late to restore what was. The only thing to do was to continue forward as though Hell were on her heels. Ihva rode on in silent turmoil, thankful that Cor made few attempts at conversation today.

The morning passed in relative silence. Ihva tried to admire the countryside. The rolling hills were slowly turning to forest. Ihva had never been west, and she marveled at the density of trees. Some of them had needles she suspected remained year-round, but she could tell those with broader leaves sprouted their splendor only in the spring and summer months. The leaves must have been about to turn colors.

After a time, as the sights around Ihva became commonplace, she grew bored. She tried counting trees as they passed, but there were too many at times or too much space between them at others. She listened for what she could hear, a bluelark's song, a squirrel skittering up a tree, a rabbit rustling in the grasses. The sounds eventually all bled together, though, and no longer held Ihva's attention, so she peered out among the trees to see what she could find. Once she thought she spotted a doe with her fawn but couldn't be sure. By midday, Ihva was staring absently ahead, her senses dulled. Then it happened.

"Ahead!"

The Prince's cry shook Ihva out of her stupor. He and Cor drew their weapon as four figures rushed out from hiding places in the brush. As the figures neared, Ihva recognized the pure black garb and kerchief masks as the garb of Shadow-sworn, most likely Shadow Bandits in their most unholy covenant with Hell's Mistress, and they were heading straight for her and the others. Ihva felt suddenly vulnerable atop Mabel and knew that if she fell, the time that it took to get up could make the difference between life and death.

The first Shadow Bandit approached Cor and his pony, slashing with his sword at Cor's mount. Cor's animal fell to the ground as a gash opened on its hind leg. It lay there thrashing. Cor leapt off just in time to escape being crushed and swung his hammer at the Bandit, knocking the black-garbed figure off balance.

The Prince faced two of the three remaining Bandits. He deftly countered each Bandit's thrusts with their swords. He made it look easy and graceful, but Ihva had little time to contemplate his prowess as the fourth Bandit approached Kronk, who was somehow between Ihva and the approaching enemy. Kronk looked frozen in place, and Ihva had to think quickly to keep the Bandit from running the woman through. She abandoned Mabel, who balked at being steered toward the swordsman, and jumped to the ground. Ihva sprinted around in front of Kronk, then stopped, panicked. The Bandit was heading straight for her now. Ihva drew the dagger from her belt, thrust it out before her, and closed her eyes tight. She was going to die.

A thud sounded in front of her, and she opened her eyes. The Bandit was on the ground, and across the body, she found Cor, a look of resolve on his face. Then she glanced behind her for Kronk and found the woman cowering. Ihva made to thank the dwarf, but he was already headed in another direction. Ihva stood in place a second, and finding no immediate danger, she surveyed the rest of the scene. As she turned her head to glance around, though, she both felt and heard something whiz past her right ear. She spun around. A fifth Bandit gazed at her as he reloaded a crossbow. She had no means of countering his attack from that far away, so she sped forward to get within throwing distance with her knife.

The figure ahead released another bolt. Ihva dodged and not a second too soon as the bolt sped through the space where her throat had been. She continued forward before her mind could catch up. Soon, she was in range to look the archer in the face. His dark eyes gleamed behind his mask with malevolence.

When Ihva came in too close for the archer to shoot another bolt at her, he drew his dagger. She realized he was coming at her too quickly and decided against throwing her own small blade. Better to have it in hand if he reached her, when he reached her. He arrived in seconds, and she twisted to avoid his knife. He caught her arm with his free hand, and it was all she could do to hold him off. She certainly couldn't match him well enough to be a real threat. The Bandit wrestled her to the ground, threatening to stab her throat with the point of his dagger. She resisted and moved to disarm or disable him. She was strong and leanly muscular for a woman, but she couldn't compare to the Bandit's force as he drove his blade forward. Ihva fought to keep her eyes open when inside all she wanted to do was cower and cringe.

Suddenly, the Prince was behind the Bandit. He pierced his rapier through the man's back, and the Bandit's body fell to the ground, threatening to smother Ihva. She coughed, trying to breathe, then felt the weight on her lighten. The Prince was rolling the body off her, then gave her a brief, unreadable look and turned heel and stalked away. Ihva rose to her knees, then her feet, dusting herself off. A sickening shock hit her as she realized the Bandit was bleeding out on the ground. He shuddered and stilled, and she averted her eyes.

His death struck her somewhere between the heart and the stomach. She began to feel queasy and willed herself not to wretch. Distraught, she turned and walked back to the rest of the group, her steps heavy and her heart still pounding.

"I can only imagine this is your first battle," Cor said as he looked at her intently.

She couldn't speak. She couldn't look at Cor. She closed her eyes and shook her head furiously, trying to drown out the world.

"You've been in another flurry?" Cor asked, surprised.

"No, no, I just... I... he died right in front of me," Ihva managed to choke out.

Cor nodded. "Remorse," he said in a knowing voice. "I am familiar, child. I do not enjoy taking life any more than you do, but I have learned there is no choice at times. There is evil in the world, and we of Oer are meant to vanquish it."

Ihva simply looked at the ground and felt shameful tears flood her eyes. She couldn't face the memory of the look on the Bandit's face.

The Prince looked taken aback, but he mounted hastily and turned to the party, saying, "Lady Cibelle is still out there. We must keep on."

Ihva thought she detected something akin to compassion in his voice, but as she looked up at him and his purposeful gaze, she decided she must have been mistaken. She mounted Mabel, still shaking.

"I have no mount," Cor reminded the others.

"Kronk not need pony. Hairy stubby man take pony," Kronk said, pointing at her horse.

"You have a horse, dear, but I suppose a horse will have to do," Cor agreed.

He looked to Jasper for help to mount his steed, but finding Jasper already mounted, Cor turned to Kronk for assistance. He was soon atop the steed, readjusting the stirrups. It was much too large for the dwarf, and he looked uneasy as he glanced down at the ground.

The Prince signaled his horse forward. Cor passed Ihva to get in line behind him, and as the dwarf passed, Ihva heard him murmuring.

"How can she bring victory if she cannot bear to slay Hell's agents?" Cor shook his head, then noticed Ihva looking at him.

Ihva smiled uncomfortably and shifted in her saddle.

"I am sorry, child," he said, his tone regretful.

"Why?" Ihva asked.

She wished she could take back her question when she saw the distress that passed over Cor's face.

63

"There are dark days ahead, Ihva. If I could guard you from them, I would. By Oer's rays, I would."

By the time Ihva came up with a response, Cor and Betti were ahead of her. Dutifully, she followed the Prince and Cor, with Kronk trotting alongside.

CHAPTER 8

JASPER WAS TIRED as the sun sank beneath the horizon. He refused to show it, though. It would only dampen the already lacking morale among the others. The girl wasn't feeling well, he could tell. She'd worn a slight grimace on her face since the battle a few hours ago. He didn't enjoy killing either, but Shadow Bandits forfeited their souls when they made their pacts with the Lady of Shadows. He couldn't help the choices they'd made for darkness, but he was still of the Light. Sort of.

The orc-blood wasn't faring much better than the girl. She was anxious and jumpy the whole afternoon. Both Miss Marchand and her orc-blood friend were unfit for what lay ahead. Jasper sighed inwardly. This was turning out exactly how he'd hoped it wouldn't-so exactly how he'd expected, he told himself wryly.

He tied Lanon to a tree, pulled some grain from the saddlebag, and let the stallion eat from his hand. The horse was not nearly as tired as Jasper since they had slowed their pace when the orc-blood had given up her mount. Kronk. He repeated the name to himself. He had to get used to referring to her by name, strange as it might have been to him. He'd never had occasion to interact so closely with an orc-blood, certainly not with an orc-blood female. This one was particularly feminine too, more so than the girl in some ways. Ihva Marchand. Her name was clear in his mind. He sensed there was little danger of him forgetting it, for some reason.

Lanon finished his grain quickly, so Jasper left him tied loosely to graze. They couldn't waste more grain when there was perfectly good grass to be found. Who knew how long they needed their supplies to last? Until they reached Irgdol, he expected.

He gathered sticks with only half a mind as to whether they were large enough for a good fire. His stomach growled. They'd had a riding lunch, and it had left him hungry. He wondered if he should hunt for some meat for dinner. Jerky sounded a lot less appetizing than roast rabbit. It was too dark now though. It would have to wait for in the morning.

But he already had plans for the morning, he reminded himself. Toward the end of his watch, he'd have to rouse the girl to teach her swordplay, of all things. He wasn't exactly looking forward to it and expected it to be discouraging at best. He hadn't seen her earlier as he took out his first two Bandits, but when he had found her, another Bandit had been about to slit her throat. She hadn't even drawn her sword. True, she'd had the dagger in her hand. Remembering her awkward grip, though, Jasper sighed again, this time aloud, then glanced around. He'd wandered from camp, and there was no one nearby to hear him. That was fortunate.

He looked down at the bundle of sticks in his hands. All too small to burn for long. Hopefully Cor had had enough sense to gather some logs. Jasper made a decisive turn and strode back to camp, where Cor was just setting up the fire. Jasper added his sticks to the thick chunks of wood lying in a pile and sat down.

Right next to the girl. He nearly jumped up when he realized what he'd done and cursed himself inwardly for not paying more attention. She made a point of watching Cor, but Jasper could tell she felt nervous just a pace away from him. He should have sat down opposite her. No, then she'd glimpse him whenever she looked into the flames. It dawned on him he felt uncomfortable. Was it the girl? Her tense deference was getting old quickly, he had to admit. Maybe that was it.

Soon a fire was blazing. Chewing the jerky tired Jasper's jaw, so he let it sit in his cheek a while to soften it. The flames leapt and pirouetted before him, mesmerizing him. The dance of light and shadows had always intrigued him, and he sat wordlessly, content to watch the fire for the rest of the evening. He flinched when Cor spoke, breaking his reverie.

"I cannot help but point out they knew we would follow."

Jasper looked over at the dwarf. Of course, they knew. Jessica's captors, the Shadow-sworn, could not have expected anything less, knowing his situation. Cor was stating the obvious, which was not like him.

"You know it is a trap, yet you march forward unswerving toward the tripwire," Cor continued.

The dwarf meant to question his plans, then?

"Sometimes the only way to avoid a trap is to spring it before it can catch you by surprise," Jasper returned.

Cor had been aware Jasper knew the foolishness of his own plan, yet the dwarf had chosen to follow him anyway. Now Jasper had questions, but he couldn't ask them here, not in front of the girl. He watched her out of the corner of his eye. Her face was blank.

"And when it is sprung, and you are in it?"

Cor wasn't using honorifics. Of course, when they were alone, the dwarf spoke to Jasper as if the Prince were his own child, no fancy titles, just "Jasper" and "son." Had the dwarf forgotten about Miss Ihva Marchand and her orc-blood, Kronk? Jasper opened his mouth to remind Cor but thought better of it. He was tiring of the girl's gross show of submissiveness, and by forcing Cor back to his public attitude, he'd only reinforce her fearfulness. Not that he wanted her calling him by his name. That was an intimacy only afforded his father, most trusted advisors, and betrothed.

His gaze came back into focus and he realized Cor was staring at him, waiting for an answer. He tried to remember what the question was. Traps, that had been it.

"I'll be exactly where she wants me, then. She'll believe she has the upper hand, so it's just a matter of setting a trap within her trap, to catch her using her own schemes."

Cor nodded slowly. Jasper knew that wasn't an answer, but he wasn't sure what his plan was exactly yet. All he knew was that if the Lady of Shadows got to Jessica before he did... He didn't want to think about that. They would retrieve Lady Cibelle before any of that could happen.

"What of you, child?" Cor asked suddenly, turning to the girl.

Her eyes opened wide. Not that look again. She looked so frightened, so small, when she did that. Her face was startled and afraid, and her eyes so big and green. Very green.

"What do you mean?" she asked, looking at Cor. She seemed more comfortable addressing the dwarf than she had Jasper at any point thus far.

"Have you noticed anything? Anything different over the past couple days?"

Jasper frowned at Cor. Why was the dwarf choosing now to interrogate her? Why was he interrogating her at all? She was scared enough as it was without the dwarf putting it in her head she was the one chosen to wreak havoc on the world. Jasper shot Cor a disapproving look, but the dwarf didn't seem to notice.

"I don't think so," she replied, then made a show of thinking for a moment. "I've not noticed anything strange or different."

Her voice was sweetly innocent. Cor nodded, and the girl relaxed her tensed muscles. Jasper would have to talk to Cor about that. This girl, Miss Ihva Marchand, had shown no signs of havoc-wreaking. In fact, she'd demonstrated a propensity for complete ineptitude in battle instead, which reminded Jasper of their lessons set for tomorrow morning. What had he gotten himself into?

He turned his eyes back to the fire, and Cor dropped his interrogation. Jasper stared into the flames for the next hour trying to think of ways to outsmart the Lady of Shadows. There had to be a way, but he couldn't come up with it, not before he grabbed his blanket and tugged it around him in frustration.

They would have to start making the girl and the orc-blood woman take watches, Jasper determined as he paced around camp on tiptoe, trying to keep himself awake. Half a night of sleep just wasn't enough.

He looked up to the sky, searching for the Star of Dawning. He found it four finger-widths from the horizon. Perfect. Time to wake

Miss Ihva Marchand. Time to play with swords. Wooden ones, of course.

He eased his way over to where the girl lay sleeping. For once, she looked peaceful. The moonlight shone on her pale face, casting soft, lovely shadows. Nothing about her was angular, not like his own features. He frowned. Many young women had complimented his looks, but he wasn't sure they hadn't been just flattering him to get in his good graces. Jessica frequently fawned over him, but even with her, he couldn't know if it was just an act. He should trust her more, he knew, but he found it difficult. He had no doubts she loved him, but he wondered if she really knew him. And if she didn't, would she still love him if she really understood? She was aware of everything supposedly. He'd told her a month previous, and she'd taken it well. Too well, almost. Suspicion crept to seize him, but he banished it before it could take hold. It was time to teach Miss Ihva Marchand the rapier, not to evaluate his romantic life.

He stood over Miss Marchand, suddenly unsure. How was he to wake her? She'd scream and likely faint if he touched her. After all, she'd fallen unconscious at the mere sight of him back in the palace. He couldn't help letting out a small chuckle. It hadn't been funny at the time, but now he found it amusing and ridiculous. The girl was so fragile. There was no way she was Oer's Blessing, whatever Cor said. Still, she was traveling with them now, so he was bound to protect her, and the best way to do that was to teach her to protect herself, which brought him back to the problem he'd had in the first place. How was he going to wake her?

Then he realized she was already awake, looking at him. How long had he been staring at her with her watching? He felt a slight flush touch his cheeks and was thankful it was too dark to see. Why did he feel uncomfortable again?

"Come with me," he whispered, then turned to get the wooden practice swords.

A way off from camp, Jasper turned back around to find the girl following him so closely she almost ran into him. He stepped backward and steadied himself, then held out a sword. She took it.

Where to start? Maybe it'd be best to see where her instincts led her, see how much he could use and how much he'd have to train out of her.

"At the ready," he commanded.

She held the sword in front of her, exactly parallel to the ground. They'd work on that later. He raised his own blade, and without giving warning, he made a strike at her side. She flailed but managed to knock him away. Somehow.

"At the ready," he repeated.

She returned to the first position. He couldn't help a slight grimace. They'd have to work on that sooner rather than later, but he wasn't finished testing her. He swung from the other side. A swing was not as effective as a thrust, and it was easier to block. She parried about as awkwardly as the first time. Not much to tell which side she was better at defending.

"At the ready."

He brought his sword up this time and swung down on her. She raised her blade, cringing, and there was a clack of wood on wood. She'd need to learn to open her eyes, but still, maybe it wasn't going as badly as Jasper had expected. Time to see how she was on offense.

"Strike at me."

She obeyed immediately, catching him off-guard. He recovered quickly and blocked her thrust. Disappointment flashed on her face and was gone.

"Try again," he said.

She swung this time, and Jasper parried neatly. She had better form on the offensive than on the defensive, he had to admit. He met her eyes again and found a sudden spark in them.

She thrust without his command. Startled, he brought his sword up just in time and glanced at her face. Her eyes narrowed with determination. Maybe he should let her hit him, give her a little encouragement.

She thrust again, and he parried, determined that he would let the next blow strike, but before he could feign a defensive move, she sliced him across his left side. He winced and met her eyes again. She looked as shocked as he felt.

Without warning, she swung again. He blocked her, but she came back at him, and her blade clacked against his. She was moving faster now. He didn't have a hard time defending against her really, not after she caught him in the side, but he felt slightly out of breath by the time he called for her to stop for a break.

He'd misjudged her, it seemed. She was no novice. Had her father given her sword lessons? Surely not, with that painful starting stance. Still, something was strange about this girl. Curiosity sparked in Jasper.

"At the ready," he whispered, smoothing his face as a smile tried to touch his lips.

He swung, and she parried. She thrust, and he blocked. Again, and again, but with each thrust Jasper continued to wonder about the girl.

Chapter 9

IHVA FELT WEARY ALREAD, and it was only noon. Her arms ached as she held Mabel's reins. The blisters on her hands had burst a couple hours into riding, and the raw skin underneath stung. It crossed her mind that Cor might be able to Heal her. She was still marveling over what the dwarf had done for the Prince that morning. She hadn't even noticed the wound on the Prince's calf until Cor pointed it out. The Prince had been trying to hide it, clearly, and had looked rather uncomfortable when the dwarf insisted on mending it. The Prince had argued it was a mere scratch, but it had looked deeper than a scratch to Ihva. She'd watched in awe as a white light sprang from Cor's hand to the affected area. The bright red hue had disappeared as the flesh knit itself back together. The Prince had winced but said nothing. Was Healing painful? Cor could Heal! All of a sudden, Ihva realized how helpful such a Power could be on the road, and she prayed they'd make it back in time for her Exchange. Not that she couldn't make the Exchange late, but she knew what Power she wanted now and just needed to figure out what she would sacrifice to get it. She wondered what gift she could bring Oer that would be appropriate for the Power of Healing, but nothing came to mind.

Her mind wandered after that, then she was thinking about the morning lessons. The Prince had said so little to her, nothing at all to tell her how she was doing. His expression hadn't changed the entire time, or if anything, it might have grown darker. Determination hardened within her. She would learn the rapier, no matter how little he believed in her.

She looked up and realized she and Kronk were falling behind. She kicked Mabel into a trot, and the woman next to her jogged to keep up. Soon Ihva was beside Cor again. She looked over at him. He wasn't smiling exactly, but the expression on his weathered face was kind and hopeful. Why had he brought her along? She realized he would have frustrated her if part of her had not believed what he was implying. As it was, he put her on edge, though in a different way than the Prince. Both men thought they could keep her in the dark, but she knew what they were talking about regarding her. She was Oer's Blessing, or so they suspected to varying degrees. The thought sent a shiver up her spine. Could Cor be right about her? Yet Cor had not originated the idea, merely verbalized it. She'd stumbled into him in the temple because she'd had an inkling of the same notion. The carvings in the temple felt more distant now in her memory. Maybe nothing had happened at all, and it was all a mistake. Even if that was true, though, and she was no danger to the world herself, she was now traveling through the wilderness with perils lurking. She wished she didn't feel so anxious at that thought.

The Prince halted in front of her at a fork in the trail. He swung down from the saddle, his dark coattails sweeping behind him, and looked carefully at the ground and foliage surrounding the two paths. The others remained where they were. The Prince's face drew tight, and he shook his head, muttering to himself. He looked again at the foliage and the dirt trail. Finally, he straightened and strode over to consult with Cor. His voice was not particularly quiet, so Ihva heard their conversation against a background of birds chirping and fluttering leaves.

"What do you see?" Cor asked the Prince.

"There are horse prints and boot prints in both directions and a wagon trail pretty recent leading to the north toward Irgdol. They're going to the capital." His voice wavered as though he was nervous.

"It is strange they are headed eastward at all. One would expect another direction."

The Prince shot Cor a sharp look. "It might be strange, but it's where they are headed."

"They are dwarven. Her captors, I mean," Cor said. "Perhaps you are correct about the northern path."

"The southern route leads toward Jinad. Dwarves would have no business on this side of Jinad, Shadow-sworn or not."

Cor and the Prince exchanged a look of understanding, and the dwarf turned to Ihva and Kronk.

"We shall travel the northern path to Eshad."

Ihva's heart skipped a beat. She'd read about the lands surrounding Oerid, but as often as much as she'd hoped to visit them, she'd never thought she'd actually have the opportunity to do so. She nodded, trying to mask her enthusiasm.

The Prince remounted his stallion and led the party along the northern route. Hours passed, and the shadows grew long, but the Prince kept a hearty pace, grueling considering Kronk was on foot. Ihva was growing sore in the saddle, but she was determined not to show any weakness. If the men could handle it, so could she. She straightened her posture and dug her heels into Mabel, urging her onward into the evening.

Hours later, the party was still traveling, and it was well past dark. The Prince was intent that they needed to outpace Lady Cibelle's captors. Ihva thought his reasoning valid-she'd heard of his engagement to Lady Cibelle and thought his enthusiasm to regain his beloved romantic. She was fine with continuing into the night, albeit no one actually asked her opinion.

Cor had produced a small sphere of light to guide them along the path. It was entrancing. It twinkled like a small star, radiant and beautiful. She didn't care about the soreness she knew would greet her in the morning but enjoyed the extra hours in the saddle riding by Cor's light. She could gaze in wonder at the orb forever. By the time they stopped to make camp a few hours after dark, though, her eyes had glazed from weariness.

The Prince suggested a cold camp. The trail seemed fresher now, and the light of a fire would convey their presence to anyone nearby. Cor dimmed the floating star, as Ihva decided to call it, and settled it in the middle of camp. Munching once again on some dried fruit and jerky, Ihva felt strangely more at ease. Perhaps she was growing accustomed to this adventure business. She fell asleep quickly in her bedroll and slept dreamlessly until morning.

The next morning before dawn, the Prince woke Ihva as he had the day before-without a word. This time she was less startled, but she still wished he could say something instead of just standing over her ominously. He had her practice balance and the basic strikes. She wondered if she was getting any better. She assumed not by the look on his face.

Everyone hurried to break down camp this morning to make up time in their pursuit. Once on horseback, the Prince took up the lead again and set a fast pace as the sun was just breaking the horizon. Every hour or so, he dismounted and inspected the ground and the surroundings.

Ihva wondered if they were getting close to catching the captors and tried to prepare herself for battle. She hoped to ease her queasiness by not thinking about the last encounter. Focusing her mind on bladesmanship, though, she realized she was far from ready to use her rapier against any enemy.

Soon, about ten minutes after the Prince had last checked the trail, Ihva smelled a hint of smoke-a wood fire. The scent wafted in and out, and Ihva grew nervous. So did the horses. It smelled old but stronger than a campfire. The Prince halted and said something to Cor, then continued forward at a slower pace. Ihva couldn't guess what was going through the men's minds, so she didn't try. All she knew was the silence of the party felt like a mixture of anxiety and dread.

Finally, smoke became visible, wafting through the thin forest, coming from a clearing ahead. The Prince held up a hand for the party to stop. He dismounted and moved forward, crouching behind the foliage as he went. As he neared the edge of the clearing, he slowed to a stop. Looking back at the party, he waved for the others to join him.

Ihva nudged Mabel forward, and Mabel reluctantly obeyed. Ihva halted her mount just short of where the Prince stood and slid to the ground. She looked into the clearing.

The scene was disconcerting. A wagon lay overturned in the center of the clearing, burned. No flames remained, and most of what was left had turned to coal. Ihva instantly scanned the scene for bodies and exhaled a slow breath of relief when she found none. She did notice, however, there were words written in the dirt around the cart.

The Prince had apparently spotted them as well and rushed over. He stopped at the foot of the writing. His mouth twisted as he read. Ihva looked to Cor, who moved to join the Prince. Ihva followed a couple paces behind. She stopped and read the scripted message.

You are fortunate our captive is worth more alive than dead. Try to regain her without our price and she will receive a dark end. She can be exchanged for your allegiance, but it will be had either way.

The captive had to be Lady Cibelle. The Shadow-sworn were holding her ransom? But, of course, they were. The message seemed directed at the Prince. What did it mean, his allegiance would be had either way?

Suddenly the Prince was between Ihva and the words, forcing her backward. He wore a dark scowl from which Ihva recoiled with the same instinct as if he'd pushed her. Whatever the message meant; it was clear she wasn't going to hear it explained. She turned and walked back toward Kronk and Mabel. It was none of her business anyway.

The Prince and Cor remained near the overturned wagon, discussing something for a few minutes. The breeze shifted and Ihva caught the Prince's whisper.

"Yet the dominion of darkness stretches farther every moment, making traitors of close friends. How long can we keep the both of them when we are faced by armies of Shadow-sworn, for surely it will come to that eventually?"

"You forget who she is. Her presence alone ensures victory. I believe you will find a certain protection in Miss Marchand," Cor replied.

The Prince's frown deepened, and he gave the dwarf an exasperated look.

"You don't know that, Cor. It's been us protecting her thus far, not the other way around. You insisted on bringing Miss Marchand, and now we must guard her, whether she is who you say or not."

"She is," Cor replied firmly.

The Prince continued to argue.

"We could leave her somewhere safe, though, while we find the captors."

Ihva was growing frustrated now, especially since the conversation pertained to her. She was still adjusting to adventuring life she'd yearned for, but she wasn't ready to be holed up somewhere for however long it took Cor and and the Prince to figure out what to do with her. Besides, if they were so worried about someone finding out about her, if she really was Oer's Blessing, wouldn't leaving her somewhere just increase the chances of something going wrong? A burst of vexation overcame her deference, and she spoke loudly enough to carry.

"If I'm so important and all, are you willing to add to the number who could betray me?"

The Prince jumped and turned toward her, and she continued.

"If you leave me somewhere, you have to trust whoever is hiding me. If the Shadow is so pervasive, why would you add to the number of potential double-crossers?"

Cor looked at Ihva and nodded, and the Prince's eyebrows raised. It was Cor who spoke.

"You must learn to fend for yourself. We cannot have you endangering yourself without some means of protection."

"I'm already training with the rapier."

"Indeed, you are," the Prince replied. "But there will be hardly enough time to go through any more than the basics before we reach a point of conflict. You must learn to disengage when you are outperformed. Hiding will be your first prerogative."

Fine, she could do that. She straightened her posture, looked the Prince in the eye, and nodded her head.

He turned to face Cor. "These tracks reveal a larger group of captors than first assumed. There must be at least eight guards on foot.

We knew we couldn't take them alone anyway, not without stealth and surprise on our side. We approach Irgdol. Might we call on those who remain true there to aid us?"

Cor puffed his chest.

"A dwarf is always ready to defend righteousness and truth." He paused. "That being said, we must ensure any who serve Arusha do not learn of our purposes. The High Counselor has been involved in more than questionable activities, though it is not well-known. Most respect him for his return from the Shrieking Summit, but I maintain suspicions his doings there were not of Oer. In any case, that can be explained later. I am sure we might find some to accompany us. I have a few good friends upon whose help I can call and trust."

The Prince nodded and replied, "We'll wait to approach the Shadow-sworn until we reach Irgdol. Once we gather some trustworthy help, we can move forward to retrieve Lady Cibelle. For now, we will travel at an easier pace so as not to come upon the captors' party too soon." He glanced at Ihva. "Be wary of ambush."

He strode to his horse without waiting for a response. Cor followed while Kronk required Ihva's prompting to stop staring at the wreckage in the clearing. They moved forward at a slower pace for the rest of the day and made camp just as the sky started to color.

CHAPTER 10

JASPER WAS BROODING, and he knew it. He just couldn't help it. The longer they were on the road, the more time he had to think, to wonder what might happen if things didn't go as he wanted. The message in the clearing had shaken him. Over the past month, he'd considered what might happen if the Lady of Shadows ever captured Lady Cibelle, since the day he'd told the woman about her role in the plan. Lady Cibelle wouldn't betray him, he knew, but the Lady of Shadows was cunning and had ways of convincing people.

He thought of Oerid, and a sense of duty dragged at him. The nation was in danger. He was its crown prince, the only clear heir, and anything that threatened him threatened his people. He was adamant to be freed from this menace to his reign. The Lady of Shadows thought she could steal his allegiance, did she? He wouldn't be won without a battle, no, a war. He trembled inside. If only it was up to him. He should have set more guards for Jessica, but that would have roused the city's suspicions. They couldn't have guessed the truth, but they would have asked questions. In any case, the four guards he'd given Lady Cibelle had been the most highly trained in Oerid, after those keeping watch over his father. No one could have gotten past one of the Keepers, much less all four. There must have been a renegade among them. Anger flared in Jasper. He'd been so certain of their loyalty.

It was no use fuming over betrayal now, though. The damage had been done, and it had to be undone. He was doing all he could do at this point. Only Oer could perform miracles, and Esh and Rawa, and the Lady of Shadows, if you could call her dark works miraculous. He supposed the Shadow-sworn and the Shrouded did.

Days passed thus with Jasper cycling between despondency and attempts at optimism. Really, the fact that he was trying at all suggested he had some hope. It didn't feel like it, though, more like he had a responsibility to try, and he was a responsible man. He didn't know any other way. It was this or die a coward, worse, live a coward and leave Oerid to fend for herself. The second was no option at all. Thus the life of a royal, according to Jasper's father, though the king embraced duty with a brighter outlook than his son. Then again, the king didn't contend with the issues his son did.

For Jasper, evenings were a welcome relief, a distraction, though he tried not to show it. Cor told stories and sang an occasional melody, and though all his songs were religious and his stories parables or fables, Jasper felt refreshed to get out of his own head. Cor was no minstrel, but he helped pass the time.

Miss Marchand didn't speak much except to explain her companion, Kronk, when the orc-blood woman didn't have the vocabulary to do so herself. Kronk managed to relate her life story in that first week. She spoke cheerfully and humorously enough, though she probably didn't intend to amuse her audience. Her story held some darkness, though. Jasper gathered that a band of orcs had carried her mother off captive during a raid. Kronk's father, the leader of the orcish tribe, however, had fallen in love with the woman and she with him. Jasper found that rather implausible, but he was also sure Kronk couldn't make up a lie as intricate as the story she was telling. Kronk's mother had become with child, and seeing her nearing the time to give birth, the orcish leader brought her back to her village. He'd been killed in the process of returning her. Miss Marchand interrupted at that point to add orc-blood woman's name came from the orc chief's final moments, when he named his son Kronk. The girl giggled, clarifying that it was a boy's name but that Kronk's mother had honored her lover's wish. The gleeful look on her face as she said it made Jasper chuckle, at which she glanced at him and clammed up again.

Kronk went on to tell them how she spent her early childhood in the village but became an outcast when her mother died. She was only eight years old at the time. A traveling man, a bard perhaps or a small merchant from the sounds of it, picked Kronk up along his way through her village and reunited her with an orcish tribe, through whose help she was able to locate her father's band. She lived with them for the rest of her childhood and teenage years. That explained her broken Common. At twenty, Kronk had decided to reintegrate into Oeridian society, traveling the countryside outside Agda. She talked about all the friends she'd met along the way. They sounded like eclectic folk, to be sure, and as she listed friend after friend, Jasper was surprised to wonder if Kronk wasn't better at remembering people than he was.

"And how did you meet Kronk, Ihva?" Cor asked the girl.

"Well," Miss Marchand said, looking up from the piece of rope she'd been fiddling with. "Father had been looking for a guard for me ever since we left from Calilla. As we were transferring our residence to Agda, that is." She looked flustered.

"And he chose a young woman of orcish blood?" Cor asked in a soothing tone.

"No." She looked over at Kronk. "No, I chose Kronk. He gave me some choices-an old man with daggers that smelled like horse sweat; a young woman who never smiled; a young man, too. He had nice eyes, but I felt uncomfortable around him." She blushed and hurried on. "And Kronk, of course."

She smiled again. It was a pretty smile, unassuming and bright. Jasper decided she should smile more often.

"Kronk was sweet and kind and wouldn't stop complimenting my shoes. Father made me wear my new slippers that day for the interviews. I wished they fit her so I could give them to her, and that's when I knew. If we took her into our service, I could buy her some slippers of her own. So I chose her."

Cor laughed and Kronk was grinning widely as she nodded along. She didn't say anything though, no one did, and when Cor quieted, an awkward silence settled in.

Jasper cleared his throat, searching for something to say. All eyes turned to him.

"I've been thinking," he started. What had he been thinking? "I've been thinking maybe we could entrust a watch to Miss Marchand and Kronk tonight. Just to see how it goes."

He was very tired, and a couple hours more sleep sounded glorious.

Cor looked at the girl, and Jasper's gaze wandered that direction as well.

"What do I do?" she asked, her eyes big.

Maybe this had been a bad idea. A yawn struck Jasper. Even if it was, he wasn't certain he'd be a much better watchman than her at this point. He needed sleep.

"Just stay awake and look around," he told her. "And wake us if you see anything. Or hear anything. Anything out of the ordinary, of course."

He was about to over-explain, so he stopped talking. She had to know not to wake them for rabbit sightings or the sound of the breeze in the trees. She was staring at him as though expecting him to go on, though, and he became flustered. It wasn't her shyness making him uncomfortable, though, as her original bashfulness was waning. What was it? He averted his eyes from her to look to Cor for his opinion.

"I believe they are ready. You two can share first watch, if you would like?" The dwarf's eyes had not left Miss Marchand.

"Alright," she accepted in a sunny voice, placing a hand on Kronk's arm. "We'll watch."

Cor nodded and glanced back at Jasper, who looked away, not wanting the dwarf to recognize the confusion that he was certain was showing in his eyes. Something about the girl's increasing boldness was getting to him, but he couldn't put a finger on why. He gave Cor his own nod and tried to sound off-handed.

"I'll take third, then, Cor. Wake me four handspans before dawn."

He waited for Cor's acknowledgement, then bid the others a good night and curled up in his blanket. Mercifully, thoughts of Oerid and his own plight didn't plague him while he was falling asleep, but he couldn't banish the image of the girl's eyes. They were deep as the Eshadian forests that lay ahead.

Two weeks passed, monotonous as they could be. Jasper and the others didn't have to fight so much as a bear, which made for boring travel. There was little to look forward to but evenings by the fireside (at which Miss Marchand was growing a bit more talkative) and rapier lessons in the morning.

Clack. Clack.

The sound brought Jasper's attention back to the present. The wooden practice swords were noisier than he would have liked. Their lessons had been getting louder as Miss Marchand improved her strength with the blade. Jasper glanced over at Cor, hoping they hadn't woken him. He wasn't worried about Kronk. The woman could sleep through anything.

Clack.

Jasper defended against Miss Marchand's strike. She was definitely getting better. She'd even managed to hit him again a few days ago. Tenderness in his ribs told him he'd bruised from it. She was getting much better, but she still had a long way to go.

He redoubled his offense, knocking her sword away. She let out a vexed click of her tongue and strode to retrieve it from the edge of the clearing. He darted in front of her and shoved his blade to her throat.

"Never take your eyes off your assailant" he told her.

"Sorry," she replied, her tone not exactly timid.

She was still respectful, to be sure. It struck Jasper suddenly that she'd been foregoing his title. When had that started? Was she just copying Cor? Jasper was thankful the dwarf hadn't reverted to their private ways of addressing each other. Miss Marchand might end up using his name if that happened. Now that would be odd. And inappropriate, of course.

She was back in his face with her blade. He struck it aside. Maybe he'd better remind her of her manners. He lunged at her, but she parried, eyes flashing. She certainly was losing her filter. He thrust again, nearly catching her in the side as she dodged. Momentary surprise flickered on her face. Then again, it was nice knowing what she was feeling. He remembered thinking that she was bad at hiding her emotions. Maybe she couldn't do so if she was trying, but her nervousness had been like a mask, concealing all she might have been feeling underneath. It was nice to find some spirit in her. She had a pretty face, and anxious looks didn't set it off in the most flattering way. Determination was what suited her best, as well as smiles. She could be rather charming when she smiled.

Something collided with his side. He stepped back, dazed. He shut his eyes a moment in the pain, and when he reopened them, Miss Marchand was standing before him with a triumphant grin. She'd hit him. Hard! He rubbed his side. He should probably congratulate her.

"Well done."

She just smiled at him. Her look was captivating, delight shining in her face.

Jasper shook his head. That blasted uncomfortable feeling again. It was getting worse, and he was getting tired of it. Maybe that was enough of their lessons for today.

"Well done," he repeated lamely, then motioned back to camp. "It's time we wake the others and get on the road."

That wasn't true. There was still half an hour until dawn. Jasper hoped Miss Marchand wouldn't notice as he strode back to camp to get Cor up. He cursed himself for not paying attention to her blade and made a concerted effort to ignore her the rest of the morning, but the ache in his side wouldn't let him forget her.

CHAPTER 11

IHVA GATHERED HER THINGS into her pack at an enthusiastic pace. She'd managed to strike the Prince, a pretty good hit if she did say so herself. She'd felt a little guilty when he'd swayed in place.

They were breaking camp early this morning. The blow she'd dealt the Prince seemed to have caught him off-guard in more ways than one. She didn't blame him for needing to take a rest from their lessons until tomorrow, though she looked forward to their lesson the next morning. The Prince gave hardly any feedback, but even she knew her strike a few minutes ago had been a sign of improvement.

Soon, the party was on horseback and trotting at a faster pace than usual. Kronk ran beside them. Did the woman ever tire? After an hour, they emerged from the sparse woods onto a cliff over a rich, emerald valley hemmed in by mountains to the northwest, garbed in thick, hazy green forests. Ihva stared in awe at the grandeur. The foothills to the east of Agda couldn't compare to this. She filed the image away to sketch in a travel journal whenever she was able to sit and write.

The Prince straightened in the saddle and kicked his stallion forward. The party continued on the path across the cliff toward the mountains. They'd have to stop for lunch soon. At this pace, the horses and Kronk would need a midday break. Meanwhile, Ihva enjoyed the ride.

A steady breeze flowed past, and the sweet scent of late-blooming flowers greeted them as they entered the lush valley. About two hours after leaving the forest, Ihva began to see farms. She recognized some of the grains that were growing in the fields, but other crops were unfamiliar to her. The small, thatch-roofed houses reminded her of riding through the farmlands surrounding Calilla.

She turned to reminiscing. When she was young and they'd lived in Calilla, her parents trusted her to leave the house unescorted. Ihva and her best friend, Anna Hadley Henderson, used to race along the path that bordered the fields, and when they could find Jack, Aliza, or Peter, they'd play hide and seek among the tall wheat. Those carefree days had ended when Ihva's family moved to Agda. Ihva slouched in her saddle, dejected at the memory of when her parents dragged her to the capital and insisted she have an escort, a bodyguard of sorts. At least they'd given her a choice in the matter. She gave Kronk a fond look, though the woman didn't notice, as she was distracted by something at the side of the road.

Ihva rode the next two hours without speaking a word. Cor instructed her and Kronk how to act properly for the dwarven king, and Ihva nodded along. It was all she'd hear about for the next week, but she didn't know it at the time and drank in Cor's wisdom.

------◆-◆------

After a few days of hearing Cor drone on, though, Ihva stopped listening. She stayed busy staring at their surroundings instead. Eshad was the most beautiful place she'd ever seen. It wasn't that she'd never seen farmland or forests before, though the mountains were a new sight. It was just that she'd never seen the countryside in such vibrance and liveliness. She felt free. Rabbits dashed through the grass, and her heart darted along after them. Pheasants took flight, and delight mounted within her. Hawks soared overhead, and it felt like her soul was gliding through the air beside them, wing-to-wing. The wonder must have shown in her face as she caught Cor smiling at her whenever their gazes met.

Even her feelings around the Prince felt unbound. His dark looks no longer intimidated her. Ever since she's struck him a few days ago with the practice sword, something seemed to have changed. Something in the balance of their relationship had shifted. In the beginning, if he'd stepped forward, she'd stepped back, and she'd never approached him. Now she felt as though he moved with her on occasion. She'd certainly never approach him still, except in rapier practice, and she never spoke to him unless he addressed her first, which was almost never. She would've liked to learn about him, but she wouldn't be so forward as to ask him anything. She didn't mind that he didn't talk to her except for a very small part of her, a small tugging, as though she was a tiny bit offended. She brushed the feeling aside. Nothing could dampen her spirits as they rode through Eshad.

They rode day after day without incident, but each morning, Ihva woke to the freshness of a new sunrise. What exhilaration would her adventure offer her today? She discovered herself smiling more often, at everyone and everything, even at the Prince, and the frowns he returned could do nothing to diminish her joy.

———◆◆◆———

A week later, the party arrived before the gates to Irgdol. The sight of the huge doors left Ihva speechless. She gazed up in awe of the two great hammers to the right and the left of the gates, though the metal gates themselves were no less impressive. They'd been molded with a relief of large, geometric shapes and straight lines, though Ihva couldn't make out much detail with both open wide for all who came and went.

Just outside the gates, a uniformed dwarf stood at each side of the entrance to the city, scanning the crowd for mischief-makers. The Prince made to dismount his steed, but Cor caught his eye and motioned him to remain in the saddle. Seeing this, Ihva remained astride Mabel and followed the other two inside the city. The guards didn't even ask their names.

Inside, Cor showed the others along the cobblestone paths. The road split left and right at even intervals, and soon Ihva made out the pattern, and realized just how orderly the city was. She marveled at how much planning it must have taken. The city was built on a switchback of streets intercepting short, dead-end paths with buildings of stone and shops of wood set along every inch. Ihva was soon glad to be on horseback as Mabel's breathing grew heavier with the incline.

The lower third of the city seemed to be the market district, and the busy crowd and numerous stalls overwhelmed Ihva for a moment. She stared in wonder. Dwarven clothing ranged from cheap, ragged cloth to embellished silks, but one thing all the clothing had in common were decorations that were exclusively geometric in nature. One woman who nearly dragged Ihva off her saddle trying to sell her some jewelry was wearing a skirt with patches like a quilt, each square a different color. Another woman called out as Ihva passed her, holding out a silk blouse with clear lines differentiating the bodice and the sleeves.

As Ihva continued forward, a male dwarf passed her wearing only a thin white undershirt and brown pants cut off at his ankles, revealing black boots with what seemed like a dozen buckles. He was carrying a large burlap sack of what Ihva supposed to be grain as a man in richer clothing directed him up the incline.

A moment later, Ihva found a skinny, young dwarven girl with red locks bouncing around, jumping up and trying to tug at her stirrups. She was begging. The girl wore a simple beige dress made of low-quality cotton and had no shoes of which to speak. Ihva started to reach for a coin but remembered that she had no purse. The girl looked up, expectant, and Ihva's heart nearly broke as she hurried past the girl.

Looking ahead and up, Ihva saw the shops give way to dwellings, either carved into the mountainside or made of stacked stones. Both looked very sturdy, leading Ihva to wonder why the homes in Agda were not built as strong. As they passed the dwellings, Ihva spotted cloth curtains in the windows with the same sort of rigid lines and even shapes as in the clothing. While she was not particular to the heavy lines and symmetry of dwarven style, she admitted that the patterns were appealing.

Continuing on, Ihva looked to her left up the mountainside. Her breath caught in her throat as she beheld what could only be the Royal Palace. They were still a couple of turns from it, but she stared in awe the whole way up. The housing around her increased in decoration and size, but she hardly noticed as she took in the palace's grandeur. It seemed it was built entirely into the mountainside with a multitude of balconies projecting out from it. What stood out the most were the gates in the wall surrounding the structure. Unlike the well-defined edges of the rest of dwarven architecture, the gates formed a group of flames when closed, as they were presently. Ihva stared at the carving and saw it shimmer in the sunlight. The flames were plated with gold, and the background was gilded with shimmering, dark metal that she couldn't place. Ihva stopped to stare at the show of riches, but Cor hurried the party along, and Ihva's sight of the gates was hidden again by a noble's rooftop.

Cor continued pushing forward, and the traffic diminished as they approached the upper parts of the city. After a few more switchbacks, Ihva found herself in front of the enormous carved and plated doors. Cor had stopped. He dismounted and seemed to be greeting one of the guards who stood at the entrance to the palace. Ihva and the Prince took Cor's lead and slipped down out of their saddles.

"Greetings from Agda, dear brothers. That the Flame finds you well," Cor was saying.

"Indeed, the Flame burns hot. What brings you seeking an audience with Eshad's Chosen?" one of the guards replied with a friendly smile.

"We come seeking audience with His Majesty, good sir," Cor informed the guard.

"No one gains audience with the King without his specific invitation," the other guard replied in an irritated tone.

"This is a matter of great concern," Cor said patiently.

Silence greeted his response. The second guard looked over the party with an annoyed scowl.

After a long pause, the same guard told Cor, "The Council of Neved decides what is important to the king." The first guard gave a Cor an apologetic look as the grumpier one went on. "What sealed letter or documentation do you have for your 'urgent' matter?"

The Prince stepped forward impatiently, saying, "We have no need of sealed documentation. I am the seal."

The frowning guard gave him a doubtful look but said nothing, so the Prince held out his right hand.

Both guards peered at it, and the one grumbled under his breath before saying, "Ah, Your Highness, you will not waste the Council's time." His tone was filled with warning. "Allow me to show you in."

The guard motioned to a servant to take the party's mounts. Then he led Ihva and the others through the doorway. They entered a hallway with lit torches mounted on the walls. The guard motioned for them to wait a moment outside the next set of doors and slipped inside the adjoining room.

The Prince turned. "Cor, you must practice your tone. You are not convincing a man but commanding him. You must remember you are no longer a temple servant, and you haven't been for years. You're a royal ambassador and advisor now. You need to start acting like it."

Cor gave a deferential nod and straightened his posture. The party waited a long moment, during which Cor turned to Ihva.

"When we are introduced, make a curtsy as you would the highest authority in Agda." His eyes flickered to the Prince, but he went on. "It would be best to not speak unless someone speaks to you. If a Council member does call on you, take care to address him as 'Counselor,' not 'Your Grace' or 'My Lord' or anything that might imply they hold anything other than elected office. Dwarves are very particular to their democracy and offend easily over it."

"But don't they have a king?" Ihva asked.

"Yes," Cor replied, then paused. "The dwarven political structure is complex. The king holds ultimate authority, but the Council holds the authority to enforce his decrees."

Ihva gave a slow nod, still confused. Why did she need to treat them with the respect due a sovereign yet address them as no better than a court justice?

Cor had already moved on and was instructing Kronk to keep still and silent. Just then, the doors swung open again, and the guard reappeared.

"They will see you," he informed the group and ushered them inside.

CHAPTER 12

THE DOORS OPENED SLOWLY before Jasper and the others. The scraping of stone against stone grated on Jasper's ears, but he stepped forward without hesitation. He remembered his conversation with Cor three nights ago as they were switching watches. The dwarf had assured him King Cherev-ad was still loyal to the Fire and the Light (to Esh and Oer, respectively) and that he would send support with them against Jessica's captors. With an extensive intelligence network, the King might even have information on Jessica's whereabouts. All they needed was to gain a private audience with him, as Arusha headed the Council and would surely interfere with Jasper's plans if they brought them forward.

Inside the room, the ceiling stood high above, and the stone walls of the room extended a good way back. No sunlight lit the space, but the number of torches made up for it. Indeed, the light from the flames bounced on the ceiling, which was an inlaid mosaic portraying a gigantic dwarf standing mightily with a flaming hammer by his side. The whole scene disturbed Jasper with its earthenness and set him on edge.

He turned his attention to the line of dwarves spread before him. They stood arranged behind two tables and a dais, six to the left behind a long wooden table, six to the right behind another wooden table. At first glance, the faces were indistinguishable, but upon a closer look, Jasper found their varied qualities. Their uniqueness lay mostly in their hair adornments, though some dwarves' wrinkled skin stood out from the rest. Jasper looked more closely at each one's jewelry, finding anything from studded earrings to a hammer beard-clasp to circlets adorning their heads.

Jasper's eyes stopped on a dwarf toward the left side. He wore a clasp on his beard in the shape of a horse. It must have been Elazar. Cor had mentioned him briefly. He owned many pastures to the west and traded mostly in equine. Dwarves did not raise much livestock for the most part besides horses, which was why they traded with Oerid for much of their meat.

Jasper's eyes moved right. The oldest dwarf he could imagine sat two seats down. That had to be Betzal. At 410 years old, the dwarf was the longest-standing member of the Council, perhaps in all history, though Cor hadn't mentioned that. Jasper could only imagine it was so, with dwarves only living to 350 or 375. Betzal was scowling at Jasper and the others, and Jasper didn't need Cor's warning about this dwarf to deduce he'd offer them no help.

Jasper moved on to the dwarf behind the center dais decorated with metallic flames. Arusha. He wore richer clothing than the rest with robes of red and bright blue velvet. He wasn't part of the royal family, of course, and his donning of the royal colors seemed rather presumptuous.

As Jasper centered his gaze on Arusha, he heard the girl beside him inhale sharply. He glanced at her. She was looking at Arusha as well, and she had that nervous look about her again. Jasper looked back at the central dwarf. He wore a heavy, disapproving frown, but Betzal's expression was far more off-putting than Arusha's. This Miss Marchand was a strange one.

A foreboding voice projected from the dais, easily heard but only a little above a whisper. Jasper turned his eyes to Arusha.

"Welcome, Jasper Thesson of the dynasty Aurdor. Welcome to you, Prince of Oerid and to your... companions," the dwarf said.

Jasper sensed the girl next to him tense. She needed to calm down. Anyway, Jasper couldn't worry about her right now. He had to persuade Arusha of private audience with King Cherev-ad.

"I am pleased to meet you, High Counselor Arusha Molech of Shelhar," Jasper replied, addressing Arusha by the title and names Cor had impressed on him. He ignored the way Arusha was sneering at his companions. "We are pleased to find you in good health, by the Flame. I apologize for my urgency, but it is imperative that we meet with His Majesty, King Cherev-ad."

It was true. They didn't have time for chatting.

"I see..." came Arusha's noncommittal response. He glanced at the others again and then back at Jasper. "I am afraid the king is not taking visitors today. He has been ill and needs rest."

"The matter is of great importance, Counselor. We would not seek to disturb His Majesty's rest without an urgent purpose to escape disastrous repercussions," Jasper explained.

He tempered his bristling impatience, keeping his features smooth. Counselor Arusha leaned forward and spoke barely loud enough to be heard and with utmost authority.

"As I told you, the King is resting and will take no visitors today, urgent purposes and disastrous repercussions aside."

Jasper drew himself up taller. Arusha didn't seem like he was going to budge, but Jessica was out there somewhere. They'd already spent three weeks in pursuit, and he couldn't afford to waste time. Arusha was going to force Jasper to strong-arm him. Jasper restrained himself from letting out a frustrated sigh.

He replied instead, "I do not believe the King would say he is too ill to discuss matters pertaining to Eshad and Oerid's welfare and good relationship, which would certainly be in danger if he does not see to the matters at hand."

There was more honey poured into Jaspers tone than he imagined possible with his souring mood. Still, the threat was clear.

Arusha looked over the party once again and gave them a sickening smile.

"You are welcome to stay the night in the palace guest quarters. Perhaps the king's spirits will return on the morrow."

Jasper studied Arusha. The dwarf was plotting something. What could it be, and how much danger were they in if they stayed? He was about to refuse Arusha's offer of hospitality when a small, reassuring hand on his arm from Cor prompted him to accept. He resisted the urge to glance at Cor.

"We would be pleased to accept the offer," Jasper replied.

"Very well," the High Counselor said as he turned to a servant by his side. "Prepare the rooms immediately." He turned back to Jasper and the others. "It will be a pleasure to serve you this evening. Dinner is served at sundown, if you would be pleased to join us."

Arusha might have thought he was doing a good job feigning a hospitable smile, but Jasper noticed the corners of the dwarf's mouth jerk as though he were far more pleased than he was letting on. Jasper smiled back, burying his suspicions behind a mask of gratitude. Whatever Arusha was up to, Jasper was one step ahead by knowing there was a plot afoot.

Servants ushered the party out of the room through a side entrance and led them to the west wing of the palace. He touched Cor's shoulder, pretending to brush something off it. Cor would know what that meant-they needed to speak, sooner rather than later. Something about their situation left them imperiled, but Jasper wondered again in what way and to what degree? Reaching the guest quarters, the servants split him and Cor from the women. That would make fleeing harder, if that was what it came to. He wished he'd signaled Miss Marchand. He couldn't have even if he'd thought of it, though. Later, they would have to agree on a sign like the one he and Cor shared.

They arrived. The servants directed him and Cor to doors across the hall from each other. Jasper entered his room without a backward glance. No need to alert the servants to his wariness in case they were in on whatever scheme Arusha had. The door clicked shut.

Jasper took a quick look around. The room was spacious and luxurious, meant to flatter and distract him. He didn't let it but instead put his ear to the door, listening for the servant's retreating steps, which soon disappeared. He turned around and twisted the door-handle in a slow, noiseless motion. Then he cracked the door and peeked out. It was a long hallway lined with dark gray stone, lit like the rest of the palace with torches. There appeared to be no one around.

Jasper stepped out and hurried across the hallway, then opened Cor's door and slipped inside.

"Hello, son. I appreciate your swiftness."

Jasper turned and leaned his back against the closed door. "What is he scheming, Cor? He was much too satisfied we chose to stay."

"You are perceptive, son, and wise."

Jasper smiled a little. Cor calling him wise. The dwarf went on.

"I do not know Arusha's exact plans, but I suggest that we find the women and make our way to the King as soon as we can. I do not believe Arusha intends for us to make it past dinner this evening without falling into some trap, whatever it might be."

Jasper inhaled quickly. "You intend for us to make our own audience with King Cherev-ad?"

"Indeed," Cor said slowly. "The King will see us."

The dwarf's "us" had the sound of referring to Cor himself. Jasper had known Cor carried a certain rapport with King Cherev-ad, but he hadn't been aware how close their relationship was. Father did trust Cor with the relationship between Oerid and Eshad. Cor was Father's counselor on all matters dwarven and his chief emissary to Eshad when a situation required more than the run-of-the-mill ambassador. Still, Jasper sensed Cor had clout with King Cherev-ad apart from his station as an Oeridian diplomat.

"How will we get to him? Surely the servants will not allow us to just wander into his chambers?" he asked the dwarf after a moment.

Cor shook his head. "No. I know another way, a more direct way."

Jasper nodded. Cor's enigmatic reply required trust. The dwarf's plans always seemed to work, though. No reason not to follow his lead now. To the King, then, but first they had to find Miss Marchand and Kronk. Would Cor know anything about their whereabouts?

"Where might we find the women?"

"I believe they are below us a floor or two. We must hurry to avoid detection."

Jasper was stealthy enough, but Cor was less practiced at such things. They would have to move quickly if they were going to see their plan through. He looked at Cor for a cue to leave, and Cor nodded.

Jasper opened the door once again and slipped out into the hallway. By instinct, his hand went to the sword on his belt, and he realized Arusha hadn't taken their weapons. For that he was grateful.

CHAPTER 13

A PALACE SERVANT-a plump, middle-aged, female dwarf with auburn hair pulled into a tight bun-ushered Ihva into a room. The door shut, and Ihva looked around. She'd never seen such splendid decorations, angular and broad yet somehow elegant. A rectangular writing desk sat in the far-right corner of the room under a window, as the guest quarters were at the front of the palace overlooking the city. On the left side of the room next to the window, centered on the wall, was the bed. A soft pink blanket and cream sheets covered it. Carved wooden bed posts held up a canopy of deep reds and dark pinks to complement the bedspread. After a moment of taking in the scene, Ihva threw herself onto the bed and found it superbly plush and supportive.

As she lay looking at the canopy above her, she couldn't hold back what had been bursting to the surface of her consciousness the past weeks. She was finally alone, and as she lay quietly, her thoughts came charging through the barrier she'd constructed inside. Her first memories were of home. She thought of her own bed. It was not as luxurious as this one, but she remembered it being somehow more comfortable. Her father's face flashed before her mind's eye. Stern and purposeful, his eyes flashed harsh authority, and he chastised her for leaving home. She recoiled from the harsh speech she imagined he'd give when she returned, but then his anger gave way, his temper settled, and his eyes became warmer and caring. He was telling her what she'd heard nearly every day of her life since moving to Agda, that he and her mother were making a future for her in which she would be in want of nothing. He pleaded with her to come home to all they'd prepared for her. For some reason, his begging broke something in Ihva that had withstood the earlier imagined tirade.

As she mulled over what must be going on at home, an image of the dying Shadow Bandit flashed in her mind. She flinched at the vision of the gruesome, bloodied rapier the Prince had withdrawn from the Bandit's back. Her parents had warned her that adventuring was not what she imagined it to be, and she was beginning to understand.

She wiped a forlorn tear off her cheek. A merchant's life might not be so bad after all. There was something her father failed to mention in his stories when she was young. What had Cor called it, remorse? A man had died, albeit at the Prince's hand and not hers, but there was no way to rectify it. She couldn't call the man back to life. She wondered if he'd had a family or if he'd been so deeply entangled in the business of the Shadow that he'd abandoned his home. Ihva imagined how his family might mourn him. She couldn't stand the thought of a young daughter weeping as she was told her father wasn't coming home. The man might have been a Shadow Bandit, but Ihva reasoned even a Shadow Bandit had a heart and a mother. Didn't he?

Somehow, they'd ended up in Irgdol without any further issues though, and for that Ihva thanked Oer. They were safe in the dwarven city now. Or were they? Were they safe? Ihva thought back to what she decided to call a viewing. Something was very off about Arusha. Cor had warned Prince Jasper against the High Counselor, but there seemed to be something deeper at play. She recalled what she'd seen standing before the Council of Neved-a dagger, bloodied, hanging over Arusha's head, and a sense that the dwarf himself would be the one to bloody it. Ihva could only interpret the image, the viewing, as an indication Arusha meant to murder someone, but who?

Ihva sensed fear creeping over her. She missed home and longed for something familiar and decided to go find Kronk. Why the servants hadn't put her and Kronk in the same room, Ihva couldn't determine. It didn't matter. She decided she would go look for the woman.

Ihva rose from the bed and went to open the door to the room. She stepped out and looked around. Kronk should be in the room next to her, she guessed. She tried the door to her left. Empty. The door to her right. Empty. That was strange.

A distant door slammed. Instinctively, Ihva flattened herself against the wall behind a tall vase. She peered around it back the way they'd come. Four uniformed dwarves were in the hallway, arguing in angry voices. They were a distance down the corridor (it struck Ihva just how long the corridor really was), and she had to listen carefully to make out their words at this distance with their strange, lilting accents.

"We must find them," came one voice, male.

"He said he'd send them here, but this floor is for women. He must have sent the other two upstairs. The girl and the filthy orc-blood should be here, though."

The guards were looking for them, for all four of them, and they didn't sound well-intentioned. Their tones were impatient and aggressive. Ihva drew herself back behind the vase and was suddenly glad she'd hidden.

"Keep your voice down," a female dwarf said.

A few more seconds of conversation and the guards split into pairs and flung open two doors opposite each other. Ihva realized she hadn't checked the door across from her for Kronk. She looked toward where the dwarven guards had disappeared and darted across the hallway. She opened the door across from her room as quietly as she could and crept inside, shutting the door behind her.

There was no one there. Ihva searched the room but still found it empty. She began to feel frightened. What if she couldn't find Kronk before the guards found them? She listened at the door, then cracked it open. The guards were in the hallway again, but two doors opened after a moment and shut again. Ihva slid out of the door, leaving it ajar, and tiptoed down the hallway as fast as she could without making noise.

Doors slammed behind her, and she slid behind another vase. The dwarves' voices were growing more irate. What did they intend to do with Ihva and the others? As soon as she heard doors open behind her again, she sprinted up the corridor westward.

She arrived at a closed door. She grasped the handle and pulled it open. Without looking, she slipped inside. Outside the door, it was silent. Good, the guards hadn't seen her. Ihva eased the door shut, but it gave a loud click as it fell back into place. A second later, there were shouts in the corridor outside, and Ihva nearly panicked.

Not before she turned around and found herself in a stairwell, though. That was fortunate. She remembered the guard mentioned the men would be upstairs. Maybe she could find them at least. Thoughts rushed through her mind as she started up the spiraling stairs.

One floor up, she jerked the door open. She had to find Cor and the Prince. Another shout sounded. Ihva caught a glimpse of another guard, this one with an ax on his back, and she turned and ran before she could think to close the door behind her. If she wasn't sure of the guards' intentions before, now she knew they intended to use force to take her and the others. Nothing that required dragging them from their rooms could be good, right? Ihva remembered the bloody dagger and redoubled her speed up the stairs. She had ascended six flights by the time she heard voices below her.

She was soon breathing heavily as she climbed story after story. Eight, ten, twelve. Finally, she reached a large wooden door. The voices had grown somewhat more distant as she was climbing, but they were still approaching. She glanced behind her, though she knew they weren't close enough for her to see, then looked back at the door. It had a lock requiring a large key. Her heart pounded harder inside her chest, and her breaths quickened.

The voices grew closer, and Ihva's thoughts became even more jumbled. She pulled out her dagger and shoved the pointed end into the lock. She twisted it, sure that it would bend or break before it would come close to opening the lock. When the dagger did neither, she jiggled it a bit. A small light appeared for a second where the dagger and lock met, the lock clicked open. The brightness winked out, leaving Ihva confused. She opened the door, stepped through, and shut it fast behind her. She had no way of resetting the lock. She had to hurry.

As she entered the room, brightness blinded her for a moment. It was sunlight, she could tell by the color, and a fresh, cool breeze told her the room was open to the outside. As she blinked her eyes back into focus, she realized the room she'd found was the dungeon, though a strange one. Windows facing south allowed an abundance of sunlight to fill the cells and hallway. Vertical bars came into focus as her eyes became accustomed again to brightness, and the bars slowly became a row of open-air cells. Why were there dungeons at the top of the palace, Ihva wondered as she took a steady step forward, careful to keep toward the center of the corridor.

"Dwarves hate the outdoors and prefer the inner recesses of homes or caverns," a sunny voice explained from somewhere down the wall of cells.

Ihva started as she realized she'd spoken her question aloud.

"It's a simple form of torture but effective," the voice continued.

"Who's there?" Ihva called out cautiously.

"Over here, lass," the voice replied. The accent definitely belonged to a dwarf. "Who are you?" it asked.

Ihva snapped a response before she thought. "My name's Ihva. Ihva Marchand." She realized she'd stopped moving through the corridor and started forward again.

"Ah, an Oeridian. What would a nice Oeridian lass like yourself be doing up in an Eshadian dungeon like this?"

Ihva walked past some dwarves who were dozing on stone benches behind bars. They were wearing tattered clothing that resembled palace garb. Strange, Ihva thought. Infiltrators perhaps? Traitors to the Eshadian Crown? As she was pondering these things, she looked up and saw a figure with red hair and a large, unkempt beard rubbing his nose. He was too tall to be a dwarf, yet the top of his head reached only her eye level and so seemed short for a human male. He had the stocky build of a dwarf, and Ihva decided he was likely an anomaly, born tall for his race. He was young and wore nicer clothing than the rest, still the garb of a royal servant but with more durable cloth that hadn't worn as much. A lumpy purple cap with a drooping blue feather sat atop his head.

When Ihva didn't answer, the dwarf continued with mock reproach, "I do hope you haven't been disrespecting Arusha and his cohorts. He'd throw you in here without a glimmer of second thought."

Confused, Ihva said, "I thought the Crown decides who to jail, not Arusha."

"Ever since Arusha returned from the mountaintop, things have been different. The king locks himself away for most hours of the day except to occasionally take his meals in the hall. And Arusha himself changed. Not that he was all that spectacular before." The dwarf trailed off.

"He went to the Shrieking Summit?" Ihva exclaimed, remembering Cor's description of the haunted peak of the Kosar mountain range.

"Indeed, the very one. He set out to liberate it, but he claimed it liberated him."

"What does that mean?" Ihva reflected.

She jumped at the sound of distant shouting. Her eyes darted to the dwarf. She was terrified.

"You better run quick, lass."

"I don't know my way!"

She looked at her dagger as she considered how well the dwarf might know to navigate the castle. He knew more than she did, in any case. Unsure why she was trusting a criminal, eyes trained on her blade, she prayed it could open this lock as well. If it worked once, it might do it again.

She shoved the point of the dagger into the lock that secured the tall dwarf's cell. A flash of light, a click, and the lock opened. Ihva hastily tossed the lock aside. Besides a momentary grateful glance, the dwarf only cast his eyes forward and sprinted past Ihva eastward toward the other stairwell.

Ihva sprinted after him. He was remarkably quick for having such short legs. They turned a corner. Just then, she heard the door behind them burst open. The dwarf in front of her reached an open doorway to a stairwell leading down. He maintained his pace down the stairs. Ihva followed, feeling how precarious her hurried steps were, certain that she would trip at any moment.

Three floors down, the dwarf made an abrupt stop. He seemed to be searching for something. Ihva grew frantic as she realized he was staring at a blank wall of stones. Suddenly, he reached out and pressed one, and just as quickly, the stones slid apart to reveal a pitch-black space inside.

Ihva followed him into the space. The stones slid back into place behind them, and at the same time, Ihva realized she knew very little about this dwarf. So very little, and now she was stuck in an inky black darkness with him in who knew how large a space and paralyzed by blindness. Ihva grew afraid and reached for her dagger. As she touched it, she heard the dwarf shift his weight toward her. She took the dagger from its scabbard and readied herself.

"No need for your blade, lass. By the way, my name's Malach," the dwarf said, and she realized he could see in the dark.

Then she felt him grab her hand and drag her through the passage. It was all she could do to manage to keep pace as the two hurtled through a web of twists and turns through the palace's secret tunnels.

CHAPTER 14

AFTER A FEW MINUTES OF SPRINTING, the dwarf finally slowed. He held Ihva in place for a second, and her mind churned with thoughts of all the things he could do to her in the dark. Then light poured in as the wall slid apart again. The dwarf reached out of the passage and grabbed a torch, then pulled it back in and closed the wall once again.

"Sorry. Should have done that earlier. I forgot human eyes don't adjust as well to the dark."

"Thanks," was Ihva's curt reply.

She looked around. The passage was narrow, and she wondered how she'd managed not to collide with the walls as they'd been running. The dwarf had let go of her arm, but she still felt the place where his hand had grasped her. His grip had been tight. They were walking much more slowly now. At this pace, she realized small talk might be in order.

"You're a servant, I take it," she began.

"Kind of. The Royal Bard, actually, the palace's very own balladeer," he told her, turning back to look at her with a grin.

"That's not an overly threatening profession, I didn't think," she noted, then went on without thinking. "How'd that land you in jail?"

The dwarf's grin faded, and Ihva regretted her forwardness.

"My apologies. I didn't mean to," she started.

"No, lass, it's fine. It's just a bit complicated." He stopped and looked at her, his eyes searching her for a moment.

104

"I've had none to share the tale with, and a poet's heart is to confide his sorrows. You look trustworthy enough."

There was a short pause as he drew in a breath.

"There were rumors of a bastard prince. The king has never taken a wife before the Court, you see, and without a prince upon whom the king could bestow his title, the royal line will end. In such a case, the Council of Neved chooses a new king. Arusha has quite a following, many impressed by his return from the Summit. Should a son of the king show up somehow, though, Arusha's claim to the throne would be null."

The dwarf paused a moment. Ihva wondered what that had to do with him. As though he'd heard her thoughts, the dwarf stopped and turned to face her. His tone was grave as he spoke.

"Let's just say your good Malach here was one of the few still trying to supply an heir to the throne, loyal to the king's supposed son." The dwarf turned forward once again, striding along the passageway.

"Where's the King's son supposed to have been all this time? Why wouldn't the King bring him forward?" Ihva asked. She thought it rather foolish for King Cherev-ad to keep his heir a secret if he believed Arusha to be a true threat to the kingdom.

Malach started and then replied, "No one knows where he is, but rumors float about, citing various small towns in the vicinity of the palace. As for the king's secrecy, many say that his heir was deformed in some way or that he was a lunatic unfit to take the throne. Others say that, for some reason, the king felt ashamed of his existence." There was something in Malach's tone that Ihva couldn't label.

"But," she started but then shut her mouth, not wanting to seem more a fool.

She wondered about this King. If his son was in truth unfit for the throne, why didn't he just marry and have a legitimate heir. There must be a way he could overthrow Arusha's plot to gain the throne.

They continued on in silence, and Ihva noticed that they were descending stairs. She had the feeling that they'd been descending for a little while. She started when Malach spoke again.

"I'm still wondering, lass, what were you doing in the dungeon? It sounded like there were guards in pursuit?"

"I don't really know," came Ihva's honest answer.

She hesitated, wondering how far to trust Malach. He'd confided in her though, so she decided to continue. She'd tell him the truth, though maybe not all of it.

"I only arrived a few hours ago, but it became clear Arusha meant to harm us, so I fled."

"Then you weren't not alone when you came?"

"Oh yes, of course. My guard, Kronk, was with me."

She was about to mention Cor and the Prince when Malach interrupted.

"Your guard is an orc?" He'd recognized Kronk's name for its origin.

"No, no! It's a long story. She's only half-orcish. And she's the sweetest person you'll ever meet!"

"You certainly are interesting, lass. What were you and your guard doing all the way in Eshad?"

"We're with the Prince. Well, we were. Him and Cor. They're looking for someone, and they decided I must accompany them, Kronk and I. I mean, the Prince didn't want us to come along at first, I'm still not sure he does, but Cor insisted. He was adamant they take us, or me really, because Cor's convinced..." Ihva trailed off, realizing she was about to talk about Cor's theory about her. Instead, she went on, "I don't see any choice at this point but to travel with them. I'd never make it back to Agda with just Kronk. Besides, maybe I can help. I don't know. I don't know much about search and rescue, but surely there's something I can do..."

She stopped again. She might have just given away some confidential information. The Prince was very secretive about the fact that they were pursuing Lady Cibelle. Maybe she shouldn't have mentioned their search.

"By the Prince, I take it you mean Prince Jasper. And Cor, you say, Cor Gidfolk?" Malach asked hurriedly. "Cor is well-known here, of course. I do believe, though, Arusha intends him harm. You say he's here?"

"I believe his quarters were a floor or two above mine in the guest wing, but I didn't have time to search for the others as I fled."

"We must find him! He hasn't much chance to overpower Arusha. His only chance is to outrun him!"

Malach sounded distressed. He grabbed Ihva's arm again and picked up his pace. She looked past him to the tunnel illuminated by his torch. Her hope that they'd find the others before Arusha did grew more desperate, and her anxiety heightened. Where could they be?

———◆◆◆———

"Kronk not understand, what trouble has beardy stubby man and frowny prince? And why it so dark in palace? Who this other stubby man with beard of fire?"

Malach and Ihva had found the woman wandering two floors above the rooms that she and Ihva had been assigned. Malach had sent Ihva to retrieve the woman and lead her back into the hidden passageway. Along the way, Ihva had informed Kronk they were going to save Cor and the Prince from some trouble they were in. That had been a mistake, as Kronk kept asking about the nature of the men's situation.

"It's complicated, Kronk, and this is Malach, the court jester. Or troubadour or something."

"Palace Bard," Malach corrected her with an amused smile in his voice.

"That too strange for name. Kronk call him Firebeard!"

"That's great, Kronk," said Ihva with lackluster enthusiasm. "Now, Malach, where would they have taken Cor and the Prince if they did locate them?"

"To the Room of Raising, eventually. It's imperative we find them before they take them there, or it'll be too late."

"What's the Room of Raising?" Ihva asked, afraid.

Raising was connected to the Lady of Shadows. Surely Arusha wasn't involved in anything that dark.

"It's a room where Arusha Raises the dead under his control. Top secret, of course. Last I heard it was still experimental, but that was some months ago. If it is functioning, to undergo its process is a fate worse than death. With one's heart in Arusha's possession, a person's soul is recalled to a life of slavery and torment."

Malach spoke with a strong note of condemnation. Ihva knew what he was talking about, but she could hardly believe it was true. She stopped breathing for a second as horror coursed through her.

"He would Raise them!?"

"He's not of Esh anymore," Malach said, his words slow and emphatic. "Arusha came back and spoke of liberation, yet who was it who liberated him but the Queen of the Mountain, or I suppose you know her as Lady of Shadows?"

"What sort of pact did he enter!?" Ihva demanded, aghast.

"There's no telling, lass."

Footsteps echoed in the passage. Immediately, they quieted themselves, and Ihva readied her dagger. She and Malach stopped, but Kronk continued forward, tripping over Ihva and falling on Malach.

"Who is there?" came a low, dwarven voice. It sounded familiar to Ihva but then, she'd learned that all dwarven voices sounded the same to her.

"Kronk here!" Kronk cried out before Ihva could quiet her. Ihva fumbled her way toward Kronk and tried to cover her mouth but only managed to half muffle the next sentence, "Ihva too!"

"Thank Oer! We have found them," came the voice as a light brightened around the corner.

"Thank Oer," came a human male's unenthusiastic mutter. Ihva immediately recognized the voice as the Prince's and relaxed, but only a little.

"Cor. Cor Leviel Gidfolk, we come as friends," said Malach, stepping around the corner into Cor and the Prince's line of sight.

"Malach?" Cor asked, sounding startled.

Ihva stepped around the corner and saw Cor with his hand on his hammer, ready to draw his weapon.

"It's okay, Cor. He's a friend," Ihva said somewhat unsteadily.

"I know, Ihva," Cor said.

"Oh," Ihva said, taken aback. "What are you two doing in here?"

"The same thing you seem to be doing, avoiding the guards," the Prince remarked in a wry tone.

Cor shot the Prince an uncharacteristic frown of rebuke and said, "It seems the Crown of Eshad has fallen to the Lady of Shadows." Now Cor was staring at Malach.

"Not all have fallen. There are those loyal to Esh still, including the Crown himself. It is Arusha and the Council of Neved who have fallen, and they have locked up any still loyal to Esh, including the king in his own chambers. The others are in the dungeon and, worse, I fear they have been taking some to the Room of Raising," Malach replied. His voice was more subdued as he went on. "I believe he is creating an army."

Malach was much more forthcoming with Cor than he'd been with Ihva. True, he could not have been sure whether to trust Ihva when he first met her, but she had trusted him with the truth about her circumstances. Most of it, at least. Anyway, Malach's manner gave Ihva the impression he and Cor had met before.

"I suppose you are one of the loyalists, then?" came the Prince's tenor voice.

"Indeed, and they were deciding whether to Raise me or simply execute me on Shol's heights. Either way, my execution was set for two morns from now, and I'd been unsuccessful in escaping, clearly. I was resigned to death until this fine lass freed me from my cell."

"How did she manage that? It is well-known that the cells of Eshad are protected from magic. Have you practiced lock-picking, child?" Cor asked, turning to Ihva.

She shook her head, suddenly wary of explaining.

"It's a mystery to me as well," said Malach.

The two dwarves stared at each other for a moment, then exchanged a firm hug and slapped each other on the back. The moment lasted longer than Ihva expected, and now Ihva wondered if, more than having met before, they'd known each other for some time.

"Now I hear you are looking for someone," Malach said.

Ihva looked at the floor, but she could feel the Prince's eyes boring into her.

"Yes, we are seeking the Lady Cibelle, Jessica Selene Cibelle of Hestia," Cor replied.

The Lady Jessica of Hestia? That was the Lady Cibelle they were pursuing? Ihva's thoughts jumbled in her mind. Jessica had been one of the kinder of the noble daughters to Ihva, at one time at least. Ihva remembered eight years before.

⁂

The girls' looks as Ihva approached were condescending and cruel. She'd asked if she could join their game of hopscotch.

The leader, a bronze-haired, blue-eyed young beauty, smirked and whispered to the girl next to her, who nodded. The leader stood upright and gave the most unexpected answer.

"Yes."

Young Ihva perked up and joined the throng in line for hopscotch.

"No," the leader said. "We won't be playing hopscotch. We'll be playing dodgeball, and the peasant will be the one dodging."

Ihva began to understand why the girl had agreed. Quickly feeling humiliated, Ihva tried to escape, but a circle had already formed around her. Someone found a small hard ball, with a diameter about the span of Ihva's hand. Ihva managed to dodge many of the throws, defying her own expectations. However, one pass caught her in the temple, and things instantly went black as she fell unconscious.

⁂

She awoke to find the crowd of girls dispersed, except for one.

"I'm Jessica," the girl with raven-black hair and dark eyes said, holding out a hand.

"Jessica?" Ihva stammered, disoriented and her head still pounding.

"That's right, Jessica. My family takes holiday here in Agda every year. I was born in Hestia. My father is still lord there but has appointed my older brother to rule while he studies and advises the king. He's very important, my father that is. As for me, I'm glad we moved to Agda. I actually have friends here, noble girls," the girl said as she lifted Ihva from the ground.

Ihva rubbed her head. She felt it throbbing. This girl talked too much.

"What about you? What's your name? Where were you born? What do your parents do?"

The girl asked too many questions, too. She was a nobleman's daughter. Why was she talking to Ihva in the first place? Ihva shifted uncomfortably.

"I need to go home. But my name's Ihva, I'm of the Marchand family. Born in Calilla just to the east, a port town. My father is a merchant. But like I said, I need to go home."

With that, Ihva hurried away.

———◆◆———

The next time she saw Jessica, the girl didn't acknowledge her. Ihva waved and waved and even shouted her name. Jessica just looked at her blankly and turned back to the noble girls with whom she was walking and laughed. Ihva was sure she was the brunt of their joke and walked away to hide her shame. She never asked to join the noble girls' games again after that.

———◆◆———

Ihva shook her head as the embarrassment of the moment washed over her once again. She returned her attention to the conversation at hand, which seemed to have finished while she was distracted. The party arrived at a dead end.

"We're here," Malach informed them. "The King will help you; I can assure you of that," he added. He pressed another indistinguishable stone, and the wall slid apart.

CHAPTER 15

JASPER TOOK A WARY STEP out of the passageway after Cor.

"I was wondering when you would discover a way out," someone said in a grave tone from the other side of the room.

"It was not I, Your Majesty, but a girl who got me out," the red-haired dwarf replied respectfully, bowing and waving a hand at Miss Marchand as she exited the passageway. Malach. The dwarf's name was Malach.

Jasper shielded his eyes from the newfound brightness as he made his way farther into the room.

"I was hoping you wouldn't have to starve to fit through the bars. After all, that's how the last escapee made it out." The dwarven voice laughed kindly.

As Jasper gained his bearings and ceased having to squint in the well-lit chamber, he looked around for the speaker. He found that the voice belonged to a majestic figure, a dwarf of course, with a smattering of gray in his hair. The dwarf's deep blue robes fell around his feet, and his dwarven locks were braided in an intricate, regal manner. He wore many rings fitted with precious stones. Jasper picked out several emeralds, diamonds, and sapphires, all set in evadium.

"And who might these lovely people be?" the figure inquired.

"To introduce ladies first, this is Ihva Marchand of Agda and her guard, Kronk. And may I present you Prince Jasper Thesson Aurdor, Crown Prince of Oerid? And, finally, you no doubt recognize the Dwarf of the East, Cor Gidfolk," Malach replied. Then, turning to face them, he introduced the dwarf. "Cherev-ad Lam Shemayim, King of Eshad."

"Enough with the formalities, Malach. These are friends, perhaps the only friends within a day's travel of us," the King said.

Malach gave the king a respectful nod. Respectful but familiar.

"I regret I cannot properly entertain you, good Prince, but I fear our time is likely limited. Arusha is unaware you are here?"

King Cherev-ad was addressing Jasper now, who searched the king quickly. The dwarf had a kind smile but worry creased around his eyes. Cor had said King Cherev-ad was trustworthy, but Jasper needed to judge for himself. He had only a moment to assess. The king's stiffened back told Jasper that he was anxious, and there was a hint of fear in his face, but his voice carried genuine concern. It had to be Arusha troubling him.

"He does not know our whereabouts, Your Majesty," Jasper said slowly. "Though the guards are alerted to the fact we are not where we ought to be."

"Indeed, we must hurry, then. He might conclude you have fled, but he would just as likely deduce you are here."

Jasper nodded. Where to begin? How much to tell? Everything he'd planned to say had vanished from his mind. He searched for the right words.

"We are in pursuit of someone, Lady Jessica Cibelle, Majesty," Cor interrupted.

That decided it, then. They'd tell the King exactly what they were up to, no thanks to Cor. There was probably no way around it. Still, if the King caught wind of the real reason they needed this woman, Jasper was in as much danger from him as he was from Arusha.

Jasper brought his attention back to the dwarven royal, who was waiting for further explanation. "She is engaged to be my wife," he explained before Cor could butt in.

"Yes, I know," the King replied.

The dwarven king took an interest in such things, then? Jasper and Lady Cibelle had become betrothed only a month before she'd been taken, the night he'd told her everything, and no message had been sent to Eshad of the engagement.

"They were taking her to Raise her," the king said.

"What?" Jasper exclaimed before he could stop himself.

There was no way he'd heard that right. Malach had mentioned Raising, too, though. The Lady of Shadows Raised people-the Shadow-sworn and men in the upper echelons of the Shadow Bandits, and some theorized that the Shrouded were powerful men from history the Lady had Raised. It was rare for creatures to Raise other creatures-humans, dwarves, elves. Very few were so embroiled in the Lady's affairs and so esteemed by her that she deigned to bestow that power on them. Cor hadn't mentioned anything like this about Arusha.

"The High Counselor likes to taunt me with information," the King replied. "It will be his downfall. He has told me much about his visit to the Mountain, explaining Hell's Mistress has his heart and that he no longer belongs to Oer."

Jasper nearly choked, but the King went on.

"I take it he was struck by her magic tricks, and he turned. He says he was liberated, but really he enslaved himself to passion and to lies when he bound himself to the Queen of the Mountain." The King took a breath. "He believes I cannot help but do the same. What he does not realize is the resilience of truth and the strength of a heart filled with love. I love my people and I will not surrender them, not for a kingdom as large as Gant itself." The dwarf's tone was forlorn.

Jasper nodded slowly as horror crept over him. He empathized with the King's attachment to his nation. What he couldn't understand was Arusha's conversion. Yet the King was still speaking.

"Yet there is little I can do as one dwarf alone, king though I am. Arusha can overwhelm me easily with his forces, and he has, locking me in these chambers. Our world has darkened, and with Malach imprisoned, I wondered at Oer's plans. It seems things have changed, though."

The King fell into silence as he looked out the window at the city below. Jasper couldn't speak. The Lady had Arusha's heart, and he could Raise.

"Have they Raised her, then? Are we too late?" Cor asked in a whisper.

"Who? Oh, Lady Cibelle," the king said as he broke from his thoughts. "No, you are not too late. A week or so before you arrived, Arusha came to me, distraught. He told me she had escaped to the south. He believed she would seek safety in M'rawa. He consoled himself that you were following and set to arrive in Irgdol within a week. I wondered whether capturing you was not his plan in the first place."

"Not all hope is lost, then," Cor said with a great sigh of relief, and Jasper regained his breath.

"There is always hope," the king admonished.

"And yet hope has a tendency to fail," came a sneering voice as the door to the chambers opened suddenly, revealing Arusha's pallid face.

A shiver ran up Jasper's back, and his head started spinning. The Lady was too near. He had to keep it together.

"Isn't this a pretty little party, now?" Arusha said as he entered the room with a smug grin. He strode toward King Cherev-ad and stopped behind the King, putting a hand on his shoulder. He turned to face the rest of the group.

"And isn't this a rude little interruption?" Malach came back bravely.

"Well, I couldn't miss the fun now, could I?" Arusha's mouth pouted as he pretended to be hurt. Still, his eyes shone with malevolent glee. "It looks like all my favorite people are here."

Jasper's thoughts raced. They needed time, time to think. They could overwhelm Arusha easily with their weapons, but Jasper was sure the Counselor had stationed guards outside. They wouldn't get far that way. He needed to buy time. King Cherev-ad had mentioned Arusha liked to talk. Jasper needed to get him talking.

"What do you intend here, Arusha?" he asked the Counselor.

Arusha turned his eyes to Jasper. "Why do you assume I have intentions? Perhaps I am simply here to check on the King's health."

He stepped over to the windowsill and turned his back. The window was open, and Jasper had the urge to push him through it. The Counselor turned back around and scanned the party.

"You look concerned, young lady," Arusha said as he turned his attention to Miss Marchand.

Jasper glanced at her. She looked sickened was what she looked. Of course, she was frightened, with everything they'd just heard. Arusha could Raise? Before Jasper could think further, he saw Miss Marchand draw herself up, looking the Counselor in the eye.

"Just confused, sir, and a little afraid," she told him in a respectful tone.

Jasper wasn't sure why she was being so open with a man who wanted to kill her. Open and polite.

Arusha laughed. "What do you have to be confused about?"

"I," she started to reply but then stopped.

Her eyes moved to the others, searching. What was she confused about? Arusha took advantage of her vulnerable look.

"You are such a sweet girl. I would hate for you to be caught in something you don't understand. It would be a shame for you to throw in your lot with those whose intentions are not what they seem." Arusha's tone was sympathetic and paternal. There was no way she could fall for it, though. "You are very important, you see. Vitally important."

Miss Marchand stared at Arusha, and Jasper was reeling. What was the Counselor saying? Miss Marchand was important? Had Arusha learned of the girl's supposed abilities somehow? Jasper thought only he and Cor knew about the Reading, her demonstration of Tongues, and he was still skeptical.

"I can protect you. Who are they?" Arusha swept a hand at Jasper and Cor. "They have no real power. They cannot preserve you when it becomes clear who you are. What, you think a single dwarf and one man can save you when they cannot guard the prince's own betrothed? I have armies at my command, child. I will not harm you."

Miss Marchand had begun to sway where she stood, and Jasper saw the conflict in her face. She couldn't truly be considering Arusha's

116

offer. Cor leaned forward, about to say something, and Malach looked afraid. King Cherev-ad stood in place, giving Miss Marchand a warning glance she didn't seem to notice.

"What are your intentions, if not to harm or destroy me?" she asked Arusha quietly before Cor could speak.

"Be careful, Miss Marchand," Jasper broke in.

She turned to him, and her look startled him. Her eyes were full of fear, her lips trembling. She was disarmed, her demeanor entirely unguarded for once, and she seemed to be begging him for an answer. Miss Marchand was entreating him, Miss Ihva Marchand, who had never asked him for anything.

"Be careful, Ihva."

Her name slipped out before he knew what was happening, but it had the desired effect. She blinked and nodded. Her gaze returned to the High Counselor, whose face gleamed something terrible, full of power and greed. She stepped backward, and Arusha's eyes flashed.

"I don't think I've misunderstood their intentions," she said.

As she spoke, Arusha was positioning himself behind King Cherev-ad. A sense of panic paralyzed Jasper as he watched Arusha close the distance. Jasper rushed forward, but he was too late.

"Perhaps, then, you have misunderstood mine," Arusha replied gravely as the King lurched forward and fell to the ground.

Behind him, Arusha held up a long, bloodied dagger, but all eyes in the room turned to the King's collapsed body lying on the floor.

"No!" three voices cried in unison. Miss Marchand dropped her knees beside Jasper while he watched the gruesome scene with horror. Blood flowed from King Cherev-ad's body onto the carpet. The king began to cough and looked up at Malach, his eyes pleading. Then he shook and stilled.

"What do you plan to do now? Your people will surely execute your King's murderer." It was Jasper who spoke, though his voice seemed like it was coming from somewhere outside him.

"Well, isn't it convenient that I have captured the assassins to ensure they face justice? Spies from Oerid sought to steal the secrets of the evadium trade and found the king loyal and unable to be bribed, so they killed him in cold blood," Arusha replied, laughing mirthlessly. Before anyone could respond, he cried out for the palace guards. "Help! Come quickly! They've murdered the King!"

Malach was already at the wall behind them, and the door to the passageway was sliding open. He pulled Kronk into the secret corridor, and Cor was right after him. Miss Marchand was still on the ground, so Jasper grabbed her arm and dragged her backward to the wall. He had just gotten her through the doorway when guards burst into King Cherev-ad's chambers. The sound of the crashing doors must have roused the girl, as she turned to run. Jasper let her go before him but wasted no time in sprinting after her as a thrown ax shattered a bit of stone near his head.

They fled through the passageway, following Malach, guided by Cor's light. Behind them, another hand-ax whizzed past Jasper's ear and clanged against the wall. Jasper shied to the left. Malach led them around corners and down some spiraling stairs, at which point things grew darker with Cor's light obscured behind the central column. Soon enough, though, they were on even ground again, speeding through the passageways and around sharp turns.

Jasper wasn't sure how long they'd been in flight when Malach and Kronk disappeared around a corner to the right. Cor vanished after them, then Ihva, and Jasper could have sworn they'd gone left, but Cor's bright orb sped right. Jasper skidded to a stop and glanced left. Cor's eyes met his, and he darted into the small corridor after the dwarf.

The passageway darkened as Cor projected his ball of light farther down the other hallway. Malach put a finger to his lips and pulled Kronk to move into the shadows. Jasper fought the urge to glance behind him as he followed.

The guards' heavy footfalls echoed behind them, then slowed. It was very dark in the passage now, with just a faint bit of the light showing in the other direction. Someone grabbed Jasper's hand, and he and the others rounded a corner. The sound of footsteps had grown more distant, and they slowed to a walk. Then there were more stairs, but a flight straight down instead of in a spiral. It was pitch black, and Jasper grasped tightly to whoever was holding him as they descended. Soon enough, the ground evened, and they stopped. Whoever had Jasper's hand let go.

"It's safe, now," came a whisper from Malach.

A small light appeared, causing Jasper to squint. They were all there-Cor, Miss Marchand, Kronk, and Malach. Kronk was still grasping Malach's hand, and Miss Marchand stood between Jasper and Cor. Malach scanned the rest of them, then looked at Jasper.

"Once we go through this doorway, we will be just outside the city walls."

At the dwarf's words, Jasper spotted a ladder in the wall leading to a trapdoor in the ceiling.

"I would be most obliged if you would allow me to join you. I'm a fugitive now, and travel is safer in numbers these days," Malach continued. "Your Highness," he added a second later.

Malach wanted to join them? Travel was indeed safer together, especially now. At least, normally it was safer, but Jasper imposed a very abnormal situation. If something went wrong, if the Lady got to Jessica before he did, things could get very, very bad. Even if they didn't, the dwarf would be privy to the situation. Jasper already wondered how he'd hide it all from Miss Marchand.

He was taking too long to answer. He looked at the dwarf and found him waiting patiently. Malach didn't have the air of one frantic or distraught like Jasper would have expected, and Jasper sighed inwardly. It made no sense, but at the same time, he couldn't leave the dwarf to fend for himself.

"You may join us," he told Malach finally.

Malach nodded as though he'd expected Jasper's reply and turned to climb the ladder. He lifted the door above him and peeked out while Jasper stared after him. Malach had expected Jasper to agree. Who did he think he was? Everyone climbed the ladder, and Malach shut the trapdoor behind them. As Jasper emerged, he saw that the sun had fallen behind the mountain range, casting long shadows over them.

Chapter 16

THE CAMP WAS SPARCE since they'd fled without their horses, taking only what they had in their packs. They had no fire, and the morning air left Ihva shivering. She looked around for the others and saw Malach asleep a few feet away. She found Cor awake and sitting quietly, a distant look on his face. His brow was creased with worry, which sparked fear in her. Cor was never worried.

Spotting the Prince took a moment longer. He was pacing at the other side of camp, inspecting the ground in places. His gaze kept returning to the river, though, his back to the others. He was so distracted Ihva felt comfortable enough to watch him. She'd never noticed how small he looked when he was nervous, how small and perfectly human. She'd come to interpret his dark looks differently over the past couple weeks. He used to look perpetually cross to her, and while she still thought him moody, she'd realized he was more sullen than angry. It confused her. The second most powerful man in Oerid, sulking? Boys were so strange.

She flushed. Stop that. She shouldn't think like that, couldn't think like that. The Prince was no boy, and she definitely couldn't lump him in with the young men she'd been chasing since she was fourteen. Her face had to be bright red now. Light in Heaven, no. That wouldn't do. She quickly turned her gaze from the Prince, who still hadn't noticed her, and found herself staring at Malach.

When had he awoken, and what was that sly smile on his face? He couldn't think... No. The Prince was engaged, and besides that, he was the Prince, all nervousness and sulking aside. That wasn't it at all. Ihva stood and turned to Cor.

"Where will we go?" she asked hurriedly.

Cor's eyes came back into focus and settled on her, and his voice was quiet when he spoke. "Prince Jasper would be the best to ask that question."

Ihva drew in a breath and made a point of not looking at Malach as she shifted her attention toward the water bubbling past. "Where will we go, Your Highness?" she asked in a slightly louder voice.

The Prince jumped and turned to her. "Well, the first thing we must do is cross this river."

He sounded breathless, and his eyes on her wavered. She just nodded and remembered they hadn't had their lessons that morning. Why did she feel disappointed? She forced herself to maintain her gaze. If she didn't, Malach would get the wrong idea again.

An awkward moment passed as she and the Prince stared at each other. She didn't want to be the first to break eye contact, and for some reason, he didn't seem to either. Finally, he addressed Cor and looked away.

"We must travel in the water for a mile or so. If they have hounds, they will certainly discover our path unless we mask our scent. A mile of wading before we cross should aid our escape."

Ihva held her breath.

"That sounds sensible," Cor replied. He glanced at Malach as though to consult him but seemed to think better of it. "We shall move through the river, then. And southeast after that, I assume?"

The Prince nodded, though his attention seemed to have drifted. There was silence for a moment.

"Right. Onto breakfast, then?" Malach's voice was bright as sunshine. He was a morning person, wasn't he? At least he hadn't made any foolish comments about whatever had just happened.

"I'll wake Kronk," Ihva interjected before he could add anything.

"That's a nice dress you're wearing, Kronk," Malach said over breakfast.

They'd all shared a bit of their rations with him, as he'd joined them with only the worn clothes on his back and the fancy hat on his head. Ihva glanced at it and fought a chuckle. Now that she knew a little more of Malach's mannerisms, the hat's flamboyance seemed fitting.

"Kronk love pretty dress. Kronk have lots at home in closet," Kronk exclaimed, then bit her bread enthusiastically.

Ihva felt Malach's curiosity emanating as he watched the orc-blood woman, and she decided to fill the silence.

"Kronk grew up in her orcish father's clan near Deepgrove for many years. She ran off from her mother's village as a small child when her mother died, but she always hoped to return to human society. She knows orcish culture but prefers the company of humans, for their fashion tastes if for nothing else."

"Oh, yes! Kronk love pretty dress!" Kronk stood and twirled her violet skirts.

"Not everyone appreciates her," Ihva added.

Malach gave a knowing nod, but it was Cor who spoke. "As much as we would like to fit in, men find a way to keep us at arm's length. I did not expect such a thing when I entered Oerid, but I have become accustomed to it after these many years."

"Where were you born, Cor?" Ihva asked.

"I was born and spent my childhood in Apul, a city on the western edge of Eshad. I was the son of a skipper and a seamstress. When I was twelve, my father was lost at sea, and my sister and I had to care for our grieving mother. She gave up her business, refused to leave the house, and stopped eating. She grew weaker and weaker, and soon she passed as well. Chana and I agreed Mother died of a broken heart. Chana could not imagine leaving Apul, and I wanted so much to stay with her-she was all I had left-but she was to marry a kind young merchant while I had no prospects. I decided at thirteen to travel back with my uncle, my mother's brother, to Agda where he was living.

"I arrived in Agda with my uncle, and he put me to work cleaning the temple with him. Being friendly by nature, I often found myself conversing with temple priests and acolytes, and it was then I converted to worship Oer. So enthusiastic was I that I would lay in bed at night, imagining I would grow up to be a priest of Oer myself."

Cor's mouth quirked.

"One day I expressed this desire to the chief priest. He only stared and told me, 'The priesthood is restricted to men. No dwarf has ever been or shall ever be a priest of Oer.' I knew not to push further." Cor's gaze fell, and his eyes had a far-off look.

The others were silent. After a moment, though, the Prince spoke. "Yet your service to Oer and to His Chosen Son became so known my father took you at his advisor. You do serve Oer, Cor."

"Indeed, I suppose I do." Cor's eyes still looked sad.

"Life hardly ever paves the path we expect," Malach mused quietly.

No one replied. Ihva tilted her head, pondering his words. She certainly had never imagined she'd be a fugitive fleeing Shadow-sworn dwarves with Kronk, Oerid's Prince, his advisor, and a dwarven troubadour. She looked around at the others. They looked varying degrees of reflective, except Kronk, who just looked uncomfortable in the sudden quiet. It was Cor who broke the silence and in a grave tone.

"It is best we depart now. Time is short, and we have wasted enough of it already."

Fear pricked Ihva again at the unsettledness in his voice. Indeed, they needed to head out sooner rather than later. Ihva's eyes drifted north as she stood, but there was only wilderness there.

They walked miles that day, resting only briefly for a cold lunch. By sundown, Ihva felt sorer than she ever had in the saddle. She thought about asking to stop a couple times, but then she saw the pained resolve on Malach's face. If he, who'd just escaped near starvation in a prison cell, could keep going, then so could she. Cor finally convinced the Prince to stop an hour after dark, and Ihva skipped dinner to go straight to bed. She was asleep as soon as she laid down.

Ihva awoke while it was still dark to a loud thud. She shot up and looked around. Nothing appeared wrong as she looked east to where the sun would soon rise, but as she looked west, her breath caught. A huge, hulking figure loomed in the dark, towering over the Prince as he dodged blows from the creature's fists. The Prince crouched to avoid being struck, then managed to slide his rapier into the creature's side.

"Hill giant!" he called out.

Ihva jumped to her feet and grabbed her blade, mustering courage to stride forward toward the battle. She circled around to the giant's back. As she did so, she passed Malach, who motioned frantically. Ihva remembered he was without a weapon. She drew her dagger from her belt and handed it to him, then dashed toward the giant again.

She didn't waste a moment once she arrived. She slashed the backside of the giant's knees, trying to force it into a kneel. She had little success before it turned on her. Suddenly faced with two swinging fists, she danced to keep from being struck. The giant's knuckles slammed into the ground beside her, and dirt exploded from the point of impact. The only way to escape being pummeled was to fell the creature. Frantic, Ihva flailed her rapier, forgetting all the forms she'd learned from the Prince.

Malach appeared to the right, but she knew there was little he could do with just a dagger. Kronk was on Ihva's left waving her club behind the creature, but the woman looked so tentative Ihva wasn't sure she wouldn't run instead. The Prince was beside Kronk, his eyes searching.

Ihva continued to dodge the giant's lumbering blows, which were becoming more aptly placed. The creature was learning her patterns. She had to do something to gain the upper hand, and soon.

Then the giant turned on the Prince, who must have struck the creature. It gave an angry roar. With a moment's relief, Ihva remembered some of what the Prince had taught her and sliced across the giant's side. She was about to pierce the same spot when she caught sight of its fist hurtling toward her.

It happened in slow motion. She dove to avoid being hit, but she knew that she was too late. The second drew itself out as she braced for the impact. The giant's knuckles connected with her side, and she lost her footing. She fell to the ground and felt something inside her crack. As her head hit the dirt beneath her, everything went black.

———◆•◆———

Ihva's eyelids fluttered open. The sky above her was tinted pink and yellow. As she went to rise, she felt a dull ache in her side. Then she remembered-the giant. She looked around her and found the creature's body slumped and motionless on the ground.

"Ihva!" Kronk was suddenly at Ihva's side.

She looked Ihva in the eyes for a moment before scanning and prodding her. Surprisingly, nothing hurt.

"Ihva feel better?" Kronk asked after her inspection.

"I think so," Ihva replied. "Just an ache right here." She pointed to her right side.

The Prince's approach startled her. "You were out cold," he said simply.

Ihva nodded, and her eyes met his. He stared at her for a moment with an indiscernible expression. She shifted. Finally, he looked away.

"Your rapier work has improved," he said, then turned and walked away.

Malach and Cor were at Ihva's side a second later. They too looked her over for injury and Cor asked, "How are you feeling, Ihva?"

"Fine," Ihva replied.

Cor gave her a doubtful look.

"I'm good, really."

"I have never performed a Healing that extensive before. There are few serious injuries in Agda, just scrapes and twisted ankles and an accidental knife cut on occasion."

"I was worse off than that?"

"Broken ribs, internal bleeding, concussion from the fall. I do not possess that great a Power, but something strengthened my abilities, something I have never felt before."

Ihva got up and was about to ask Cor to explain when Malach interrupted.

"It was a close encounter. As for me, I feared you were lost."

Ihva glanced at Malach, then all of a sudden, she saw an ephemeral crown fall above him. She was startled but tried to contain her surprise. As she continued watching, a small image of Malach picked up the crown and donned it. He looked much more regal in the viewing than he did standing before her. In the image, his tattered clothes were exchanged for royal robes. Slowly, the vision faded.

"What did you see?" asked Cor. He was peering at her.

Ihva rocked from one foot to the other and tried to lie, "Nothing."

"What you see has meaning, child," he told her.

Malach blinked at Cor's words but said nothing.

Frightened, Ihva spoke barely above a whisper. "It's Malach. He wore royal robes, and he picked up a crown that had fallen and was wearing it."

What could it mean? Her viewing of Arusha had been fulfilled obviously enough, but the one of Malach seemed absurd, if she was interpreting it correctly. Malach would wear a crown? Palace Bards, though highly respected among servants, stood nowhere near royalty, not in Oerid at least. She could only guess it was the same in Eshad.

Cor was waiting for her to continue, so she said, "That's all."

He shared a glance with Malach, who looked troubled. Ihva hardly cared to know the meaning of their looks. She was more interested in how Cor had discovered she had these viewings.

"The Beholder's Sight does not lie," was his only explanation and seemed more directed at Malach than her.

What was the Beholder's Sight? Cor gave her a sympathetic look but walked away before she could ask anything. She rose slowly, perplexed.

The question nagged at her the rest of the day. Cor knew about her viewings, and he believed they reflected reality in some strange way. Did it have something to do with being Oer's Blessing? She lifted a desperate prayer that it wasn't so. Her plea to Oer not to be his vessel was ironic, and she knew it, but her prayer was instinctual. Light in Heaven, let it not be true!

CHAPTER 17

FIVE DAYS LATER, Jasper found himself on a road headed south. He'd been nervous to take it, as it was clear from how beaten the dirt was it saw a good deal of traffic. Cor was adamant, though. They indeed passed a few wagons along the way, but even Jasper had to admit the passersby looked harmless enough.

Meanwhile, rations were running low, and they'd spotted a few farms along the way. They conferred over a late lunch whether they should stop at the next steading for the night. Malach and Cor agreed that news of fugitives and their descriptions couldn't have traveled this far yet, seeing as they'd set a rather grueling pace and cut across the countryside and forest. Malach pointed out the road they were on led north to Lochemesh, a smithing city in the east of Eshad, and that it would take over a week for news to travel here by horse, if the message was traveling on beaten paths. Jasper was not as convinced, but their supplies were running out. He could hunt with daggers, and he suggested as much, but Cor pointed out they'd waste a lot of time that way. Better to spend part of one day stocking up at a farm than a couple hours every day gathering provisions. Besides, then they'd have to cook, and they'd avoided starting a fire up to now. Jasper reluctantly agreed.

An hour before sunset, they came upon some planted fields-a farm. It was a unanimous decision to take refuge there for the night. They found the farmhouse five minutes later and quickly decided on fake names before they approached.

Cor and Malach led the way and found the farmer, a dwarf of course, and some of his children on their way back from the fields to a small, sturdy house with a thatch roof. Cor greeted the farmer and introduced the party, calling each person by their alias.

"Greetings, good fellow. I hope this evening finds you well. My name is Lanar, and these are my companions, Esther, Grucka, William, and Mathar. We seek shelter for the night, if you would be so kind." He motioned at Ihva, Kronk, Jasper and Malach in turn.

The farmer looked taken aback and kept glancing at Kronk. He wasn't the only one. His younger children ogled the orc-blood woman until the farmer gave them a reprimanding look. Then he looked back at Cor and replied cautiously.

"Welcome, travelers. My name is Eruach. We are graced by your visit." He looked over the party and went on, "I would be obliged to take you in for the night, and I'll tell my wife to add more to the stew for supper." He bowed and took his leave, making quick strides toward the farmhouse.

The children, meanwhile, quickly forgot their manners and began talking over each other.

"Where are you from?" came a middle child's inquiry.

"Have you ever used that?" another asked, pointing at Jasper's rapier.

"Have you ever killed anyone?" the youngest boy wondered.

If the boy only knew, Jasper thought. Malach laughed and started answering the questions, skipping the one about where they were from.

Cor moved to fall in step with Jasper as they headed toward the house. Under his breath, only loud enough for Jasper to hear over the noise of the children, he explained, "There is a tale that teaches us dwarves to take kindly to travelers. It is told like this: one day, a farmer refused shelter to a beggarly old man traveling along the road near the farmer's field. It was nearing dark, and the old man had stopped at the farmer's house, asking to stay for the night. The farmer denied the old man to sleep in his home or even in his barn. The next day, the farmer found his crop ruined by locusts and his barn collapsed. His children and his wife were gone. He looked around and found the old man at his side. The farmer asked the traveling man if he had seen the culprit, and the man only pointed his finger at the farmer's chest. As the farmer blinked, it was Esh himself standing before him, finger still pointing at him. Esh's voice came like the rush of flames through a forest, and he told the man that his inhospitality had been his undoing. In another blink of an eye, Esh disappeared. The farmer lived a beggar from that day forward. Now, we dwarves are careful to give the most attentive care to strangers on the road, telling each other Esh might be among them."

Jasper nodded absently as the story finished. They were nearly at the farmhouse. He looked around and counted five children, from a little girl around age eight to a boy of about sixteen. The oldest boy was tall and kept glancing at Miss Marchand. Jasper stiffened. He'd have to keep an eye on the boy.

They stepped through the wooden door into the house, and Jasper was surprised at how roomy and comfortable it was inside. He looked for the farmer's wife and found her in the small kitchen, stirring a delicious-smelling stew. He inhaled gratefully. He'd tired of jerky, bread, and dried fruit two weeks ago. If nothing else, this stop would be worth it for the meal.

As he continued to look around, he found three doors branching off the living room. He wondered where the farmer planned for them all to sleep. Anywhere would be better than the ground they'd been laying on the last few nights.

Jasper took a seat at the table, next to Miss Marchand, and glanced over at her. She had her eyes directed across the table at the oldest son, who flashed her a flirtatious smile. What was with this kid? Miss Marchand smiled back, not exactly returning the sentiment, but her look was not discouraging either. Jasper bridled a sudden urge to round the table to reach the boy. He wasn't sure what he might have done had he gotten there, but either way, there was no need for that. Miss Marchand could fend for herself.

An hour later, everyone was still sitting cramped around the table conversing. Eruach's wife, whom Eruach had neglected to introduce, ladled generous portions of leek and potato stew. Jasper brought a small spoonful to his mouth with it still piping hot, and it was nearly impossible not to gulp down the rest. Maybe it was all the travel rations of late, but the stew tasted like it had come from the royal kitchens, even without any meat. He was about to accept a second helping when he noticed the rest of the pot's contents would just barely feed the family.

As dinner for the party drew to a close, Eruach lit the fireplace and motioned to four chairs cramped together near the flames. Jasper and the others made their way in that direction. Jasper heard a bit of whining as the youngest daughter was apparently denied a second bowl of stew. She looked thin for a dwarf. His own stomach pleasantly full, Jasper wondered how often the girl went to bed hungry. With King Cherev-ad dead, he wondered how many other dwarven children would do the same before Eshad steadied herself from her reeling. He sat holding the melancholy thought, only vaguely aware of when the family finished their dinner and joined the party near the fire.

It was Miss Marchand's voice that roused him. She was sitting some paces away at the edge of the group, but her tone was sharp and carried over the other conversations that had begun.

"And you are rather tall for a dwarf." Her words held distaste.

Jasper glanced next to her. The oldest child, the dwarf boy with the eyes for her, was seated hardly two feet from her. The boy was chuckling.

"I don't suppose you've fallen in love with a dwarf already?" he said.

Jasper cringed. Where had this boy learned to flirt? Suddenly he was less afraid for Miss Marchand. Rather, he felt sympathy for her. He'd never seen her around another boy, but somehow he knew the young dwarf had met more than his match in her. Jasper held back a tickled chuckle of his own as he turned his attention back to the boy and Miss Marchand.

Her eyes flashed as she returned, "I haven't, and neither do I intend to fall in love with anyone until my journey is complete."

The dwarf's eyes gentled, and his playful manner turned milder. Good. She'd put him in his place. He was quiet when he spoke again, and Jasper had to strain to hear his reply.

"I don't suppose you have much time for romance on the road. The interesting ones seem always to be too busy being interesting to settle down and bother with love." The dwarf's face fell, and he sounded sorrowful. Jasper almost felt bad for him. Almost.

"It's not that I have no interest. Really, all I lived for back home was to fall in love. Well, that and adventure."

Interesting. Miss Marchand, the boy chaser. She certainly didn't seem it to Jasper, even if she'd grown bolder around him over the past weeks. She'd never come remotely close to flirting with him.

The dwarf looked up at her. His eyes shone more softly than before. "Tell me about your home," he said.

Then Miss Marchand was peering back at the dwarf. "Well, I lived in the capital of Oerid. Agda. It's busy much of the time, people milling about, barely avoiding running into each other. Everyone goes about their business with little interest in anyone else. My father is a rather wealthy merchant, one of the wealthiest in fact." She paused, her eyes turned to the ground in seeming embarrassment, but quickly recovered. "It's not very interesting, really. For all the people around, I have no friends. No commoners are confident enough to engage my interest for all my riches, and nobles snub their noses at me for being a commoner."

Her forlorn sentiments sounded oddly familiar to Jasper, though it was his royalty that scared everyone away rather than his common-ness.

"I hated Agda," she declared forcefully after a moment, her emerald eyes aflame.

There was silence. She hated Agda? Jasper wasn't sure why the statement felt like a blow to his stomach. The way she'd explained it, she seemed embittered. Who was it that she resented? The nobles, from the sounds of it. Did she resent Agda's royalty as well? He didn't have time to think further as the boy replied.

"Whoever would reject you like that doesn't deserve your grace."

Miss Marchand shot the dwarf a suspicious look, but he just gazed back at her intently. Jasper watched in suspense. A moment passed with the two staring into each other's eyes, then something in the way she was sitting and looking at the dwarf changed, allayed, untethered. She looked suddenly vulnerable. And beautiful, very beautiful.

The dwarf's stance had changed too. He appeared possessive, downright proprietorial. All at once, he raised a hand to her cheek. He was going to kiss her.

Before Jasper knew he'd risen from his seat, he was across the room.

"I need to talk with you, Esther."

What in the name of Oer was he doing? At least he'd remembered her alias. Miss Marchand looked up at him. At first, she seemed like she would flee, then as though she wanted nothing more than to melt into the ground, then a spark of anger appeared and winked out. A mere second later, a mask of indignation hid it all. What had he done to her?

A moment later, they were in the kitchen with the table between them and everyone else. He stopped, and he turned to face her.

"We are not here to make romance," he whispered, trying to take a sharp tone when all of a sudden all he wanted to do was sink into the floor. Uncomfortable was not a strong enough term to describe his emotional state. He couldn't have let the boy kiss her, but this wasn't going as planned. Not that he'd had a plan. What had he done?

She looked down and muttered in a defensive tone, "I didn't start it."

"I don't care who started it."

He didn't care, he told himself. Then she glanced up at him, her eyes shining with tears, and he recognized some sort of pain in her face. He'd hurt her. Something inside him felt like it died. He couldn't do this.

"It's not that I thought you meant any flirtation," he tried to console her.

Suddenly, he realized he was holding her hand. She must have discovered it at the same time and jerked hers back. Her eyes turned down for a brief second.

"Is that all?" she asked without emotion.

Oer, what was wrong with him?

"Yes," was all he could manage to reply.

She met his gaze again. Though her look was dutiful, there was something defiant in the way she spun and strode back to the group. She chose a place between Cor and Kronk instead of returning to her previous seat. Jasper stared after her.

What in the name of the Light had just happened? His breaths were halting, and he was sure his face had flushed. He was thankful that no one was looking at him. She'd addled him to such a degree he was having a hard time standing up straight. The wounded look she'd given him still dizzied him. If he hadn't been so busy being appalled at himself, he might have mistaken himself as languishing over her. He tried to steady himself. That was lunacy.

He gave an emphatic shake of his head and marched over to rejoin the others. He made a point of joining an animated conversation between Malach and the farmer, Eruach. It was madness, Jasper repeated to himself. With great effort, he managed to immerse himself in idle chatting for the next hour until Eruach showed them to their rooms. The farmer put Cor and Malach in a room together, and Kronk and Miss Marchand in the largest bedroom, and finally Jasper in the smallest bedroom by himself. Thank Oer, Jasper wouldn't have to face anyone until sunrise.

CHAPTER 18

A ROOSTER CROWED, yet Kronk was still fast asleep. Ihva jostled the woman's shoulder, and soon enough Kronk was stretching with a loud yawn.

Ihva stepped out of the bedroom and saw Cor emerging from the room he'd shared with Malach. She smiled a greeting. Looking for their hosts, she found the farmer's wife in the kitchen stirring what looked like oatmeal. Ihva still didn't know her name, so she simply said, "Good morning, ma'am."

The farmer's wife looked up briefly and gave a polite nod. With nothing pressing on the agenda until the party gathered, Ihva sat in a chair at the table and watched for the others to emerge from their rooms. Cor sat down by the ashes of the fire and put on his boots. A door opened, and Ihva looked up to find the Prince looking directly at her. Her heart raced as she remembered the previous evening's conversation. She changed her expression to a frown to hide her confusion.

She was thankful a moment later when Malach came through the other door, loudly proclaiming, "And Oer's smile and Esh's blessing shine down on us another day."

Chuckles sounded throughout the room, though the Prince maintained his dark expression. Ihva tried not to see him. Soon, the party was eating a breakfast of porridge with honey and berries. The farmer and his children came through the front door in the middle of the meal, and between that and their wrinkled clothes and the bits of straw dangling off them, Ihva knew they'd slept in the barn. They were carrying provisions, for which Ihva prayed her gratitude to Oer. She saw wheels of cheese, cured meats, and some bread among other things. The family stood waiting silently while Kronk licked her bowl clean. Was the family going to eat? Ihva realized there was nothing left of the porridge and rubbed her stomach guiltily. The children looked more than hungry.

Cor stood first and thanked the family for their hospitality. He shook Eruach's hand and patted his back in a manly hug. Malach thanked them similarly and prayed Esh's blessing on them and their crops. The farmer seemed to relax at Malach's words. The Prince shook the farmer's hand after that but didn't say anything, and Ihva stood beside Kronk and thanked the farmer, gently nudging Kronk to follow. Kronk jumped, startled, and then proceeded to express profuse gratitude to the family.

Soon, the party was filing out of the farmhouse, packs on their backs newly stocked. The family followed to see them off. Ihva waved, then turned to follow Cor and Malach, but she felt someone gently tug at her hand. She looked back and saw the oldest son.

"Good travels to you, Esther," the boy said. "My name's Aaron, by the way."

Ihva thought she could sense the Prince glowering behind her. She stiffened. As much to spite him as due to her own feelings, she held Aaron's hands in her own and tried to formulate what she supposed would be a proper salutation.

"May the fires off Esh illuminate your way." With that, she smiled and turned to follow the others. She made a pointed effort not to look at the Prince. With the farewell behind them, the party strode along the path toward M'rawa.

The day passed, and Ihva was pleased to find herself less sore at the end of it. The next week or so was much the same way. On the fourth evening, though, something odd happened that split up the monotony.

Around twilight, they stopped to rest for the night. They'd decided to make a fire, and the flames seemed to brighten everyone's spirits. When Cor had finished his meal, he turned to Malach.

"Why don't we have some music, son?"

Malach produced the small flute and asked, "What shall it be? A jig, a pipesong...?"

"Let us have a pipesong," Cor replied, smiling.

Malach grinned, and the music began. A lively melody soon filled the air. Kronk stood and awkwardly hopped from foot to foot mostly in tempo, which made Ihva laugh. Across the fire, she caught the Prince's eye and was surprised to see a small smile on his face as well. He'd reverted to taciturn silence during their rapier lessons the past few mornings, but tonight he seemed to have relaxed a little. Ihva smiled back at him. She'd been worried the night at the farmhouse had ruined whatever semblance of friendship had been building between them, but now she wondered whether the camaraderie might be returning. She hoped so.

The music was so cheerful and vibrant she couldn't help but sway a bit in her seat. Without thinking, she began to hum along to the tune of the Traveler's Ditty Malach had switched to. Soon she was singing the words to herself:

The sun, it rises strong this morn,
As I don clothes I've already worn,
This not a day for me to mourn
For this is the road I travel.

The path's ahead, and I'll not tarry,
I'll only take what I can carry,
Today's the day when fears I bury,
For this is the road I travel.

Her voice tapered off. There were still more verses, but the flute had quieted, drawing the song to a close.

Applause split the air, and Ihva started clapping herself. Then she saw the others were looking at her, and Malach was clapping too. Her cheeks grew warm as she realized she'd been singing loud enough for the others to hear. What was she even singing about? Silly, childish ideas of adventure. She hid her face.

"This is lovely!" Cor exclaimed. "Let us have a reel next!"

"If I play a dance, we must have dancers," Malach replied.

He turned his gaze to Ihva and grinned. There was something knowing about his smile that put Ihva on edge.

"Someone dance with the lass," he demanded.

"I am afraid I have little practice dancing. Very few Oeridian women desire to dance with someone a head shorter than them," came Cor's reply as he chuckled. "His Highness, on the other hand, has studied dance." He looked at Jasper with a glint of merriment in his eyes.

"Oh ho, then our Prince it is!" Malach exclaimed. He rose, strolled over to the Prince, and pulled him up by the arm.

The Prince struggled a bit but gave in, most probably to maintain his royal dignity. Ihva grew nervous. Of course, she knew how to dance, at least well enough to follow a man's lead. However, to dance with the Prince... She struggled against the confused feelings bubbling up inside.

Yet, a few moments later, she found herself standing face to face with the Prince. As Malach began a reel in a minor key, the Prince and Ihva circled each other in frigid solemnity, each looking past the other into the shadows capering outside the fire's light. The Prince closed with Ihva and clasped her hands with an awkward grip, still refusing to look her in the eye. His feet shifted beneath him, and as abrupt as the way they'd been pushed together, Ihva found they were dancing. The Prince looked stiff to her, though he had perfect form. Ihva moved in time as well.

The reel picked up speed. Ihva glanced down and watched her feet. She found herself more graceful when she took her eyes off the Prince and his passionless motions. She followed his movements out of the corner of her eye, and her own grew livelier as the song continued. The strain of the music moved something within her, and her heart swelled. Enthralled with the melody and the movements, she forgot to keep her eyes down. She caught the Prince's gaze.

His grim expression had morphed into a look of concentrated enjoyment. Indeed, Ihva thought she saw the corners of his mouth turn up slightly, if only for a split second. As her eyes met his, though, his steps faltered. He recovered but seemed a bit frantic as he started circling her at a faster pace. She gave him a small smile and almost missed a step when he smiled back. He was rather handsome when he smiled.

They continued around the fire for some time. Ihva was surprised when the Prince took her hand into the air to twirl her. Then, taking both her hands more firmly, he dropped his stiff manner. He led her in more complex patterns, and she didn't miss a beat. Sharing his gaze thrilled her, and she realized the dancing was not the only reason her heart beat fast. Caught in the moment, she didn't care to wonder what it meant. It was enough to rest in the pocket of joy they'd found in a strenuous and fearful journey.

Too soon, the crackling of the fire filtered with the echoes of the song's last notes. Ihva spun around, laughing. She looked at the Prince and grinned as the others clapped their enjoyment. He looked back at her and smiled for a moment, then a distracted frown overtook his face. Ihva quieted her laughter and sat back down at her place by the fire, listening to Malach's melodies. Her heart was still pounding, but she refused to decipher its significance. Even after Malach had put the flute away and the party laid down by the fire, Ihva's head was filled with song, and she drifted off to sleep.

CHAPTER 19

THIS WAS RIDICULOUS. Absolutely downright ridiculous, Jasper fumed as he led the group through the forest. The girl wouldn't leave his mind. Miss Ihva Marchand, he seethed. For the love of Oer, go away!

She'd struck him four times that morning. With the rapier, that was. Even if she was improving, four times was excessive. He'd been distracted trying not to look her in the face, but that was no way to fight. You had to look at your opponent's face. Even novices knew that. He cursed himself.

He had to pull it together. He couldn't waste precious time and energy worrying about a girl, definitely not this much time and energy. There were so many things wrong with this situation and too much at stake for his attention to be diverted. There was too much that could go awry.

He hoped the others didn't realize he was stomping. No one could see his scowl, since he was at the front, but his posture no doubt gave away his mood. He'd avoided Miss Marchand the rest of the morning since the moment their lesson had ended. Still, no one could have guessed the reason for his demeanor, at least he hoped.

He drew in a deep breath. Calm down. Nothing had actually gone wrong. In fact, they were rather fortunate. They'd made it to the lush forests of M'rawa just a week and a half after they'd left the farm and without interference. It was almost as if no one was coming after them, but that couldn't be it.

Yet there was still so much to lose. Jessica was out there, somewhere, in who-knows-what state, and with her fled his salvation-Oerid's salvation. With Lady Cibelle, the kingdom would rise or fall, and it was all because of him. He balled his fist. If only there was some other way, any other way. But there wasn't, and he knew it. He had to find Jessica.

His pace slowed as he wondered about the woman. His fiancee, his betrothed. He ought to have been feeling something, he knew. He did feel something-protective. And affectionate. He was fond of Jessica. She was devoted and doting, even if not the most soft-hearted toward those around her. She did show sympathy toward him, though, and was always concerned and attentive in their conversations. She seemed to remember every detail of things, every word he'd spoken. It was kind of disconcerting. But no matter, he loved her, and he would marry her, and that was that, but first he had to locate her.

Which brought him back around to another worry-what was his plan once they did find her? Other than marrying her, of course. How could he protect her when she was to steal from the goddess of Hell herself? He considered heading straight to the Shadowed Realm once they found Jessica so they might catch Hell's Mistress off-guard. It was clear she meant to steal Jessica for herself, and Jasper with her, but certainly she'd expect them to return to the safety of Oerid once he'd retrieved his betrothed. The Lady of Shadows would not expect them to strike so soon. But what if that was her scheme in the first place? Dejected, Jasper mulled for a while, unaware of anything around him.

After some time, Malach's voice broke Jasper from his thoughts as the dwarf asked in frustration, "Where are we?"

Jasper looked around. The forest was dense and particularly green and almost lifted his spirits. Green was his favorite color, after all, and it was present in all shades in the foliage surrounding them. Large, exotic insects buzzed by with wings as wide as the length of Jasper's hand. Jasper was glad they didn't seem the biting kind, though he still batted at them when they came too close. Bright flowers of all colors-sun-yellow, crimson, sky blue, burnt orange-dotted the scene as well and added vibrancy to the verdant backdrop. It was damp in the forest, and strands of Jasper's hair were sticking to his neck. He wiped sweat from the side of his face.

"Seriously, where are we?" Malach moaned.

"We don't have a map, Malach, so I can't show you, but we're in M'rawa," Jasper shot back with impatience.

Jasper was supposed to be tracking, searching for Jessica's trail or any trail really and following it. He didn't want to admit to the others there was no trail. Instead, he was heading toward the center of M'rawa, where the elvish capital was located, or at least so he'd heard. One couldn't call it a capital, though, really. The elves were comprised of large bands in a decentralized network of tribes, and they dwelt in settlements built in the trees. Jasper had never visited M'rawa as he'd never had occasion to, but the few transplanted elves he'd met had spoken of a towering metropolis in the heart of the country, so that was where he was heading. He was certain Cor didn't know any more than he did, or he'd have asked.

"It so hot!" Kronk whined.

It was hot. Jasper preferred cooler temperatures himself, and the heat here was stifling, but what use was complaining about it?

"Kronk hungry! Kronk tired! Kronk need water!" Kronk was losing it.

"Shush, Kronk," came Miss Marchand's voice, sounding at least a little annoyed. That wasn't like her. The difficult forest path was getting to them all.

Jasper continued to pick his way through the trees, weaving in and out, as the argument behind him escalated.

"Ihva have water! Ihva give Kronk water!"

"What'd you do with yours, Kronk?"

"Kronk was thirsty. All gone now."

Miss Marchand sighed. "Fine, have mine, but leave me some."

Miss Marchand was right to conserve water. Despite the humidity, finding more of it would be difficult. They'd passed a few streams along the way, but if they wanted water in between, they'd have to collect if off leaves, which would take more time than they could afford.

"Perhaps we ought to take a short rest, drink a little and take some rations," Cor said calmly. Did the dwarf never fluster?

"Fine," was Jasper's response. It came out more curt than he'd intended, but he couldn't be bothered to soften it by adding anything else.

They stopped in a small clearing, and Jasper gave a slight glare to no one in particular as more drops of sweat streamed down his forehead. He wiped them away. The greens here really were nice. They even included the deep shade of beryl he found most appealing. It was the color of emeralds and of Bradinholt, a region in the southeast of Oerid. Jasper's gaze wandered and found Miss Marchand looking at him. And of her eyes. It was the color of her eyes. How could he forget Ihva Marchand's eyes, deep and fathomless? They were a part of why'd he'd avoided looking at her the past week and a half. Disgusted with himself, he stood and strode to the edge of the clearing, pretending to inspect the ground and plant-life there.

At first all he saw were the same old ferns and bright flowers he'd become accustomed to. These flowers were crimson with butter-colored tips and bright orange strands bursting from the center. They dangled on their stems like bells. It took Jasper a second to notice that the flowers were crumpled and wilting. He looked again. The ferns around them were crushed as well. Someone had been this way.

"Someone's been through here," he said in a loud voice, glancing back at the others.

Malach's gaze drew his eyes first. The dwarf looked confused. "Yeah," he said. "Someone's been through everywhere we've been going, I assumed?"

Oh, right. Jasper was supposed to have been tracking. "Look at this," he replied instead of trying to explain. He waved the others over, and they came.

They peered at the place where Jasper was pointing, and he looked again at the mess of broken stems and drooping flowers. He felt foolish. It really should have been nothing to comment on. He stared on, though, to allay suspicions, especially Malach's.

They'd been standing there a moment when something caught Jasper's eye. A faint white light appeared, and the ferns and flowers were changing in some almost imperceptible way. The morphing quickened, and Jasper watched as the stems slowly came unbent and the petals smoothed from their wrinkled drooping. The ferns regained their life and pliable bounce. They'd been Healed.

Jasper looked at Cor. The dwarf was sentimental in some ways, but Jasper didn't know him to have a particular affection for flowers. He was a dwarf at heart, and though he'd adopted the Oeridian religion in which all life was sacred, he'd never demonstrated a particular interest in plant-life. Aside from that, though, he'd just ruined the one clue Jasper had for a heading. About to comment, Jasper opened his mouth, but the words never departed his lips as he watched the dwarf. Cor's eyes were wide and his mouth slightly agape. He hadn't been the one to Heal them.

What had happened then? Jasper followed Cor's gaze, but instead of returning to the foliage, it landed on Miss Marchand. She had a subtle, concentrated look about her and seemed unaware of anyone around her. Her eyes focused on the flowers, and after a moment, her mouth crimped in a self-conscious smile. Had she been the one?

"The mystery goes deeper, it seems," Cor said softly.

Miss Marchand's eyes widened and darted to Cor. "I didn't," she started.

"You did indeed," Cor interrupted.

She shook her head as though to ward off his words. Jasper couldn't blame her. The whole thing was very strange and a bit off-putting. She had no Power, yet she'd Healed. Why was Oer blessing her with such abilities when she hadn't made the Exchange? No one received magic without the Exchange, not even the King of Oerid, thought he was known as Oer's Chosen Son. Something didn't add up.

"I didn't mean to," Miss Marchand said quietly.

"No one is upset with you, Ihva," Cor replied.

That was true. Jasper was not upset, just bewildered. She'd Healed.

"This explains how you were Healed before," Cor went on. "It was not only my doing, Ihva. Your own magic merged with mine. From how badly you were injured and how well you recovered, I suspect your abilities run deeper than my own, much deeper."

Her expression was a mixture of awe and dismay. "How?" she stammered.

Cor gave her a steady look. "You are Oer's Blessing, Ihva."

Somehow, the idea sounded less preposterous than it had back in Agda, and that frightened Jasper. Could Oer be blessing Ihva Marchand because she was, in fact, his Blessing? Jasper shivered despite the heat.

Miss Marchand was staring at Cor, her eyes big and pleading.

"Not everything you have heard about the Blessing is true, Ihva," Cor said.

She didn't say anything. Cor was about to speak when something whizzed past Jasper's ear and buried itself in the tree. Another whizzing, and a crossbow bolt was sticking in Cor's leg just above the knee. The dwarf kept his eyes on Miss Marchand as he fell to the ground. Bolts began to shower the party from above.

Jasper drew his rapier and faced the trees where the bolts had originated. He struck a few of them out of the air, but it wasn't enough. Just seconds later, a bolt found itself in his calf, then he was on the ground. Falling unconscious was a lot like how he imagined it felt to bleed out-he was helpless, absolutely helpless, then everything went black.

CHAPTER 20

AS IHVA'S EYES ADJUSTED, she found herself suspended between two creatures. From the way they were carrying her, she figured they walked on two feet. She opened her eyes but could see nothing but a vague, filtered light. They must have blindfolded her. She listened and began to hear quiet voices.

"The big, bulgy one is waking up," said one voice.

"The orc, you mean?" came the voice beneath Ihva.

"Half-orc, I think, but yes," the first voice beside Ihva replied.

"What if it tries to eat us?" the second voice squeaked.

"It won't," the first voice said, which began to distinguish itself as female. Her words sounded a little unsteady, and Ihva wondered what they really would do if Kronk were to attack.

"Shhh. It might hear you!" the second voice cautioned, a female as well from the sound of it.

"I'm pretty sure orcs can't understand Common, but we can speak the Ancient Tongue if you'd like," the first voice whispered.

"You said it's a half-orc."

Ihva didn't understand anything else after that, as they switched to another language, the Ancient Tongue, as the one had called. That was the elves' name for the language only they understood, an older language, wasn't it? Elves had captured them, then. At least they'd found the elves. The elves could help, surely.

She tried to remember where they'd been when they'd been taken. Pursuing Lady Cibelle, of course, the Prince's betrothed. Ihva had never give much thought to the Prince's chase, she realized. She'd taken it for granted. When a maiden was captured, the young knight, or young prince in this case, went after her to save her. He would brave danger and intrigue to find her, and he wouldn't stop until he brought her back and married her. It was in every fairy tale she'd ever heard. Of course, the Prince was pursuing Lady Cibelle. Of course, he was.

The memories trickled back into Ihva's mind. They'd been seeking Lady Cibelle, and the Prince had found a trail, some broken ferns and crushed flowers. Then Ihva had Healed them. She, Ihva Marie Marchand, had Healed without a Power to speak of, without any right to magic at all, much less to Oer's favored ability. Was Cor right? She'd pushed the notion out of her head for so long, but now it assaulted the whole of her consciousness. Could she be the bearer of the world's catastrophe? Could she be the carrier of disaster to Gant and to everything around her? Surely not. Surely not!

Ihva's captors came to a sudden halt. The next thing she knew, they set her gently on the ground, unbound her, and removed her blindfold.

Green-tinted light flooded her eyes. She was in a clearing, staring up at a forest canopy, which towered hundreds of feet overhead. Lower to the ground were platforms connected by ladders, and rope bridges spanned the clearing in every direction. Color blossomed everywhere-yellows and blues and pinks and reds and oranges in all the flora surrounding them-but as much as they thrilled her, it wasn't the colors that captivated Ihva. It was the elves. They tread the bridges, graceful and elegant, and wore loose clothing of various greens and browns. Ihva couldn't make out individual faces from as far away as she was, but she detected a luminosity about them. They'd found the elves!

Remembering the others, Ihva glanced around for them. To her left, she spotted Kronk and Cor, and to the right the Prince and Malach. They were at various stages of consciousness. Before Ihva could speak to them, though, a small being came into view, an elf. It had an effeminate face with soft features and dainty, pointed ears. She (Ihva thought she must be a girl, and seeing the pale green shift the girl wore over her breeches, realized she was right) looked at Ihva curiously with her blue eyes and asked in Common, "Are you hungry?"

Ihva's stomach felt worse than empty.

"Very much so," she replied.

The young elf nodded, then held out a hand to help Ihva stand. Once she was on her feet, she found herself following the girl to the base of a tree where a ladder hung to the ground.

"My name is Linara," the elf said as she climbed the ladder, motioning for Ihva to follow.

Ihva looked back at the rest of the party and saw that they were getting up and finding their balance. Cor was bowing to the young male elf that stood before him, and the Prince was busy dusting himself off. Malach's purple hat had fallen to the ground, but he snatched it quickly and refit it snug on his head. For a split second, he looked around as though nervous, but the look was so fleeting Ihva wasn't sure she'd seen it in the first place. Kronk must have just stood up as she was wobbling a little. A young girl elf said something to her, and she jumped, then stared at the elf, wide-eyed. The elf spoke again, and Kronk visibly relaxed, which allowed Ihva to relax, too. It was Kronk she'd been worried about. Satisfied the others were okay, Ihva turned and followed Linara up the ladder.

When she reached the top, she found a platform supported by intersecting tree branches, the floor woven of huge, waxy leaves. As she pulled herself up, she found a large cloth laid out on the floor with delectable-looking treats. Ihva walked over and, seeing Linara sitting cross-legged before the beautiful spread, bent her knees and sat cross-legged herself beneath her flowing skirts.

She looked at the wide array of foods before her. There were bowls with broths and leaves floating inside as well as breads of all kinds sliced and laid out on leaves. Fruits spilled out of a horn made of greenery, and vegetables covered the spread, arranged with a sense of artistry. Not wanting to disturb the beauty and colors, Ihva hesitated. Eventually, Linara handed her a piece of dark, nutty bread.

Kronk came stumbling up onto the platform. Uncoordinated, her eyes darted back and forth as she walked on the swaying branches. After a few fearful steps, she knelt down and crawled over to the tablecloth. Malach came behind, attempting to maintain dignity, though he looked uncomfortable being that far above the ground, as he kept glancing down. Cor looked similarly uneasy. Last, the Prince appeared, graceful as ever, and took a seat between Cor and Malach.

The rest of the party followed Ihva's example and began to eat. The foreign setting must have made Kronk forget her table manners, as she scooped up a quarter of a loaf of bread and drained a bowl of soup in seconds. Ihva couldn't blame her-she herself hadn't had a full belly since the night on the dwarven farm. Still, she caught Kronk's eye and motioned for her to slow down.

Meanwhile, Malach looked almost refined, taking fastidious bites of the fruit he held. Cor was concentrating hard on the spoon in his hand. He must have been thinking about something. They were all eating well, though, except the Prince, who nibbled here and there, just enough to be polite. His brow was furrowed, and he had that small look about him again. Ihva knew she didn't understand everything that plagued him, but a profound sympathy swelled in her, and she was surprised to find that she wanted nothing more than to comfort him. A desire to take his hand and speak soothing words subdued her for a moment, though she had no idea what consoling thing she could say. With the impulse came a tingling throughout her body, a very unusual experience.

The Prince glanced over at her while she was reflecting, catching her eye. He must not have realized she'd been looking at him as surprise flashed on his face. Ihva's gaze didn't waver though, and she continued to wonder at what she was feeling. The Prince appeared transfixed as well. He looked ill at ease, and a moment later, his mouth quirked, and something oddly unguarded filled his eyes. Ihva froze. The tingling intensified, but the desire to comfort became the impulse to flee. Instead she blinked and looked down.

Why was she nervous all of sudden? Flustered even. Searching for something else to focus on, she looked around for Linara. She didn't find the girl but did spot another elf watching them from a branch slightly elevated above the platform. It was a male, Ihva could tell, because it had on tawny pants and a cream top instead of the short sage dress with generous sleeves that Linara had been wearing. How she remembered all the details of Linara's outfit, Ihva didn't know. She blamed Kronk's fashion awareness rubbing off on her, and chuckled to herself, releasing a tension she wished she hadn't felt in the first place. Not that it mattered. She went back to studying the young male elf.

Each of them, the male and Linara, had the same amount of straight, blond hair. Ihva remembered Linara's hair had been plaited along the sides of her head into an intricate bun at the back of her head.

The male elf broke into Ihva's recollection as he addressed the party. He spoke in a soft voice that nonetheless commanded attention. "Welcome to you all. Welcome to M'rawa to the city of Rinhaven. May Rawa bless you in the night. I am sure you have many questions, and our elders would be pleased to answer them now that you have had some sustenance. If you would accompany me." He climbed up another short ladder to a larger platform above them.

Ihva stood and followed the others as they ascended. When she reached the second platform, she found herself facing a number of elves with solemn looks on their faces. They all looked older than Linara and the male elf who'd led the party there. Ihva counted seven, both male and female, sitting cross-legged before the party. They wore long gowns and robes and their skin, still soft and smooth, didn't give away their agedness. Only the gray in their hair betrayed that.

"Welcome, friends," the male elf in the center said. "I am Laithor, High Elf and head of this council."

"Greetings to you all, by Oer's Light." It was the Prince who spoke.

"We shall begin with your names," Laithor said. His voice was tranquil and reminded Ihva of rain upon leaves.

"I am Jasper Aurdor, Prince of Oerid," the Prince began, then paused.

If Laithor was at all surprised, he didn't show it. The only gesture he offered was to rise alongside the other council members and incline his head respectfully. As the Council sat back down, the Prince went on.

"And this is Cor Leviel Gidfolk, the Emissary and Advisor to Oerid's King."

Laithor dipped his head at Cor in acknowledgement.

"This is Miss Ihva Marchand of Calilla."

Laithor's eyes moved to Ihva and he nodded at her.

"And Kronk of Deepgrove."

He'd remembered Kronk's hometown. Ihva hadn't realized he'd been paying that close attention.

The Prince glanced at Malach, and instantly Ihva recognized his dilemma. Malach had said nothing more to introduce himself since they'd fled the palace. He had no surname to their knowledge. Ihva looked at Malach, but his eyes were on Cor, who nodded. Then Malach drew himself up, took a breath, and spoke.

"I am Malach Lam Shemayim, son of King Cherev-ad of Eshad." His eyes darted to the Prince, then settled back on Laithor. "I have claim to the throne which has recently been vacated by my father in his death, may he rest in the halls of Esh."

Malach paused to take another breath, and Ihva's jaw dropped. Malach was the Prince of Eshad?

CHAPTER 21

JASPER WATCHED as Malach retrieved the raggedy hat from atop his head and pulled out something sewn into the inside. Jasper was close enough to see it was a signet ring. Malach held it up. It had a seal, presumably the royal seal of Eshad.

"Forgive me," Malach said, looking at Jasper.

Jasper just gaped.

"Yet you are no dwarf," a female elf to the right of Laithor said.

Really now? Of course, Malach, Prince Malach, was a dwarf.

"It is true. Only my father was a dwarf," Malach answered. "About thirty years ago, my father fell in love with a beautiful maiden while he was taking holiday in Genna in Oerid. Her name was Isolia, and she was as beautiful as the sun is bright, but she was a human noblewoman, and low-ranking, passed over by many men in their search for wives."

A human mother would explain Malach's height, of course.

"My father returned to Eshad and requested the High Counselor to put before the Council of Neved to allow him to marry her and make her Queen. It was not only for love's sake but also to sow peace between the kingdoms. At the time, though there was no war, there was a level of animosity between Eshad and Oerid, a certain, well, mutual envy of a sort."

Jasper nodded at the last statement. Father had spoken of a time when relations between Oerid and Eshad were not entirely friendly.

"But to continue my tale, the High Counselor refused, and without his support, my father knew the Council would surely refuse as well.

My father was devastated, and he decided to marry his love in secret. He reasoned the concealment could be broken, when the time was right, and his pursuit of peace would see itself through. My mother agreed.

"They required a man with ties to both kingdoms to officiate. The lovers conferred and chose a dwarf born in Eshad named Cor Gidfolk, who was advised the king of Oerid.. I must note the irony that their confidence in Master Gidfolk ended up improving relations between the two nations. Their trust in him and his own uprightness eased communication between Eshad and Oerid. Their marriage indeed sowed peace before an heir was ever born."

Malach looked at Cor briefly with a smile. Jasper could hardly believe he'd missed the relationship between the two. He'd known they recognized each other, but even he'd not understood the level of familiarity between them. He'd missed the history there, figured it had something to do with their common dwarvenness. Their shared glances from the past two weeks made more sense. Had Jasper been that distracted?

"Cherev-ad and Isolia were married, and my father protected his new wife from the Council and from the Eshadian people in a remote winter palace. He visited her as often as he could find legitimate excuse to travel there. During one visit my father made to my mother, she conceived. She bore a son, and my parents named their child Malach, gifted from heaven to their loving hearts.

"Always aware of my father's whereabouts, the High Counselor grew suspicious at his many days spent in the winter palace. When I was in my fourth year, a small company of spies and assassins followed my father there. The High Counselor had sent them, we know now. This was before Arusha visited the Shrieking Summit. He followed Esh then, but with stringence and cruelty. He did not approve of my mother's humanness. My father was playing with me out in the garden while my mother watched from the window. I remember her laughter in the distance. Then her laughter turned to screams, and a moment later, she quieted. My father ran to her, but he was too late. She was gone."

Malach stopped, eyes shining. Jasper saw uncertainty flicker in his face, then he continued with mustered steadiness in his voice.

"He did not remarry. Dwarves only ever marry once, and he would not profane her memory like that. He brought me to the palace in Irgdol after a time and had me trained as a court bard, giving me reason to remain close to the throne. He confided his strategies and plans to me in midnight lessons. He had no other children, no one but myself to take the mantle he wore.

"So, indeed, I am only half-dwarven, but I am nonetheless heir to the Eshadian throne. As hard as I have studied my instruments and ballads, I have studied the governing of Eshad with twice the devotion. There are none whose mind knows the things of Eshad like mine and none whose heart belongs to Esh and his kingdom like my own."

Malach finished and bowed his head with respect toward the elvish council. His expression was uncharacteristically subdued as he awaited the elves' response.

Laithor stood and bowed his head. The rest of the council members followed in rising to their feet and remained standing for a moment. Malach looked up, eyes widened a little, even as the council sat back down. The female elf who had addressed Malach earlier spoke again.

"Your dignity indeed is reminiscent of the posture of Eshadian royalty. As for us, we offer you the respect we would give a sovereign of any nation. What aid do you seek of us?"

Malach dignified? Jasper remembered the dwarf's jig as he'd played what he'd called Rayon-Rai on his silvered flute, a variation on a tune Jasper knew by some other name he couldn't recall. It definitely wasn't Rayon-Rai, though, something more Oeridian. Anyway, the Malach Jasper had known up to this point was spirited and light-hearted, teasing even, but not dignified. At least, Jasper hadn't believed so, but as he looked at Malach, he recognized a certain submission in him, a yielding to something higher as though he carried a weight far heavier than he could hope to bear. Jasper recognized it because he knew it. It was his burden, too, after all. Jasper broke from his thoughts as he heard Malach speak again.

"I require assistance in claiming the throne of Eshad. I have very few allies among my people. By now, Arusha has likely claimed the throne himself or stationed one of his puppets there. I regret to inform you; he is building an army of Shadow-Raised. He will soon become a threat to more than just my own nation."

Some of the younger-looking elves jerked slightly at the mention of Raised beings while the others furrowed their brows. Jasper himself felt fear wash over him, though he'd known about the army already. Hearing of the Raised did that to him. It'd do that to anyone, he assumed, but most especially to him.

"We will discuss it," Laithor promised. "You will not go unaided to retake what is your own." He gave Malach a steady look, then turned to Jasper. "I presume you have come for your own reasons, Prince of Oerid."

All eyes moved to Jasper.

"Indeed, I have. I seek a woman." He paused. Cor would tell him to be open, he knew, so he went on. "Lady Jessica Cibelle of Hestia."

Jasper tried to justify his forthrightness to himself. The elves seemed to know things, many things. They'd known Jasper and the others were coming, for example, and it wouldn't surprise Jasper if they'd known the group's identities beforehand as well, though he had no idea how they might have gained that information.

"Lady Jessica Selene Cibelle. Beautiful by human standards, I have been told. Flowing dark hair and dark eyes like your own. Dwarves were chasing her into Rawa's forest, if I am not mistaken," Laithor said.

"Yes, that is correct."

Laithor had known about her. He must have known her whereabouts as well, then. Jasper fought to maintain a calm demeanor and asked simply, "Do you know where she is?"

"She fled into elvish lands, it is true, but then she turned toward Jinad. Her decision surprised our scouts. Perhaps she intended to escape to a place where no dwarf has set foot in hundreds of years. Indeed, dwarves do not dare take a step onto Jinadian soil even in Alm'adinat. Similarly, we dared not track this Jessica past the border,"

Laithor answered, but Jasper couldn't determine if the slight edge to the elf's voice was more reproach or unease.

The elves wouldn't pursue her, then. Of course, they wouldn't. They had no need for the young noblewoman, not like he did. Still, he realized he'd hoped she was with them. He'd been counting on their chase ending soon. Now it seemed it had only just begun. She'd headed toward Jinad? That made no sense, unless perhaps she was hoping to find a dwarven ship in Alm'adinat and use it to travel back to Oerid. Could that be it?

Laithor was looking at him. He needed to answer the elf. He'd have to tell Laithor he planned to pursue Jessica, and sooner rather than later.

"Perhaps you will not pursue Lady Cibelle into Jinad, but I will," Jasper replied, his words coming out terser than he'd intended. "I must," he added in a quieter voice.

"We did not say that we would not aid you, only that we will not send our people into such danger as Jinad presents. We do have other methods of assistance."

Interesting. Maybe Laithor could provide an escort through the forest, or at least supplies. Either one would be more helpful than Jasper cared to admit.

"In return, however, we must lay down our own request for your consideration," Laithor went on.

The elves needed something? They'd proven themselves self-sufficient through the years, never sending to Oerid for aid. If anything, it was Oerid that sent for the elves, for their wisdom.

"What assistance can we provide the Children of Rawa?" Jasper asked, curious but cautious.

"There is a Horn we possess. It calls on the power of the goddess of the Moon when sounded. We will need you to retrieve it."

A mission to seek and find an artifact. Interesting. Jasper wondered just how much information the elves had concerning the Horn's location.

"I take it you will need us to find it," he ventured.

Laithor looked at him seriously. "No, we know where it is. We may only journey to retrieve it at specific times."

Jasper frowned as he replied. "And how soon might we make that journey?"

"A fortnight from now is the accepted time. If you recover the Horn, our knowledge and gifts will be at your disposal."

A fortnight! Jessica could be anywhere by then! But Laithor wasn't finished.

"I must apprise you, there is a member of your company who would do well to remain until the Horn is retrieved. Only the bearer of the Horn may wield Darkslayer, and the End of the Age requires he be wielded. Without Darkslayer in the hand of the Appointed, the cycle will only persist."

Laithor's face was inscrutable. What was Darkslayer? Some sort of weapon, clearly. And the Appointed? Jasper had a sinking feeling he knew where this was going. The elves were as bad as Cor. Jasper hoped none that of the others had caught on, though he was certain that Cor understood. Just let Laithor not tell Miss Marchand what he was implying.

Thankfully, Laithor chose not to explain himself. Instead, he simply stood. "We will await your decision."

The rest of the Council got up as well. The meeting was over. Jasper stood and nodded his head at Laithor and the other elves, but his thoughts were churning, and he was only half-conscious of descending the ladder to the ground.

His mind went to Jessica. Two weeks! Fourteen days, and they had to be already a week or more behind her. There was no way. Especially if all they were waiting on was some weapon. Miss Marchand had a weapon already, a perfectly acceptable sword, and she was learning to use it with greater strength and dexterity every day. Besides, if she really was Oer's Blessing, arming her was the last thing they wanted to do. The very last thing.

But she wasn't. She'd been learning swordplay with miraculous speed, and she'd Healed, and she might even have Read the Prophecy, but there was no way Miss Marchand with the deep green eyes was fated to destroy Gant. She was much too endearing to be the catastrophe the world had been awaiting with bated breath.

He saw the others were looking at him, and he realized Cor had been telling him something.

"Sorry, I was thinking about something else," he said.

Something else, indeed. He found himself a touch breathless. He really had to stop this.

CHAPTER 22

IHVA WAS WATCHING the Prince as Cor addressed him.

"I was simply saying we have much to discuss, but perhaps it would be better to consider the matters tonight on our own and confer for a decision tomorrow."

All of a sudden, the Prince looked very focused on what the dwarf was saying, though he didn't respond. Prince Jasper didn't, that was. They had another prince in their midst, Ihva reminded herself. Prince Malach. That sounded so strange.

Cor waved a hand at the ground. "On the other hand, we might discuss our decision tonight."

Ihva didn't wait for the others to sit to do so herself. The sun had gone down, she realized, as the light was no longer green coming through the trees. Instead, dim rays shone forth in all sorts of bright colors. Ihva looked closer. The light was coming from the bodies of insects floating in the cool evening air.

"Under normal circumstances, the decision would be yours, Highness, but there is another among us whose judgment carries as much weight as your own."

Suddenly, Cor had become very formal with Prince Jasper. Maybe he was afraid of the Prince's response to what they'd just learned. Cor had known the entire time who Malach was and hadn't mentioned it. Ihva knew he'd only been protecting Malach, but she still felt a small jab of betrayal. She remembered Malach had requested the elves' aid. Did that mean they were about to lose a member of their company?

"Stop it, Cor," Prince Jasper said, his voice strained with impatience.

Cor just gave the Prince as dutiful a look as Ihva had ever seen in him.

"Stop," the Prince repeated, more frustrated this time. "There's enough going on without you becoming suddenly obsequious, Cor. And don't think your servility will convince me of your hypothesis. We need to find Jessica. That is of first importance. We don't have time for their quest. That is my decision."

Cor straightened, and his tone became as commanding as the Prince's, maybe more so. "Do not be so blinded by duty to Oerid you let Gant fall in the process, Jasper."

The Prince's eyes flashed defiance at the dwarf. Time slowed as the two stared at each other, and Ihva held her breath. She realized she didn't exactly know what they were talking about. About her, she realized, with all that about Gant falling "in the process." But what was the Prince's duty to Oerid? Ihva thought he was going after Lady Cibelle because of, well, Lady Cibelle. She guessed marrying his betrothed could be construed as "duty to Oerid," kind of.

"Fine. I'll think on it," the Prince finally replied, his voice hard.

He and the dwarf stared at each other for another moment until Malach spoke up. Prince Malach.

"Right," he said. "On that note, maybe we should get some sleep."

No one replied, so he glanced around, then changed subjects, his voice serious for once.

"It seems we have a few notable individuals among us." He turned to Ihva. "You are more extraordinary than you let on, lass." He smiled at her and added, "Welcome to the club."

She didn't know what to say, so she just gave the lame reply, "Thank you, Your Highness."

He burst out in roaring laughter, and she jumped. After a moment, he settled and said, "Now, now. None of this, 'Highness' and 'Prince' business. I'm not used to it, and I don't know that I'm ready for it. Besides, I'm below eye level for you, nothing high about me."

Ihva couldn't help laughing, too, as relieved as she was tickled. "Only by a few inches," she told him.

He grinned and winked at her.

"Malach is right, though. We must get some sleep," Cor said.

Malach smiled at Ihva again, then turned to look for a place to lay down. As he was searching, an elf approached him and asked him a question. He glanced up into the trees, then shook his head, and the elf nodded and slipped away.

Ihva looked at the others. Cor was watching Prince Jasper. Though seeing as Malach didn't want any titles, she could call Prince Jasper just "the Prince" again, she realized. The Prince had a distant look about him, his eyes gazing out among the trees but likely seeing nothing. He didn't look small this time, but then, he didn't appear nervous either. More determined. Apprehension gripped Ihva for a moment until someone tugged on her sleeve. It was Kronk, looking to her for direction. Ihva shook her head and followed Malach, motioning for Kronk to come with her.

As she was falling asleep that night, she wondered about Malach some more. Would he leave them to try to reclaim his throne then? Part of her realized, was certain, though she could not explain her confidence, that he wouldn't leave. The thought comforted her. Malach had become a crucial presence. His music and stories and jesting brought a smile to her face even when everything else seemed tedious and dull. He broke the tension in the party, especially between the Prince and Cor. Ihva wondered how the Prince's relationship with Malach might change now that he realized Malach was his equal. He'd always respected Malach, but maybe he'd give the dwarf's comments more weight now. If Malach started making comments worth giving weight to, that was. Something told Ihva he would.

Her thoughts turned back to the party's original intent. Lady Cibelle was heading toward Jinad. Ihva shivered at the thought of going there, too. However, much parents described the Shadow-sworn and the Shrouded as menacing and horrid to their children, they only mentioned the Jini in hushed tones with a terror reserved for Hell itself.

Ihva cared to go home, and a journey leading into Jinad seemed it would accomplish the opposite.

She dozed off remembering again she hadn't told her parents where she was going. They'd never approve if they knew what had happened even thus far. Tell them she was heading to Jinad and they might have chained her to her bed until she was old maid, at the very least. At the very least.

———◆◆◆———

The next morning, Ihva woke to harsh whispers, not angry but unyielding. Cor and the Prince were arguing.

"You know it's impossible without her, Cor. Oerid will fall as surely as I stand before you if she is recaptured before we can find her."

"Gant will fall without this Darkslayer, Jasper. You will have no Oerid left to defend if you neglect this."

"We don't have time to go chasing some mystical weapon."

"Counselor Laithor said we seek the Horn, not Darkslayer."

The Prince threw his hands in the air in exasperation. "Great! So we get the Horn, after a fortnight, might I add, and then they'll send us on another little mission, after who knows how many more weeks. We don't have that kind of time to waste, Cor."

The Prince caught Ihva's eye and clamped his mouth shut. Cor turned and saw her as well.

"Good morning, Ihva," the dwarf said, his tone much gentler than the one he'd taken with the Prince.

"Good morning," she replied.

Awkward silence. Even Cor could be caught off-guard, it seemed.

"Um, do you know if there's breakfast?" Ihva asked.

Maybe food would diffuse the stress they were all feeling. As the words departed Ihva's lips, Linara appeared.

"We have prepared the morning meal, if you would join me," the girl informed them.

Ihva smiled her. She was so slight and slender, her movements as graceful as any of the elves they'd seen so far. She was soft-spoken, too, but that seemed to be an elvish thing as well.

"We'd love to," she told Linara and glanced at Kronk, who was still asleep.

"We will show them where to join you when they wake," Linara told her.

Them? Ihva looked again and saw Malach was lying there too, snoring softly.

"Okay," she said.

Linara led Ihva, Cor, and the Prince up a different ladder than before, then across a bridge. They arrived at another cloth laid out with bread and fruit and sat down to eat.

The meal went well except that they didn't speak, and the Prince was glaring slightly into his drink every time Ihva glanced at him. She wondered if he'd eaten anything. Cor was silent as well, but his demeanor was one of a patient sufferer rather than one of anger.

Ihva looked back at the Prince. He was particularly surly this morning. As she watched him, she realized he wasn't just afraid. He looked helpless. She wondered again how the Prince, the second-in-command of the most powerful nation in Gant, could feel deficient at all. Yet she could tell that he did, and she pitied him for it. Well, pitied wasn't the right word for it. She felt for him. Her heart went out to him. What was this man contending with that made him feel so powerless and insufficient? It had to be related to this duty he had to Oerid. He'd connected Lady Cibelle to the fate of Oerid a couple of times now. He had to find the woman, had to, or something would devastate the nation he was to rule. No one had the power to do that but the Lady of Shadows or maybe Eshad, and the second only if the dwarves concentrated all their resources on the task. Besides, the Prince had seemed as surprised by the situation in the dwarven kingdom as Ihva had been. It had to be the Lady of Shadows who was threatening Oerid, but what did that have to do with Lady Cibelle? What did the Lady of Shadows want with the Prince's betrothed? Lady Cibelle was just a woman, noble-born as she was. Wasn't she?

CHAPTER 23

COR HADN'T SPOKEN to Jasper since their argument that morning, and Jasper knew the dwarf wouldn't until Jasper addressed him first. Cor knew not to talk to him when he was like this. It wasn't that Jasper would lash out or anything. He knew how to be civil. It was just that talking to him would only make him dig his heels in further. Cor was wise and resolved, and he was using every trick he knew to persuade Jasper. Jasper hated to admit the dwarf was succeeding. He was a little torn, but that he was torn at all indicated Cor's strategy was working.

So much was at stake, though. One mistake could cost them everything, could cost him everything. Something inside reminded him how lost he would be if they failed. He wasn't afraid for himself, though. He couldn't afford to be. He didn't matter, as long as Oerid survived. The thing was, if Oerid lost him to the Lady, Oerid herself would be lost, too. Guarding himself was guarding his kingdom. He hated how self-regarding that made him.

What if Cor was right, though? About Miss Marchand and the prophecies? And if the elves were right, too? There would be no Oerid if all of Gant went to pieces. Could it be that protecting Miss Marchand was protecting Oerid as well?

⬥━◆━◆━⬥

Clack.

Miss Marchand knocked away Jasper's strike with ample deftness. He'd been having to try their past few lessons. She was beginning to develop a style of her own, a style that reminded him of the lanky

163

young Easterner he'd faced off on multiple, memorable occasions. Come to think of it, Jasper remembered wondering if he'd see the young man at the Copper Carafe the day they'd left to follow Jessica.

Clack.

He parried as she brought her blade across, and just in time. She was getting better, much better, but even so, more practice couldn't hurt. Still, he wasn't sure why he'd called her to lessons that afternoon. He'd wanted a distraction, as he was tired of the internal monologue consuming his thoughts. He'd needed a break from the anxiety of trying to figure out what to do. It was hard for even Miss Marchand to distract him, though, but that itself was a relief, in a way. Maybe he was getting over that ridiculous infatuation he'd been developing.

Clack. Clack.

He warded off two strikes in quick succession. That was enough of her almost hitting him. Time to force her to the defensive.

He jabbed at her left side, but she knocked away his blade. He stepped back with the force of her parry, and she smiled. Not so fast, Miss Marchand. Overconfidence led to mistakes, and mistakes could be deadly.

He stabbed at her again, and she dodged. Her smile faltered a little. He thrust at her left side with greater force than usual and realized a split second too late his aim had been true, too true. His sword struck her. She cried out and jerked back. He'd hit her, hard, and now she was looking at him, eyes wide, bewildered. He stared back at her, unmoving. Her mouth twisted a little, and she looked to be in genuine pain.

He'd never struck her before. He'd been afraid of hurting her, not to mention he'd been taught growing up not to hit girls, unless they were going to kill him, of course. He'd known it'd be awful if he ever struck Miss Marchand, but he hadn't counted on this. She didn't look upset or angry at all. No, she looked dazed, astonished. As she should have been. He'd hit her. This was terrible.

"Sorry," he muttered.

"No, it's okay," she said quickly. She turned her eyes down.

"No, I didn't mean," he started.

164

She interrupted before he could finish. "It's okay. I was getting too self-assured."

Jasper swallowed what he'd been about to say. She had been a bit puffed up. Still, he'd told himself never to connect a blow while training her, and he had.

"I promised never to hit you, and I did. I'm sorry."

She gave him a strange look, and he began to feel uneasy, uncomfortable. An awkward silence followed.

Jasper cleared his throat. "Let's be done for today," he suggested.

"Okay," she replied almost before he'd finished.

He gave her a slow nod and turned to walk away, then glanced back. She was rubbing her side. When she caught his eyes on her, she stopped and gave him a reassuring smile. She was going to have a bruise. Jasper wondered whether Cor might Heal her but realized then he'd have to tell the dwarf what had happened. Miss Marchand seemed resolved to pretend nothing was wrong, so she might be offended if he said something. He decided against informing Cor.

As he left, he fought the temptation to look back at Miss Marchand. He wondered if she was watching him and was suddenly conscious of the way he was walking, like he was slinking away. He drew himself up and marched the rest of the way across the clearing, looking for Malach and Cor.

Chapter 24

THE FIRST FULL DAY in Rinhaven was smooth enough, given that the Prince spent the rest of the afternoon after their lessons sitting, glowering, on the ground while Cor and Malach sat off to the side discussing something in secretive tones. As for Kronk, the woman had disappeared for the entire day. Besides that, Ihva's side had throbbed with pain since the Prince had struck her in practice. She couldn't let him see it, though. She didn't want to make him feel worse than he already did.

It had caught her off guard, his comment about how he'd promised not to hit her. First, he'd never told her any such thing. Perhaps he had promised himself that? Did that mean he thought about her more than just to parry her with the sword? But it hadn't been his words so much as his tone that surprised her. He'd sounded attentive, concerned, warm even. The look he'd given her had been strange, too, like he minded her. It was tender, if that was even a word one could use to describe the Prince and his expressions. Thinking about it made her feel odd-her heart beat faster and it stole her breath. It wasn't like she thought he'd meant anything by it. She just wished. She'd been wishing things like that ever since the night at the farm with Aaron. The dwarf had been nice enough, but it had been the Prince's aside that had set her heart racing. It startled her to realize-she really did wish there was something behind his looks and words. With that came another realization, a comprehension-a confession.

She liked him. Liked him. It was liberating and thrilling to admit. She felt something flutter in her stomach, and the breathlessness came back. It scared her, too, though, but not for the reasons she would have guessed. It had nothing to do with his station. She was becoming comfortable with him, too comfortable, if she was honest. She was no longer intimidated by his princely-ness. Being on the road had taught her even that the most titled man was just a man at the end of the day, with concerns and worries and flaws like the rest. She had none of the illusions concerning him that she'd so often believed about other boys, that he was perfect. He was much too gloomy and pessimistic most of the time for her to make that mistake. It wasn't even the fact that he was already in a relationship. He belonged to Lady Cibelle, and that was that.

No, what scared her was that somewhere deep inside, she liked him. She'd never felt like this before. Sure, she'd "liked" other boys, but her feelings back then had been so one-dimensional. There was something deeper to this, something more intense about it than a run-of-the-mill crush. She felt powerless and defenseless to stop it this time. The knowledge that a boy didn't return her sentiments was enough to quash any infatuation she'd had in the past. This time, even multiple levels of impossibility did nothing to squelch her feelings. Even if she told herself it was pointless to entertain such emotions, and she would tell herself that, she knew there was something enduring to them. It didn't make sense, it was illogical, and it struck fear in her. To be at the mercy of someone else, that was what it was. But that was what it had always been, what she'd been wanting her whole life, though that was just half of it. To be at the mercy of someone who loved her in return was the full of it. Loved. Now she was thinking about love.

She shook her head. This was going nowhere, nowhere good at least. It was pointless to entertain these emotions, these thoughts. See, she'd reminded herself like she'd promised to. Anyway, it was time for dinner. Time to get out of her head. Just then, Linara appeared. Ihva just smiled and followed the girl up into the trees once again.

———◆·◆———

The food at dinner was much like what they'd had the first night, though with less variety. Everyone was quiet and subdued, and the atmosphere was tense. They spoke little more than to ask someone to pass a piece of bread or a cup of juice. The air felt heavy without Malach's usual banter, Cor's attempts to contain his amusement, and Malach's occasional jab at the Prince.

Kronk, who'd already been at the table when Ihva arrived, must have felt the weight of the silence too and spoke in a whisper.

"Ihva like Kronk's dress? Kronk pretty! Kronk wear pretty dress!"

Kronk had shown up wearing a gown after the elvish style. How the elves managed to find a dress that size was a mystery. It was beautiful, loose and flowing, a mixture of light blues and green fading into one another. There were flowers woven into Kronk's hair as well.

"Kronk spend day with happy forest people. Happy forest people like Kronk. Kronk happy too," the woman continued.

That explained how the elves had found the outfit. They must have stitched it today.

Ihva gave a half-hearted smile. "That's great, Kronk," she said, trying to sound enthusiastic.

Kronk grinned. "Ihva need pretty dress, too! Happy forest people make her one!"

That made Ihva laugh. "Maybe I'll get them to make me one tomorrow," she agreed.

Kronk gave an energetic nod, then the conversation hit another lull.

"Speaking of tomorrow, what's everyone have on the agenda?" Malach asked suddenly.

Ihva started at his voice, then looked at him. His eyes were on the Prince, who met the dwarf's gaze and answered steadily.

"If it were up to me, we'd leave at first light."

Malach didn't say anything (for once) but waited for the Prince to go on and go one he did.

"Cor has heard my arguments, and I assume you have as well, now." His tone held a hint of accusation.

"I've only heard you hope to pursue Lady Cibelle as soon as circumstances allow," Malach replied, his tone sharp and defensive.

The Prince glanced at Cor and gave him a searching look.

"He's told you nothing more?"

"Nothing."

The Prince relaxed a little.

"Is there something he ought to be telling me?" Malach asked after a moment.

The Prince's expression turned perturbed. "No." He turned back to Malach, a flustered look on his face now. "These matters concern Oerid and her keepers."

"Then forgive me for intruding. I hope you know I'd never impose myself where I'm not welcome." Malach's tone was different than Ihva had ever heard it. He was stern and sounded a bit aggravated himself. Nothing ever irritated Malach.

The Prince rounded on Cor, inflamed. "You put him up to this, didn't you?"

"I did not, son," Cor replied calmly. He sounded truthful enough, but of course he was being honest. Cor didn't lie.

"I can't believe a simple weapon is worth everything we could lose waiting for it, Cor. You don't have any proof this Darkslayer is even necessary. What do your prophecies say about such an instrument? If you have something definitive, then tell me. If not, I don't see that it's worth arguing anymore, and we should be on our way."

Ihva watched as the argument escalated. She hated conflict. It upset her. She saw Cor and the Prince staring at each other but wasn't listening when she decided to try to slink away. They wouldn't notice her leaving if they remained as engrossed as they were now. Besides, even if they did, she didn't have a vote in what they'd do next. She was just a merchant's daughter in a company with two princes and a king's advisor. They wouldn't mind her going even if they did notice. She slowly rose and made her way over to the ladder, then looked back.

"I don't see how elvish wisdom has anything to do with it," the Prince was saying as Ihva descended.

She was thankful she was able to slip away before she had to listen to anymore. The Prince was so flighty, so afraid. That much was clear. Ihva didn't know exactly how Cor was interpreting Laithor's words about Darkslayer and it being necessary for one of their number, but she was smart enough to realize he and the Prince were arguing over her again and the Prince found something about retrieving his betrothed more pressing than dealing with this Oer's Blessing business. She wondered again about Lady Cibelle. What about this woman was so important the Prince would ignore what was becoming clearer, to Ihva at least? Healing was not something people just did. Oer had bestowed magic on her, and as much as she hated to admit it, she was starting to wonder if it was true that she was his Blessing. She must learn more about this Blessing, she decided, and determined to ask Cor more of what he knew and had read. Better to be educated, even if it turned out to be false. She wouldn't ask Cor in front of the Prince, of course. She didn't want to upset him further.

Absorbed by her thoughts, she realized someone was standing in front of her and stopped just in time to not run over Linara. She backed up until she could see the girl's face.

"I thought you might like to join me in the trees before it's time to sleep," Linara said.

"Oh, um, sure," Ihva replied. Did Linara need to talk to her about something? From the girl's unconcerned demeanor, Ihva guessed not. Maybe Linara just wanted to spend time together. In the trees, as an elf would be wont to do.

"Good," Linara said, smiling now.

She turned and led Ihva up a ladder to a platform, then along a series of long rope bridges. Then Linara ushered Ihva up some ladders until they reached a high platform, the highest around that Ihva could see. She looked down and was that grateful heights didn't dizzy her like they did her mother. Even so, the distance between her and the ground was long. She turned back to Linara, but the girl had disappeared.

"Follow me," came the girl's voice from above.

Ihva looked up, and there was Linara, climbing even farther up the tree. Thick branches supported her ascent, and seeing them, Ihva decided to listen to the girl.

Twenty feet higher, Linara and Ihva reached the top of the tree. They emerged from beneath the leaves, and the sight that met them stole Ihva's breath.

The sky was clear, not a cloud in sight, and the stars shone as brilliant as Ihva had ever seen. The moon was so white and luminescent she couldn't look at it. It hung low in the sky and seemed like it was resting on the distant forest canopy.

"I like to watch them," came Linara's soft voice beside Ihva.

They were beautiful, the stars. Ihva hadn't seen them since they'd entered M'rawa.

"I missed the starlight," Ihva said.

"The night below is so dim compared to this." Linara sounded sad. Indeed, Ihva thought she detected even a hint of despair in the elf's voice.

"There's light enough to live by," she said to Linara.

Linara turned to her with a question in her eyes, and Ihva went on.

"Your people have those insects that give light..."

"The firewings?"

Ihva nodded.

"They are not like the stars, though," Linara said, pins of light from the night sky reflecting in her eyes as she watched Ihva.

Ihva shook her head. "No, but they are light nonetheless."

Linara didn't say anything, so Ihva went on.

"Some people say the night is very dark, Shadowed even. A lot of people at home do. They rush inside as soon as they can after sunset and won't peek outside again until daybreak. I only see light. The light of many suns, distant, but shining just as bright."

Indeed, it was told among Oeridians that Oer had created many suns with many worlds, but he had chosen Gant for his residence. He was out there, somewhere, guarding Gant and tending to this world as he did nothing else in all Creation. Some even said he created the other suns just for Gant to see by at night.

"Perhaps that is why you are appointed." Linara's voice was almost inaudible. Appointed? By whom and to what? Did Linara know something about Oer's Blessing?

"What do you mean?" Ihva asked.

"You carry the Power of Life in you."

Ihva waited for Linara to continue but she received only silence. Finally, she asked, "What does that signify?"

"Every race has them. I am Appointed, too."

Linara sounded sad, and Ihva realized the girl was using the word, Appointed, as a title.

"Appointed to what?"

"Appointed to the Journey, for me," Linara answered, then looked at Ihva and continued. "You see, we elves are not a race without enemies. There are creatures in the forest, creatures with minds but no bodies, creatures alive but without souls. For as long as we remember, they have hunted us.

"Night after night, except when the moon is full, they appear to steal us away. We began to sleep in the trees, closer to the stars and the moon, closer to Rawa who lives in the sky. We built our cities in the trees, ate and drank among the trees, and lived among the trees, as we continue to do to this day. We called the creatures that haunt our nights the Shades of Twilight."

Ihva watched the girl shudder and look away.

"The Shades emerge from, or rather extend, the shadows the night casts. They creep along the like tendrils of some dark tree. While we tried to protect ourselves and our kin, each his own, one child, High Elf Orla's daughter, Erithen, was left behind one night over three thousand years ago. She fled along the ground. The Shades cornered her and drove her out of the city. While many wept with despair, Orla leapt from branch to branch, tree to tree, just behind the Shades, following.

"The Shades reached the great river to the west, where they turned on Orla. She pulled the Horn from her belt and sounded it. You see, the Horn was wrought by the hand of Rawa herself the night Orla defeated the Black Monocero on the night we thought it might all end, when the creature that drove us toward the Shades fell to Orla's spear. It was the destruction of the Monocero that earned Orla the position of High Elf in the first place."

Linara stopped a moment and shook her head, and Ihva waited for her to go on.

"In any case, Rawa answered Orla's call the night Erithen was taken, but it was not in the way that Orla had hoped. Her daughter was lost, and she barely made away with her own life. The Horn was also lost in the river to the west.

"Orla returned to Rinhaven the following morning, defeated and heartbroken. She remained among the living, cared for by her husband, Abron, but her mind was elsewhere. Perhaps she blamed herself for her daughter's fate, or perhaps she simply mourned her daughter's disappearance. In any case, Orla joined Rawa in the stars within a year.

"Meanwhile, knowing he could not bring back his wife or his daughter, Abron sought to retrieve the only thing he could-the Horn of Orla, as he named it. He sent a young elf, the first Appointed, to take back the Horn, but she did not return. Rawa visited Abron in a dream that same night and instructed him to carry out the search every hundred years. Rawa told him that the Appointed must be a young girl, around Erithen's age, and must be her parents' only child. Now, every hundred years, we make the Journey of the Horn. One is Appointed to take the place of Orla, to find the Horn and sound it. If the Appointed succeeds, it is said Rawa will come rescue us and drive the Shades out of M'rawa for good. If the Appointed fails…" Linara trailed off.

"If she fails, what?" Ihva asked.

"If she fails, she is lost, her soul forfeits to the Shades, and we must wait another hundred years."

Horror crept over Ihva as she realized what Linara was saying. The stakes for the Appointed were so high-the young elf would either save her people or die trying.

"How many times has this happened?" Ihva asked.

"This next new moon will mark the thirty-sixth Journey of the Horn. None has returned, but each time, we hope," Linara said, her eyes on the moon.

Ihva stared at Linara, aghast. "You realize what you're doing, right?"

The girl would become a living sacrifice. Ihva was not one to give up hope easily, but this situation seemed impossible. Already 35 young girls Appointed and lost. Suddenly Ihva was sure they could not accompany Linara to find the Horn, and she couldn't let the girl give herself up so readily, either.

"You will forfeit your life to the Shades, Linara!"

The girl replied calmly, "I know."

What was going on? Had they brainwashed the child?

"Who Appointed you, anyway?" Ihva asked, trying any angle to dissuade the girl.

"Laithor and the Council of Elders. Rawa came to Dalen in a dream the night my mother disappeared and told him I was chosen. They Tested me and confirmed it. It is an honor bestowed once a generation, and they crowned me the Appointed the next evening."

Linara touched the braids in her hair, which Ihva now realized looked like a coronet. The girl was insane.

"You can't do this, Linara. It's certain death!"

Linara glanced back at Ihva, resolve shining in her eyes. "There are things worthy of death, and my honor is one of them. Nobility and grace adorn the heads of those who sacrifice, and victory visits only those who lay down their treasures for it. You will learn."

Ihva was struck dumb. Linara couldn't be serious. What an austere creature! She couldn't look at the girl any longer and turned to process her words. What good would honor do Linara in the grave? What victory would she have if she was dead? It didn't make sense. Ihva would learn? Linara spoke as though Ihva were the younger, foolish, as though she possessed wisdom Ihva had yet to attain.

She looked back at Linara and started to ask her whether Rawa had even promised success when she discovered the girl was gone. Ihva searched the vicinity. Linara had disappeared.

Ihva shook her head. This was crazy. There was no way they could let Linara go, much less join her on the hunt for the Horn. She tried to decide how to tell Cor, the Prince, and Malach that she'd just learned they were being sent on a suicide mission. She found herself in sudden agreement with the Prince. They had to leave, and fast. Maybe they could take Linara with them, but that sounded dangerous as well. What could they do?

Ihva puzzled over the situation a while longer. It distressed her that such a peaceful people as the elves could be beset by such evil, at the mercy of such darkness. She was certain this was the Shadow. Ihva hadn't realized the Lady's influence penetrated even the forests of M'rawa. Rawa must be weeping with the tragedy of her people. Rawa, Oer's daughter, created to give life to the elves, was said to care for them as her children. It made sense, though, that Rawa would allow the Shades to beleaguer her people. She was not a strong deity, being a creation of Oer herself, but why didn't Oer himself step in at that point? What concerned Rawa concerned her Father. He had some stake in the matter. Why didn't he send something, someone, to deal with the problem instead of letting 35 young elf girls and innumerable other elves fall to the Shades? That was when it dawned on Ihva. What if, in fact, he had sent someone?

She remembered that Linara had called her an Appointed as well. Not by Rawa, Ihva reasoned, but by Oer. Could she be the one Oer was sending for the elves? She shivered, for the answer was clear to her. Oer's Blessing was for the elves as well. She, Ihva Marie Marchand, was meant to save them.

It struck her that she'd just identified as Oer's Blessing, and without reservation. She felt the truth of it somewhere deep inside. She was Doomspeaker. Cor's insistence that she was unique, chosen to define the present condition of the world, had broken through the barriers of denial she'd been fighting to hold up. As they came crumbling down as last, she recognized the wake of destruction that lay behind her. Accompanying the Prince, she stole away with one nation's sovereign, leaving Oerid's throne vulnerable to usurpers. With Malach, she'd taken another prince and had left Eshad in the charge of a powerful Shadow-sworn and his minions.

Disaster lay behind her, and she knew it, but she wondered if there wasn't something she could do to change the future, to steer in a different direction. She couldn't leave the elves in the same position as the other nations. She might be called the Dread Prophet by men and dwarves, but she would make a better name for herself among the residents of Rinhaven. If Oer was really bestowing on her talents like Tongues, viewings, and what Linara had termed "the Power of Life," surely she could use her abilities to bless rather than curse. Surely, if it was up to Ihva, she would fight the Shadow with all her might and come out victorious.

Chapter 25

RINHAVEN WAS EXPANSIVE, Jasper discovered. He'd decided to take a walk that morning before everyone else woke up. As he'd stood to leave, he'd seen Miss Marchand lying next to Kronk. She'd been sound asleep, Miss Marchand that was. Kronk, too, but that was hardly a surprise. Miss Marchand had to have come back late last evening, as she hadn't been there when he'd gone to bed. He'd hardly been aware of stopping to watch her. He'd roused himself quickly, though, and left for his walk, but his thoughts kept straying back to her.

Little moments kept replaying in his mind. As soon as he distracted himself from one, another would arise. He hadn't realized how much time they'd spent together and how many memories there really were. There had been the time she, Malach, and Kronk had found him and Cor in the secret passages of the Irgdol palace and she'd been trying to tell Cor that Malach was a friend. Little had she and Jasper known at the time how well Cor already knew that. Jasper felt a strange sense of camaraderie in their ignorance. There'd been the time she'd fallen into boisterous laughter at some joke Malach had made. She'd turned red, appearing embarrassed at her outburst, but couldn't stop laughing, and Jasper had had to restrain himself from laughing with her. There had been their dance. She was a good dancer, nimble, and she'd looked as though she'd been enjoying herself. It had caught him off-guard, and even just the memory of her face, her giggling at the end, was unnerving. There was something about her expression in that moment, the joyful glint in her deep green eyes, the unhampered delight in her smile, the abandon of her laughter, that mesmerized him, and he couldn't banish the scene from his mind.

That was when it hit him full force. She was lovely. Lying there just this morning, her golden hair spread around her, she'd looked serene. And beautiful, so very beautiful. It wasn't even just her eyes that enchanted him anymore. It was all of her. The way she moved, more graceful than any elf he'd seen; her soft features; her slender figure; the looks she gave him, so alluring in their innocence. Ihva Marchand had enraptured him, and he was beginning to realize there was nothing he could do about it. Denying his feelings only seemed to make them worse. Resisting them only seemed to make them that much more inescapable. Maybe it was better that he just stop trying. Maybe, just maybe.

He experimented for a moment, just let himself be. At first, a torrent of emotion dizzied him. She was enchanting, and the mere thought of her overpowered him. Ihva Marchand was captivating and winsome, and her gentle beauty fixed him with an elation he'd never experienced until this moment. It was how learning to fly might feel-absolutely terrifying and unsteadying at first, but after a moment, a long moment, it became more manageable, and after that, sublime. He wanted to kiss her-her hand, her cheek, her lips, her mouth. He wanted her. It was an ache like he'd never felt before.

He tested the waters again-he loved Miss Ihva Marchand-and it was delightful and intoxicating to admit it. He loved her. All he wanted was to hold her, to feel her resting in his arms, to tell her what he felt. He didn't even care if she felt the same way. It was just something he needed to say, no matter the outcome. Letting go, uninhibited by "shoulds" and "ought tos," he realized he felt more defenseless to this than he'd felt to any danger or enemy-he was powerless to change it-but for some reason, he didn't care. He'd never been happier than in this moment. It was magical.

It took a few minutes, but then the fearsome deluge subsided until only a quiet joy remained. He couldn't be with her, he knew. She wouldn't be his, and he wouldn't be hers, but something about this was changing him. Things looked brighter, and though everything had just become more complicated than ever, he felt strangely untroubled.

He'd have to figure out how to handle it all. Yes, he'd definitely have to figure out how to handle it all. He wasn't going to betray Jessica. Did she feel this way about him? He couldn't betray her like that, not if she felt this way. He'd have to figure out what to do with this new information, but it was like a blindfold had been lifted and he was seeing everything for the first time in, well, forever. He felt hopeful. Jasper Thesson Aurdor, hopeful.

⸻ ◆ ◆ ⸻

Rinhaven was a three-dimensional web of interwoven walkways and platforms and ladders. Nothing existed on the ground. Instead, the elves had built everything in the trees many feet above the soil. The greens of M'rawa had struck Jasper before, but this morning they seemed even more vibrant and full of life. The elves were already awake and gliding their way along the bridges. They looked down at Jasper, and he found himself returning small smiles for their polite nods. It was an odd feeling, being so light-hearted, but pleasant.

He wandered for a good forty minutes before turning back. The others might worry about him. Not that much could happen to him in Rinhaven, but they might wonder if he'd gone. He hadn't. Obviously.

He strolled back the way he'd come, contemplative. He'd tried thinking further on what to do about his epiphany, but emotion overwhelmed thought whenever Ihva Marchand was the subject. It was rather useless to try to decide anything in that regard.

Instead, Jasper turned his mind to their next steps. To leave M'rawa in pursuit of Jessica or to remain until the hunt for the Horn and obtain Darkslayer, those were their options. Jasper had been so set on leaving. Even now, he wasn't sure if that wasn't the more logical choice. Yet something about his new openness brought more bearing to Cor's arguments. What if Ihva, Miss Marchand that was (it felt much too reserved and detached to call her by the second name now, but he realized he needed to), what if Miss Marchand was Oer's Blessing? If so, maybe Cor was right about the rest of it, the whole she's-not-as-bad-as-it-seems thing. And if Cor was right, and the elves as well, then they needed Darkslayer. Maybe they had to stay.

With less reluctance than he'd imagined possible, he decided he'd remain until the hunt. Except for the fact it would put them two weeks behind, it seemed like an innocuous choice. What could happen to them in M'rawa, in the sheltered land of the elves? It occurred to Jasper that Jessica would have done much better to find Rinhaven or let the elves find her than to turn toward Jinad. The woman had strange ways of thinking. They would find her, though. His newfound optimism had not worn off yet. They would find her. They just had a little errand to run first.

When Jasper arrived back where they'd slept, he found the others awaiting his return and Miss Marchand rocking back and forth on her feet. She looked anxious. He watched her a moment, then shifted his gaze to Cor. She was beautiful, and he could lose himself in her emerald eyes, but now was not the time (nor would it ever be), and he needed to apologize to Cor. Before he could open his mouth to speak, though, Cor made an announcement.

"Ihva has something to tell us. She says that it is important that we know what she has learned. Perhaps we ought to sit."

Jasper looked at the dwarf, confused, but from the look on the dwarf's face, it seemed Cor had no more idea than he did what Miss Marchand wanted to say. Interesting. What had she learned? She'd learned something, something significant from the sound of it. She didn't seem the spying type, though. Jasper caught himself before he smiled at her, though inside he was grinning. Miss Marchand, the intelligence collector. He wondered if he could ever plumb the depths of this girl. He sat with the others in a circle and waited for her to speak.

She seemed unsure of herself as she began, her voice wavering. "I was talking to Linara last night, the young girl that's always around. You know…"

Jasper remembered the young female elf. A child, really, she couldn't have been more than a human fourteen-year old's equivalent. He nodded, though Miss Marchand wasn't looking at him.

"She told me some things, important things, about the Horn we are supposed to retrieve. It turns out, she's coming with us."

Miss Marchand glanced around cautiously.

"Linara said she is the Appointed and has been tasked with retrieving the Horn as well. She said a young girl has gone every hundred years to try to do the same." She faltered. "She said none has returned."

Miss Marchand's eyes darted to Jasper, then fled back to Cor and settled there. In the split second her gaze was on him, Jasper detected a profound unrest in her. He tried to get his mind off her expression to process what she'd said.

Linara was the Appointed (it was a title, it seemed) being sent after the Horn. She wasn't the first. There was an Appointed every hundred years. They'd all had the same task, but the rest hadn't returned. That sounded bad. Really bad.

"How long has this gone on for?" Malach asked.

Miss Marchand looked at Malach. "For thirty-six hundred years."

She looked down, and Malach nearly choked. Jasper's stomach dropped.

"As in three thousand, six hundred years, lass?" the dwarf asked.

She nodded, now shifting her gaze to Cor.

Malach sounded strangled as he asked, "And we're supposed to accompany her on this search, this martyr operation?"

The dwarf sounded like Jasper felt. So much for his resolve to stay. This was mad. The elves were deranged if they thought they could send Jasper and the others on this suicide mission. How could the elves even consider asking this, knowing the party contained two men of royalty, the next leaders of Oerid and Eshad? If the group failed this task, no one would survive, from the sound of it. This was insane. The elves were deluded.

"We can't, just plain cannot, do this," Jasper managed to say.

Miss Marchand had a powerful look in her eyes as she turned to him, and he realized she meant to disagree. What in the world was she thinking? Was she insane, too?

"Hear her out," Cor said patiently.

What did Cor know? What could persuade Jasper this was worth the risk? They'd all die. Oerid and Eshad would succumb to turmoil.

Gant would fall apart at the seams. There was nothing that could convince Jasper now, nothing. Still, he waited for Miss Marchand to speak, which she finally did.

"Linara is not the only Appointed. There are two this year."

What difference did that make? One more elf would be lost to some unknown force of destruction. What was keeping these elves from returning? It couldn't be good.

"The other Appointed is myself."

Miss Marchand was no elf. How could she be Appointed?

"I believe Oer has Appointed me to the same task as Linara. I." She stopped and looked at Cor. "I think you're right, Cor. I think I'm Oer's Blessing."

Cor gave her a solemn nod. "I believe you are, Ihva. One does not come by such abilities as your own by happenstance. Oer does not bestow magic without consideration and never without sacrifice."

Miss Marchand tilted her head at Cor. "But I haven't made the Exchange."

"No, you have not. In most cases, the Father gives only once an offering has been received. However, I believe that as He grants Powers to you, at the same time as He imparts a duty, an obligation to Gant and to Him. The magic you have received is a deposit, a goodwill offering, that once you have used requires your devotion to Oer's cause. I guarantee you, you will sacrifice, and seeing as the potency of one's powers reflects the value of one's offering, I foresee you shall offer something very precious."

Miss Marchand stared at Cor, silent. It was a heavy moment, and everyone felt it. Even Kronk looked upset, and she remained still and quiet, too. For Jasper, it was baffling. What Cor had said made sense. It was logical and well-reasoned. Miss Marchand had magic with no explanation, and the dwarf's theory made more sense than any explanation Jasper could come up with. As much as Jasper wanted to argue, he realized he believed Cor to some degree. Miss Marchand was likely Oer's Blessing. Doomspeaker. The Dread Prophet. Jasper's breaths became halting.

"I've left disaster behind me," Miss Marchand said. "The king of Eshad is dead, and both Oerid and Eshad are in danger, if not already in turmoil."

It was true. He hated to admit it, hated it, but Miss Marchand was right. Her wake looked much like what the other Dread Prophets had left behind, or how they'd started at the very least.

"I can't leave Rinhaven the same way," she continued. "I must have some choice in the matter. There has to be some good I can do for all the destruction that lies behind me. I've been denying the truth of it, and that has only turned out to prove it more true. I am Oer's Blessing. Now I just want to bless."

Cor nodded, his expression grave but pleased, and Malach was staring at Miss Marchand in wonder. Kronk had a proud look about her. She might not have understood the whole of what Miss Marchand had just said, but she must have grasped the courage and nobility in Miss Marchand's tone. Jasper felt overwhelmed. It had to be true, that Miss Marchand was who Cor had taken her to be. It had to be true, but then that had all manner of terrible implications.

"You are coming into your own, Ihva," Cor said softly. "Many of those called Oer's Blessing have denied their identities, fleeing those who persecuted them, fleeing their very selves, but even closing one's eyes does not banish one's shadow, only blinds the individual to truth and Reality. Even Aria Aderyn, who confessed herself to be Oer's Blessing, did not do so until too late."

Aria Aderyn. She was one of the Blessings about whom they had more records, though she was a thousand years dead. After six months of uprising in which she'd led an army of resistance against King Derrick of Oerid, she'd shown up with a white banner to Agda and revealed herself as Doomspeaker. They'd executed her. The rebellion would have succeeded, too, but she'd explained something about uniting against the common enemy with cryptic references to judgment and renewal. If the present situation hadn't been more dire, Jasper would have been curious as to what Cor knew about Aria Aderyn from histories and contemporary journals. As it was, Cor continued speaking, and Jasper gave him his rapt attention.

"You have recognized yourself sooner than any other of Oer's Blessings, Ihva. There is wisdom and knowledge, hidden in parable and poetry, that suggests you are much more than a prophet of doom and much better than just a bringer of destruction."

"Can you teach me?" Miss Marchand asked meekly.

"Yes, Ihva. I will tell you everything I know."

She nodded. Jasper was reeling. That was that, then. He knew he'd run out of arguments, even to dissuade himself from the inevitable conclusion.

"We're staying, then?" Malach asked. He'd recovered quickly.

"Yes. Well, I am," Miss Marchand replied. She looked around at the others. "You can go if you need to. I don't want to keep you."

And leave her behind? Jasper's rationality was teetering on a narrow edge. He couldn't leave her, not now. Jessica's face flashed in his mind. He had to find Lady Cibelle, yet he was starting to understand what Cor had been telling him. If he let Gant fall, he'd have no Oerid left to defend. He should stay. He should go. Oer above, he didn't know what he should do.

"Kronk stay!"

Of course, Kronk would stay. Her exclamation was soon followed by Malach's own pledge, though.

"I'll remain with you." The dwarf gave no explanation, and Jasper realized he didn't need one. Malach believed Cor. It was probably part of what the two had been discussing yesterday. Malach would stay with Miss Marchand.

Cor was quiet, and Jasper realized the dwarf was waiting for him to answer. Cor was his advisor after all, or the Crown's, but not Miss Marchand's. Cor would follow him, not the girl, yet Jasper could only imagine the dilemma in the dwarf's mind. Both Jasper and Miss Marchand needed Cor desperately. Jasper wouldn't make it far without the dwarf's support, and he'd need him to help devise a plan to overcome the Lady of Shadows. Yet Miss Marchand needed him as well. The look of distress on her face as she gazed at Cor revealed that she knew it, too. She'd need Cor's wisdom and knowledge. Cor was the only one Jasper had ever met who believed Oer's Blessing was meant for blessing. Miss Marchand wouldn't make it far without Cor's exhortation and guidance. A grave decision faced Cor right now, graver than any Jasper hoped he'd ever have to make. Unless Jasper stayed. That would solve everyone's dilemma. He'd have to remain in Rinhaven until they found the Horn. He drew in a breath.

"I'll stay with you."

He was looking at Miss Marchand, then realized he'd addressed her apart from the rest of the group.

"With all of you," he added quickly. "You'll have to stay with me, Cor."

The dwarf gave Jasper a grateful look, then they were all looking at Miss Marchand.

"We should tell the Council," she said.

Everyone nodded.

"You ought to be the one to inform them, Ihva," Cor said.

She looked frightened.

"Can't one of them do it?" she asked, glancing at Jasper and Malach.

"No. You are the Appointed."

She swallowed and nodded. There was a silence.

"Alright," she said after a moment. "I'll go now." She flashed them a mustered smile, nodded again, and walked off toward the nearest ladder. Jasper guessed she was looking for Linara. Soon she was up the ladder, across a bridge, and out of sight.

Cor turned to the rest of them. "We must guard her. She cannot be lost."

Malach nodded, and Jasper just looked at Cor.

"This is as vital as your own task, Jasper. Without her, you will have no kingdom. With her, you will still contend for Oerid, and it will demand much of you, but she will make it possible."

Jasper nodded, too, now. This was all too much to handle. He could hardly believe it was only an hour ago he'd been floating on the wings of adoration for the girl he now knew as Doomspeaker. He saw her face in his mind, so brave and noble, and endearment welled in him. Her identity was unnerving, but what he felt for her was strong.

She was the Dread Prophet-one more reason he could never hope to have her-but he felt less afraid of her and more afraid for her. Could her heart handle the horrors to come? Could he?

CHAPTER 26

IHVA STOOD ON A LEAF PLATFORM before the Council, all of whom were also standing respectfully. As she nodded her greeting to Laithor, he rested his gaze on her and seated himself. The rest of the council members and Ihva followed in kind.

"Good morning, Elders," she said to them.

They murmured their salutations in reply.

"I have come to inform you of our decision. We will make the journey to retrieve the Horn of Orla. We will accept your offer of aid in return."

Laithor looked at her intently for a moment before addressing her. "Some would say we take a great risk sending you, whom some call the Dread Prophet, to accomplish the task we have entrusted to you. Perhaps you know this."

Ihva dropped her gaze and nodded. Her heart began to sink, and she felt a crushing weight come down on her. The elves believed like men and dwarves then.

Laithor went on, "We know, however, while many see you as a ill-fated and dangerous individual, Oer seeks to bless all his children through you. Men live a short-sighted existence, understanding only what is immediate, which is no understanding at all. Rawa has blessed the elves with longer memories and keener eyes. While men remember only the catastrophes that accompany each Blessing's existence, the elves see the patterns that led to such events apart from the Blessing's influence. We notice the choices men have made to incite the Shadow, and having Rawa's sight, we recognize the ways in which the ones called Oer's Blessing have attempted to mitigate the destruction of such dark times."

Ihva looked up, processing Laithor's words slowly. So, they didn't think her an uncontrollable force of chaos.

Laithor went on. "Perhaps our situation will grow more dire before we see our confidence fulfilled. We do not know, only Oer does, and Rawa as far as her Father has informed her. We know; however, your presence cannot ultimately harm us. Indeed, you are a blessing to us."

Ihva felt confused for a moment, even suspicious. As much as she had reasoned with herself earlier, convincing herself she could bless rather than curse, these words were in conflict with all she knew. The elves were welcoming her and expressing gratitude for some benediction she was supposed to have brought with her.

"Thank you," she started, shifting in her seat.

Laithor was not finished, however. "If you are to face the Shadow, you will need a weapon. Creatures of the Dark are not wounded as normal creatures. Those of the Shadow hardly fear the weapons of man."

Ihva nodded, but Laithor didn't stop speaking.

"Hundreds of years ago, a star fell just outside Rinhaven. Some of us watched it descending through the sky. We knew it was a gift from Rawa and so recovered it from where it fell. We considered what we might do with it. One younger council member received a vision that day that a champion would come in power and defeat the Shadow with a sword fashioned from the Sidereal Stone.

"We have few weapons besides spears and crossbows and even fewer weapon smiths. One of our number, Alexander, had been sired by one of your race and lived his early days among men. He trained as a weapon forger. He returned to us when his mother died. With his skill unsurpassed by most men, he offered to forge the weapon. He took the Sidereal Stone, the fallen star, and formed the blade, calling it Darkslayer. Our champion had not yet arrived, and so we passed Darkslayer down through the years, awaiting the one who would come." Laithor fixed Ihva with a solemn look. "Today, our champion has arrived."

Ihva's breath faltered. "How do you know?" she asked, mustering an outward calm.

"When we found you wandering in the forest, we wondered, or hoped, as you might say. Life bends around you. It became clear when our scouts reported you possessed the Power of Life. Our Appointed, who was one of the scouts, knew the signs and understood almost as soon as we did. The recent days have only confirmed our suspicions," Laithor confided.

They believed her, believed in her. Moisture gathered in Ihva's eyes, but she willed herself not to let the tears fall. She wouldn't allow emotion to take over, she promised herself. She looked back at Laithor, who spoke again.

"You shall wield, Darkslayer, Appointed, but first you must sound the Horn. You shall defeat the Shades and proceed to greater victory. With the blade of Sidereal Stone shall you defeat the Shadow."

Somehow, Ihva felt smaller than she ever had before while at the same time understanding how very significant a role she was accepting. This was no self-degradation or shameful self-effacement. She was not nearly the woman needed to fulfill these duties, and she knew it, but somehow it was falling to her. She would have to learn, like Linara had told her.

She drew herself up and spoke. "I am honored by your pronouncement, and I pledge to do everything possible to defeat these enemies of yours."

She hesitated a moment, seeing Laithor's eyes soften toward her.

"Of ours, Daughter," he corrected her. "Though you find your origin among men, you are making yourself a place among us as our Defender. You may not be a daughter of Rawa, but Rinhaven offers you a refuge and a home among the elves."

His words felt like an embrace. Tearful, Ihva nodded, as she didn't trust herself to speak. Laithor stood in respect for her, giving her the same reception as he had the Prince and Malach. The other council members followed in kind.

"You are Appointed by Oer, and Rawa smiles upon you as well. You hold a unique place in history, Daughter. You face a darkness hitherto unknown, and we offer you all we have in support," Laithor told her, bowing his head. "May the peace of Rawa mark your steps."

The council members quietly made their parting greetings as well. Ihva didn't know how to respond, so she just curtsied like she would before a king and thanked them. The meeting was over.

She turned and descended the ladder to the ground. As her feet met the dirt below, the tears she'd managed to keep at bay began to fall. She avoided meeting elves or any of her companions for the next few minutes. Perplexed still, she also felt the first hint of pride about her position as the Father's Blessing. She'd been insisting on hope before, but the promise of good and Light and victory had now taken a life of its own. She now believed what had been her curse might be something else, something blessed, and this new faith didn't stand on some feeble desire within her. No, this faith found its source in something deeper and more profound, something more certain, on the words of the elves and of Rawa. If the prophecy of a goddess wasn't enough to bolster Ihva's conviction, she wasn't sure what could. Her tears became less of confusion and more of exaltation and humility-exaltation of Rawa and her wisdom and humility that she, Ihva, had been chosen, of all people for such a task. It was all a mystery, an unsearchable mystery, to Ihva, and she allowed herself a moment to wonder at it all.

Some minutes later, she came to herself and found herself sitting with her back to a large tree trunk covered in soft, plush moss. She looked around, folding her marvelling thoughts into a neat bundle and tucking them away for later pondering. She had to go find the others, though she decided in that moment she wouldn't tell them all she'd learned from Laithor. It was fragile knowledge to her still, and she wanted to protect it. No, she would tell Cor a little about the conversation and leave it at that.

She nodded and rose from her seat at the base of the tree and headed back toward the others.

In the days that preceded the Journey of the Horn, as Ihva had discovered it was called, she found herself rather busy. Her lessons with the Prince had resumed the day after their decision to stay in Rinhaven, though they waited until later in the morning to commence practice. No reason to rise before dawn if they didn't have to. He didn't hit her again, which was good. It had hurt when he had. She continued to improve her skills and strength. She didn't strike him again either, but she could tell he was concentrating harder now. He fended off her blows, but she knew she was moving faster every day, surprising him on occasion such that he blocked only just in time. His arched eyebrows told her when he was taken aback and impressed, which was strange for a couple reasons. First, she'd never been so good that she impressed him, or so she'd assumed. Second, he now had facial expressions beyond the normal glowering and sulking.

Of course, he'd smiled before and laughed even, but never with her. He still didn't with her, not exactly, but something was different. He seemed more casual and more contained at the same time. The fear that had exuded from him was subsiding, and though Ihva still caught him with his brow creased with worry, he didn't look as helpless anymore. He didn't look small, far from it. Now he was the same strong, compelling figure he'd been when she'd first seen him, no longer brittle. He was striking like this. Ihva wasn't sure how to handle it, so she tried not to think about it.

Soon after their lessons ended each day, it was time for lunch. Ihva ate with the party and Linara and other elves in the trees. Over the meal, they talked to the elves and amongst each other, and over the two weeks before the Journey, Malach resumed his normal banter, which gained small smiles from even the elves. Ihva felt a growing affection for her companions. They offered support she was realizing she was desperate for. She'd told them they could leave that day, but she'd been clinging to the hope that they'd stay with her. She'd a hard time containing her relief that they'd agreed to remain.

After lunch and maybe a few games of Cats in a Bag, a card game Malach had taught the others and even managed to rope Cor into on a few occasions, Ihva would join Linara in the trees. The girl became

Ihva's guide to elvish life and society. Ihva felt a deep connection to the elves and their culture, and she drank in all that Linara told her. From elvish greetings to stories of Rawa and her relationship with her children to elvish hairstyles (which reflected everything from a person's age to how many children they had to their role in society) to daily life in Rinhaven, Ihva should have been overwhelmed by the barrage of information, but instead she listened and asked questions, hungry for more. On their fourth day in Rinhaven, Linara even took Ihva to have her hair styled by a woman named Ridara. When Ridara handed Ihva a mirror, she was surprised to see the woman had braided her hair in a coronet like Linara's. Yet of course she had. They were both Appointed.

The nights changed after they decided to accompany Linara on the Journey, but Ihva realized it had little to do with their acceptance of the task. The elves had brought the party into the trees to sleep the night she'd met with the Elders. The moon was no longer full, and the Shades would be out. She didn't alert the others to this fact, just let them believe in the hospitality of their hosts. She had to hem Kronk in with the light blankets the elves provided to assure her he wouldn't fall from the platform while she was sleeping, but after that night, they stayed in the trees, out of the reach of the Shades of Twilight. It wouldn't be too long before they had to face the Shades, though, and Ihva had very little idea what to expect. Best not to think about it, she told herself. Imagining would only invoke fear and no real sense of what they were to fight. It wouldn't gain her anything, just set her on edge, and she was enjoying her time in Rinhaven too much to let thoughts of the Shades spoil it.

Still, it was a creeping thought in the back of her mind, and the evening before the Hunt, she couldn't fall sleep. She tossed and turned all night and only pretended to be asleep when she heard the Prince awaken. It had to be the Prince. He always woke early. She made herself wait a while to check, though, and when she did, she was startled by what she found.

CHAPTER 27

JASPER AWOKE EARLY the morning they were to leave to find the Horn. He'd been waking up early every day and had been taking advantage of the time alone to think. This morning, Jessica was on his mind.

He was wondering how she'd managed to escape the Shadow-sworn dwarves, flee through the whole of Eshad, and brave the forests of M'rawa all on her own. He'd known her to be capable of handling herself, of course. He'd sparred with her a couple times and knew her favored weapon was the longsword, which had given him an automatic disadvantage. Her father, Lord William Cibelle, believed in training women to fight to entrust a portion of their safety to them. Lord William's manor was located in the mountains to the south of Oerid. It was clear why the Cibelle women had to be able to protect themselves, as their border was with the Shadowed Realm and orcs were wont to venture north and carry out raids at intervals. Jessica could hold her own in battle, and Jasper liked that about her.

Still, it remained a mystery to him how she'd managed traveling on her own for so far and so long. She couldn't keep watches by herself. She needed to sleep sometime. If she'd been strategic about where she laid down to rest, though, that made it more feasible, and of course she had. The fact that she'd made it to M'rawa was encouraging, really. Her journey was good preparation to face the enemy she'd inevitably come to. The Lady of Shadows wouldn't be easy to defeat. In fact, it'd be impossible by brute force. If they made it past the orcs and Shadow creatures into the Shadowed Realm, they'd still have to find the Lady's lair. They'd have to rely on stealth after that or a distraction or both. All Jessica needed was to find the box, that precious, precious box, and take what lay inside. Father had described the box a thousand times, so often Jasper had dreamed of it in great detail. It was too burdensome to make it past the Lady of Shadows with the box. That was why Jessica had to go. Jasper decided he'd send some of the Masks, a dangerous group of warriors trained in remaining unseen, to accompany her. He'd instruct them to sneak along just well enough that the Lady would think she'd discovered Jasper's plan if she found them. That would give Jessica the best chance to move along unspotted herself and make it out alive. A plan to divert attention from the real plan was always a good idea.

Jasper realized he was smiling a little. He knew why, in this instance, but he'd been doing that more of late at things that never would have sparked a hint of one before. He looked around. No one was awake. He wasn't sure if the others had noticed the change in him. He'd been trying to hide it, but he felt like the bonds on his mind had come loose ever since that moment a couple weeks ago. He could think straight again. Things were clearer to him, and though it was a strain to keep his thoughts from tangling with his feelings, he'd been managing much better.

The key was that hour before the others woke. He had an hour to think about Miss Marchand, to wonder about her, and to push her out of his mind before anyone else could notice. For an hour, he would lean against the tree trunk with his eyes closed, acknowledging that truth, that enduring thread in the fabric of Reality, that he loved her, then try to free himself from it.

On the fourth day he'd come up with a strategy. For some reason, he'd been thinking about the Exchange, the sacrifices young men and women offered to Oer. He'd watched a few Exchanges, and he'd always wondered what happened to the sacrificed items once Oer took them. Whatever they might have been disappeared forever, and with them, all they signified. That was the point of the Exchange, to offer one's best in hopes of something better. Oer took one's good-will tribute, and it'd never come back. That was when it came to Jasper. He would offer these sentiments to Oer to be taken and never returned. He would imagine this love as that sacrifice.

From that morning on, every day he conjured the image of Oer's altar and laid it there-his affections, his yearning, his adoration, his near worship of this woman, this Ihva Marchand. He imagined it all wrapped together in a neat package, wrapped in paper, tied with a string. It wasn't that Jasper was religious, just that he didn't know anyone else to offer this to who could remove it. He'd never made the Exchange, so he didn't know what it was like to offer oblation, but it dawned on him if he had to choose one thing to give up to Oer, this was very precious. He thought the altar imagery rather appropriate. After he'd laid his offering down there, he'd imagine turning and leaving. He always willed himself not to look back, to continue forward without so much as a peek behind him. It became a daily ritual for him in the hour before dawn.

Once everyone awakened, he'd lay it all aside-the feelings, the thoughts, the longing, the pain. There was pain to it. Every time she looked at him, he felt like everyone else disappeared, and he wanted nothing more than to go to her. He delighted in rapier practice for the mere fact he had her undivided attention for that hour. It was a sweet misery, knowing she had no idea and she could never find out. Sometimes he consoled himself their journey would be over soon. Then he could depart from her and forget her, he told himself. He knew that wasn't true, though. Even if she traveled to the farthest province in Oerid to live out her days, he wouldn't forget her. It wasn't that easy.

He realized he was thinking about her again. Time for the rite he'd designed for moments like this. The rite of a heart undone. That sounded so poetic, so tragic, so rending. He realized now why poets so often wrote about love. It touched the depths of one's soul. Oer, he sounded dramatic. How had emotion come to drive him so entirely? He'd always prided himself on being logical. He'd prided himself on being able to push aside what he felt for the sake of doing what was right. He was doing so with Jessica. Father wanted him to marry Lady Cibelle, for some reason or another, and though Jasper didn't feel like he wanted to marry the woman, he did want to please his father, and that was enough. He'd even convinced himself that he loved her, though he knew better at this point, but he and Lady Cibelle were betrothed now, and it was a matter of honor. He had to follow through on this pledge, or Oerid could not trust him for any promise he made. Besides, it was Jessica and not Miss Marchand who would complete love's task and face the Lady of Shadows for him. He shouldn't be thinking about Miss Marchand at all.

He noticed a creeping feeling up the back of his neck. Someone was watching him. He opened his eyes and looked around. Miss Marchand, the very last person he wanted to see him.

She was staring at him, unblinking. How long had she been looking at him? He fought the abashment threatening to subdue him and tried to think of what to say to get her to stop. She appeared concerned. He hoped she wouldn't ask any questions. He spoke before she could.

"Good morning, Miss Marchand."

"Good morning," she replied softly, sounding distracted. Her eyes were still on him, but he could see her thoughts churning behind them.

"It's the Journey today," he reminded her. He had to get her to stop wondering whatever she was wondering.

She started. "Oh. Yes, it is. Are you ready?" she asked quickly.

"Yes. Yes, I'm ready," Jasper replied.

He was. He was ready to be done with the Journey and onto his own task. Who knew where Miss Marchand would end up, but he couldn't follow her after they'd found Jessica.

"Yeah, me too," she said.

Right. He should have asked whether she was ready too. Well then. He hoped someone else would wake soon.

"I'm going to go find Linara," she told him after a moment.

Thank Oer. He nodded and watched her go. Soon enough, Cor woke, then he and Jasper woke Kronk and Malach.

Jasper felt unnerved and discomfited the whole time. That was when he realized he hadn't completed his ritual. Miss Marchand was still on his mind, and he wasn't sure he could banish her from his thoughts without more time on his own, which he wasn't going to get. Today was the Journey of the Horn.

CHAPTER 28

IHVA ADMIRED THE LIGHT BLUE CLOAK Linara wore this morning. The elves with the Elders at the front surrounded her, Ihva, and the others on the ground, speaking solemn prayers. For the most part, Ihva lowered her gaze, acknowledging the gravity of the words raised to Rawa. Every so often, however, she would look up. She caught Laithor's gaze on her, shining with hope and expectation but shadowed by concern.

Kronk stood next to Ihva, understanding enough of the situation to stay silent and keep her head down with respect. At one point, Ihva exchanged glances with Cor and found his eyes betrayed uncertainty. Ihva had mentioned to him some of what she'd learned in her meeting with the Council. She wondered what the dwarf had deduced from what she'd shared. Most of her talks with Cor had been her explaining her understanding of Oer's Blessing and him walking her through the prophecies to show her another interpretation. He hadn't talked about the Council's words to her. Maybe he was still working through what the elves had said. They'd have time to discuss them later, in any case, Ihva was sure.

Laithor stepped forward and spoke. "Today, we entrust you, Ihva Marchand, Linara Ellenlithe, Malach Shemayim, Jasper Aurdor, Cor Gidfolk, and Kronk of Deepgrov, with the protection of our people. Tonight, you shall face darkness unlike any you have ever encountered. May Rawa bless your steps and accompany you on your path, and may you return to us by her favor."

With that, the crowd dispersed into the trees until only Ihva, Linara, and the rest of the party remained. It was time. Ihva looked to Linara to lead the way, and the girl began a brisk walk westward. Ihva didn't look at the others, just took Kronk by the hand and started after Linara.

It took over an hour to reach the edge of Rinhaven. The ground travel made it harder, but Linara had explained the Appointed was not to leave the soil until her task was complete. In the daytime, that was fine, and they were safe enough, but Ihva feared for once the sun set. The Shades would appear with the dark of night, and then walking on the ground would be far from safe. She hoped they'd make it to the river before dusk.

She didn't get her wish. They traveled the day through, speaking very little, and before Ihva knew it, it was nightfall. The firewings that illuminated Rinhaven seemed to have disappeared, so Cor produced his orb of light. Linara had a spear at the ready, and the others took her lead and drew their weapons.

Thirty minutes of navigating through the underbrush after the sun had set, Ihva heard the sound of running water. Linara quickened her pace, and they reached a clearing with a large stream running through the middle. Linara stopped at the edge of the treeline. The clearing was so wide that Ihva could see the night sky above them through the space in the canopy. With the darkness of the new moon, the stars were even more brilliant. Their light didn't do much to comfort Ihva tonight, though.

Linara motioned for the others to be quiet and follow, and she eased her way over to the stream, where she knelt. Ihva followed close behind, and the rest of the party surrounded Ihva and Linara protectively. Ihva watched as the girl reached into the stream, which was deeper than Ihva had suspected, though not very wide.

"It is said Orla dropped the Horn here in these waters. I cannot be sure where along their length we will find it, though," Linara whispered.

Ihva nodded and headed north, hugging the water's edge. She couldn't see into the stream, so she reached down and felt along the bottom. She drew her hand through the sludge and drew in a breath every time it brushed something only to draw out a stone or branch fragment. She watched the clearing as she searched. No sign of the Shades. Still, they had to hurry. There was no guarantee the Shades would not come bursting from the trees at any moment.

Ihva glanced around at the others. They were probing the waters, too. Cor and Malach appeared on edge, the latter muttering under his breath. Kronk was standing in the stream with both hands in the water, watching everyone else. The Prince was the closest to Ihva, between her and Linara, and wore a look of resolve. Ihva wondered again about how she'd found him that morning, sitting and leaning against the tree, his eyes closed, his face pained. He'd been so flustered when he'd realized she'd seen him. She hadn't been able to mask her surprise or concern very well. She'd never seen him in such a clear state of suffering. It had transfixed her, which only seemed to make him more uncomfortable. She knew he was hiding something now. A cry from Linara interrupted her thoughts.

"The Horn!" the girl gasped.

Ihva looked over and saw her holding up a small instrument with a loop of tubing connecting a flared bell to a tapered mouthpiece. It was made of a dark, matte material. Ihva could tell it was beautiful and intricate, though she couldn't make out the particular carved patterns. The others joined her as she talked to where Linara stood.

"That was too easy," Cor breathed.

Linara looked at him and back at the Horn, then replied, "It was. It cannot be this simple, or the Appointed of the past would have retrieved the Horn of Orla easily."

Ihva looked at Linara, saying, "They're not here, though? The Shades of Twilight?"

Linara glanced around, then shook her head. The others relaxed their grips on their weapons, but only a little.

"Let us hurry on our way, then, if indeed our way is clear. The Elders, at least, ought to be present when the Horn is sounded," Cor said quickly.

199

Indeed, it seemed appropriate that the elves be able to witness their salvation. The others agreed as well, and Linara led the way back across the clearing toward Rinhaven, carrying the Horn in a small pack at her side.

All was well until Ihva was just a few strides from the edge of the clearing. Linara had turned her head to look back, and her eyes grew wide as she called out, terrified, "The Shades! The Shades of Twilight!"

Ihva turned and saw that the shadows on the other side of the clearing had grown and were moving steadily toward the party. Malach and Cor turned and jumped between the girls and the growing darkness. Ihva turned to escape toward the city, but more black was creeping in from before them.

"They're in front, too!" she alerted the others.

Weapons already readied, Cor maintained a firm grip on his war hammer and Malach brandished his dagger in front of him, prepared to slash anything that came near. The Prince had moved up beside the dwarves with a tense grip on his rapier. Kronk was next to Ihva, seemingly petrified.

Linara bumped into Ihva as she backed away from the ethereal dark in front of them. She was wide-eyed and panic-stricken. Where had the girl's courage fled? She'd acted so brave and ready to give her life in their conversation two weeks ago. But Ihva was horror-struck, too.

The Shades advanced, pushing the party back toward the stream. Ihva's heart constricted as lonely terror overtook her. Certainly, Linara was feeling it as well, but as strong a unit as they made, they'd each die alone-isolated, helpless, and alone.

The inky blackness was gliding more quickly toward the party now. It had already cut off their escape and pushed them toward the stream in the center of the clearing. She looked back. The Shades would force them into the water. The Horn of Orla. Ihva had to sound the Horn.

"Linara," she called out. "Give me the Horn!"

Linara glanced over. Ihva's words must have startled the girl back to consciousness, as her face showed a moment of recognition, and she immediately drew the Horn from her pouch and tossed it to Ihva.

Ihva tried to catch it with her left hand, since she had her rapier in her right, but it bounced out of her grasp and splashed into the water. The Shades were only twenty paces away now. She had to get the Horn!

She stepped into the water and reached for it. Her fingers closed around the looped tubing and she pulled it out of the stream. It was dense and heavy, and she felt the indentations of the carvings on its surface, but there was no time to look at it. She put her lips to the mouthpiece and blew hard.

Nothing happened. She tried again. Still nothing. She'd never sounded a horn before. The Shades inched closer as the group huddled in the center of the clearing, half of them up to their calves in water. Kronk struck out at the nearest shadow with her club. She hit the ground, and the club almost shattered with the impact. Cor and Malach attempted to drive the Shades back too, to no avail. Ihva remembered Laithor's warning about creatures of the Shadow. Normal weapons wouldn't harm them. She looked at Linara.

"They are trying to enclose us! They'll cut us off from the light," the girl cried.

The darkness began to rise into a wall surrounding Ihva and the others. Soon the wall was reaching its way inward above them, and the stars in the sky started to disappear from view. Linara dropped to her knees, murmuring something in Elvish.

Ihva brought the Horn to her lips again and blew. Again, nothing. At the same time, the Prince reached inside his shirt and pulled out a small, red-stone amulet. He whispered under his breath, and violet light burst forth from the stone toward the Shades. The Shades halted, but only a second later the darkness moved to close the space above the party again, its speed redoubled.

The space above became smaller and smaller, just enough to fit Ihva's body through, then only her head. As the last few stars were about to vanish, Ihva tried the Horn one last, panicked, desperate time.

That noise proceeded from the bell should have jarred her, but instead it sounded subtle, comforting, and delightful. It was a strange feeling to listen to it, like she'd been hearing it her whole life and had only just noticed. The Shades shuddered and receded, allowing more and more of the night sky into view. Ihva breathed again, then took a deep breath and sounded the Horn again. A moment later, the sound faded, but she still felt it inside. The Shades withdrew to the edges of the clearing, then disappeared.

She hardly noticed at first as the others shifted their attention from the Shades to her. It wasn't until Linara spoke Ihva became fully aware of their stares.

"I told you, you're Appointed," the girl said as she rushed to enclose Ihva in a hug.

"Indeed, she is," a woman's voice echoed through the clearing.

Ihva turned to find its source. From the northern edge of the clearing stepped a tall, bright figure, and though Ihva had never heard anyone describe the deity, Rawa, she immediately recognized the figure as the great elvish goddess of the sky.

Chapter 29

DESTROY HER. Take your blade and pierce her.

A voice hissed in Jasper's mind. It had struck him so suddenly. All these years later, it was still there inside, bidding him to evil. The scene around him started to spin, and he shut his eyes tight against it.

Strike her.

The voice only sounded louder when he closed his eyes. He'd known that, but he'd forgotten. It had been so long.

End her. Erase her.

He knew who the voice was talking about, but he was terrified to acknowledge it. He had to keep her safe. Even if it meant...

Only one shall remain. It must be you.

Even if it meant enduring the threats, the ultimatums, he wouldn't touch her.

"I told you, you're Appointed," came Linara's voice.

Jasper opened his eyes. He had to get it together. It was because he'd used his Power, that Oer-forsaken Power. She was back in his head because he'd used the Power.

"Indeed, she is," came another voice, one Jasper didn't recognize. It was real, though, not that the one in his head wasn't real, but that one was different. This other voice had a substance and presence to it that the one in his head lacked. He looked for the speaker.

"She is the Appointed foreshadowed these thousands of years," the voice went on.

That when Jasper caught sight of her-a tall figure with feminine physique. Unlike any woman he'd ever seen, though, she shone with white light that reminded Jasper of the brightness of stars and color of the moon. She was hovering three feet above the ground at the northern edge of the clearing. Her voice was silvery and conjured memories of the small bells they used in the palace to call servants. She went on.

"This is the woman foretold by poets and prophets, Linara Ellenlithe."

"Rawa, worthy of a thousand praises," Linara said from the ground to which she'd fallen.

This was Rawa, then. Had Jasper not been so discomposed, he would have guessed so the moment he'd seen her. Rawa, goddess of the sky. He'd heard the elves whisper she dwelt among the stars. Others had said she was the moon herself, though they'd been speaking poetically, and Jasper had believed it was only a metaphor. Seeing Rawa like this, he wondered if he'd been wrong.

"You have done well, child," Rawa said to Linara. "Whom you seek is not here, though."

Linara looked up, her face startled, then sorrowful.

"Kenia Ellenlithe's soul is still imprisoned beyond the reaches of the forest, along with the rest," Rawa went on.

"Mother," Linara murmured. She had a distant look on her face, but a moment later, her eyes had refocused, and she was gazing at Rawa again. "Good and gracious Rawa, it has been passed down among us that the day the Horn is sounded would be the day of their deliverance and return. Please tell us where they might be. I will seek them myself."

"Daughter, you do well to desire to pursue them, but it is not yet the hour of their emancipation. There is a task yet to be completed." Rawa turned her attention to Miss Marchand. "You believe you have accepted your role, child, but you do not know what your purpose entails." Her voice was kind, but her words struck Jasper with apprehension.

"I'm not sure I understand. What is my purpose?" Miss Marchand appeared so calm in the light of the portentous glimmering.

"It it not for me to explain to you. My Father has called me to aid you in what way he has allowed, not to tell you your way. You will learn in time. I can only exhort you to remain firm in your resolve for good. The pressures of the Shadow are enough to turn many a soul, and it is devious to do so without many realizing they have been converted."

What was that supposed to mean? Jasper was starting to feel aggravated. Rawa meant to warn against the Shadow's guileful ways and mention some grand, mysterious purpose and then not elucidate in the least? What was Miss Marchand to do with that information? Jasper had to remind himself that he'd be parting ways with Miss Marchand soon enough. He'd help as he could, of course, but he had Oerid to save.

Rawa continued, saying, "You have proven yourself worthy of the Horn of Orla, Ihva of Oerid, and to wield Darkslayer, just as you will prove yourself worthy of the powers you possess. You must continue on your journey."

"My journey to where?" Miss Marchand asked.

Indeed, where was Miss Marchand supposed to be going? She'd been following Jasper this whole time. Now she had some destiny of her own, and unless she knew something she hadn't told the others, she had no idea how to fulfill it.

"These are answers you must seek. I bequeath to you a companion whose knowledge is both wide and deep, expansive and profound. Her name is Yidda. She had studied Oerid for many years. She knows more than I do in some ways, less in others. I entrust her to your service. Yidda, may the Father's blessing go with you."

Rawa spoke as though this Yidda was present, but Jasper didn't see anyone. He looked around the clearing again when he heard another woman speak.

"I greet you in the name of the Father, Oer. Might I find myself welcomed by you?"

Miss Marchand was looking around now, too.

"You have heard her voice," Rawa said. "She possesses no body, for the time being. Treat her honorably, and she will impart her knowledge to you, for she is but a creature like you, desiring respect and kindness."

Rawa paused as Miss Marchand nodded slowly. The latter looked like she'd swallowed something unpleasant, and Jasper couldn't blame her. An invisible, immaterial guide for a journey with just as little explanation. It was all very bizarre and disconcerting. Yet Rawa was not finished.

"As for your journey, you must make haste. The Shades have only fled. They are not destroyed. The souls they have captured remain parted from their bodies. The Shades will return in one year if not defeated before then. You, Ihva of Oerid, must vanquish them if the elvish kin are to be released from their captivity.

"Take heart, Ihva of Oerid. Take heart and be strong in hope." Rawa stepped backward and began to fade. Her shining grew less intense until it finally shimmered into nothingness. The party was left staring to the north.

"We must be going," came a woman's kind urging. Yidda. Maybe it was Jasper's discomfort about her being immaterial, but her voice seemed to have an otherworldly undertone now that he was listening. He suppressed a shiver.

Still holding the Horn, Miss Marchand nodded and turned to head back to Rinhaven. Jasper and the rest followed. It struck Jasper how little they knew about Yidda to be taking her word as command. Rawa's endorsement of the mysterious, invisible woman did little to calm the fears that were rising in him. He only knew of one creature that could travel incorporeally, but Yidda couldn't be one of them. She couldn't be a Shrouded.

He realized the voice inside was gone. He desperately hoped it would remain that way.

They arrived back in Rinhaven as the light of dawn began to show through the canopy. A small elvish boy was the first to see them, and he cried out, "They're back! They're back!"

He tugged on his mother's sleeve, and she turned to look. Marvel and veneration showed in her humble smile. She whispered something in her son's ear, and he took off running along a bridge to the east.

Other children began to shout and squeal. The adults, however, were silent, staring at the party as they continued along the ground. Linara had told them to wait until the Elders invited them to ascend back into the trees. They walked the first ten minutes amidst this hushed anticipation, watching the elves watch them in solemn wonder.

After those ten minutes, Jasper heard a sound from behind them. Someone had begun to sing. Others joined in the song as the party continued to make their way toward the Council's meeting place. At first, the elves sang wordless syllables, and their voices melded into a beautiful harmony. There was triumph in the tune. Soon enough, the syllables became words became quiet lyrics, and Jasper listened closely to decipher them.

She holds the sun in her palm,
She grasps the moon in her hand,
She holds her sword like a balm,
For Healing's her command.

She speaks the way of the wild,
Her words are words of the free,
Her heart strong, her manner mild,
Hers the attended plea.

Oer's Appointed is she,
Deemed worthy of the calling,
M'rawa's salvation she'll be
As all the world is falling.

It was clear to Jasper that they were singing about Miss Marchand. This was what they thought of her. Jasper was surprised to find that he identified with them, though maybe not about the details. He wasn't so sure about the holding the sun in her palm part. That sounded blasphemous, but maybe they meant something other than what he was interpreting. He didn't understand the moon imagery either, unless she somehow held the power of Rawa in her. In any case, the song was adoring, full of adulation. They treasured her. She was precious, and they knew it. A sudden affinity for the elves welled in him.

By the time Jasper and the others came in sight of the Elders, the Council was waiting in a clearing on the ground. Jasper found it odd that they'd abandoned their normal platform for a place on the forest floor. The party arrived before the elders, and Jasper looked at Laithor. His face was serious, but his mouth twitched slightly as though he were holding back a smile. The elves' song around them slowly faded to silence.

"We have returned, Laithor!" cried Linara.

"Indeed, you have!"

Jasper was startled to hear the exclamation in Laithor's voice. Elves were often so reserved.

"We have returned successful," Miss Marchand said, holding up the Horn.

Linara was grinning. Laithor's eyes creased as he smiled. He looked around behind Miss Marchand and the party, and his smile faltered.

"Where are the others, our brothers?"

Linara looked at the ground. "They are still captives of the Shades," she replied.

Behind Laithor, the other elders' smiles quickly faded to fearful frowns.

"We must defeat them before a year's time. If we do not vanquish them then, I am afraid the Shades will have possession of our brothers forever," Linara said.

"Have you any idea how to defeat them, Linara? If the Horn did not conquer them, in what can we hope?" Laithor's tone was grave.

"I don't know except we must look to Lady Ihva to defeat the Shades. She sounded the Horn of Orla."

"All will be told in time," Laithor said softly as he shifted his gaze to meet Ihva's, "Daughter Ihva, will you aid us in our battle? It is the final stand in a war we have fought for as long as we can remember. The fate of the elves depends on your assistance."

Miss Marchand looked taken aback. She must not have expected this. She thought a moment, then replied, "The world is not yet falling."

Laithor's face fell, but he looked as though he understood.

Miss Marchand continued, "The world is not at its end, and I have a journey I must continue. Rawa confirmed it was so."

"Do you mean Rawa, the Ever-Praised, spoke with you?" Laithor's eyes widened.

"Yes."

"Indeed, you are blessed, Daughter. Hold tight to the words of Rawa, for they are trustworthy."

It seemed Laithor didn't intend to ask what Rawa had said. Instead, he went on. "Your journey must be pressing if Rawa indicated you must continue. We will not hinder you, but we ask that you find your way back. Darkslayer is yours to take with you, of course, for you have sounded Orla's Horn. I suspect you will have need of this Darkslayer before too long."

Miss Marchand looked resolved, but Jasper could tell Laithor's words unsettled her. Her voice wavered as she spoke. "I have been deemed worthy by Rawa to carry this Horn, and I pledge to use it when M'rawa's need is most dire. I will not tarry in my travels, and I pledge I will do everything I am able to return within a year's time to free you from the terror and grief of the Shades. All that I ask is that you pray for safe passage to... Well, to wherever we head next, Jinad, maybe?"

Miss Marchand meant to accompany Jasper, still, then. He hated that the idea pleased him.

"Very well. Daughter Ihva, we will see you off on your journey. We will send a party to guide you to the edge of Jinad, but I am afraid we cannot accompany you farther."

"With Shades at bay, I believe we'll be safe," she replied. "I believe we have a guide already."

She was speaking of Yidda. What did the elves know about this mysterious woman without a body?

"Very well," Laithor said. "Join us this evening for a celebration. We will present Darkslayer tomorrow morning, and you can be on your way."

Laithor looked thoughtful and didn't wait for Miss Marchand's response before standing. The other council members followed, and they all made their way back up into the trees, leaving Jasper and the others on the ground. Jasper looked at Cor, who was looking at Miss Marchand. Miss Marchand's eyes were on Linara, though.

"We must sleep," was all Linara said.

"Sleep sounds like an excellent idea," Miss Marchand replied.

"Indeed, it does, lassies!" Malach said as he stifled a yawn.

Linara went with them to the platform that had become their sleeping quarters and left them there. Jasper had hardly just laid down when he fell fast asleep.

CHAPTER 30

LINARA WOKE IHVA with a gleeful greeting about an hour before sunset and led her up to a platform high in the trees. From one of the branches hung a beautiful elvish dress the girl said was for her. The dress was flowing and deep green in color. Ihva dressed herself in it. It fit tight in the bodice and flowed more loosely around her hips. The sleeves were long and had extra material hanging down, giving Ihva the illusion of having wings when she raised her arms. She twirled once to see the fabric billowing around her, then headed toward the ground. Celebratory sounds-crackling fires, voices, and music-came from below.

She reached the fireside and found a gathering of elves with more trickling in. She spotted Kronk to the side having her hair redone by a few older female elves, including Ridara, and Malach laughing with some nice young elvish women with whom he seemed be getting along charmingly. Cor and the Prince sat on the outside of the circle, drinking a beverage that steamed as they held it.

Linara left and came back with a crown of flowers. She placed them on Ihva's head, then brought her to a circle of joyful dancers.

"You look as beautiful as Mother," Linara said to Ihva.

Ihva smiled back. She'd learned a few days previous that Linara had lost her mother to the Shades when she was thirty years old, which Ihva calculated to be around six if Linara had been human. Linara's father was lost a week later in pursuit of his wife. According to Linara, her mother was the most beautiful of all the elves. Ihva felt the weight of the girl's compliment.

As they joined the circle dance in progress, Ihva tried to copy the elves' graceful movements. She stumbled a bit while she was learning the steps. The elves crossed their feet behind their legs and swayed in the air in complex patterns, and it took intent observation to copy them. Soon enough, though, Ihva was keeping up with the other dancers splendidly, albeit a bit less fluidly. She caught Linara's eye and smiled. She couldn't remember a time she was more at ease than in this moment. She felt at home. Soon the music turned into a couple's dance, and Ihva tried to sit down.

Linara stopped her, saying, "You and I are guests of honor tonight. We must dance. The men believe they receive blessing from our presence, and who's to say they won't with smiles as bright as ours?"

Ihva nodded and found her first partner, a tall, lithe elf who looked about thirty, at least, if he had been a human. He introduced himself as Amhain. He was nimble and an excellent dancer, and it was a joy to be his partner. Ihva spun and danced in his arms with perfect contentment for a few minutes until the dance ended. Another elf approached her to ask her for the next dance.

After a few more songs, Ihva excused herself in search of food. Her stomach complained of emptiness. She found the celebration spanned more than one clearing, with many smaller fires blazing in other spaces and elves milling about everywhere, eating, drinking, and dancing. When she found an enormous spread of fruits, breads, and soups, she had to restrain herself from rushing toward it.

"I'm usually more for stews and meat, but this elfy fare is nothing to turn my nose up at."

Malach's lilting voice came from beside her. It was muffled as though his mouth was full.

Ihva turned and smiled when she saw Malach with half a slice of bread in his hand, the rest presumably the reason for his bulging cheeks. Crumbs littered his beard.

"They're kind folk, aren't they? There's a sort of beauty to them. And the womenfolk are really quite attractive. Not that you would have much to say on that matter." He stuffed the rest of the bread in his mouth.

Ihva's polite smile turned to a grin as she laughed, and she nodded. She hadn't realized Malach had such an interest in women. Of course, he was probably only twenty-five years old or so, of marriageable age to be sure.

Ihva looked back at the wide range of food options before her. She picked out some of the same dark bread Linara had offered her when she had first arrived in Rinhaven. She had already developed a nostalgia for its rich, nutty flavor. She also took one of the fruits shaped like an apple but with a taste like the candies she loved back home.

"Have you found any of the menfolk to your liking?" Malach asked. He was still standing next to Ihva, and his eyes glinted impishly. He nudged her with his elbow.

"Um, no. Not really," Ihva replied. It was the truth.

Malach's joking manner made her feel relaxed, and she was surprised to find herself willing to confide in him. If indeed she had found anyone to her liking, she might have even told him. She thought of the Prince. On second thought, perhaps she wouldn't tell Malach anything.

"I suppose most are a little too tall and pretty for you." Malach sounded disappointed.

"I mean, I guess." She wasn't sure whether to be offended by his comment.

Malach must have interpreted her noncommittal response as hiding something and teased her. "Oh, there is one then? Who is he?" He scanned the crowd around them.

"No. There's no one." She was such a bad liar, there was no way he believed her.

"Uh-huh," Malach said doubtfully. His voice became a whisper. "Don't worry, lass. You can tell me later." He took another three slices of bread and bounced off.

Ihva shook her head, chuckling. She ate and then grabbed a cup of the steaming liquid she'd seen the Prince and Cor drinking. She took a sip. It was bitter and earthy. She made a face and looked for something else to drink. She found a translucent pink liquid in another large bowl and dipped her cup in that, then tried it. It was cool and tasted much

213

sweeter, kind of like the fruit she'd just eaten. She took another cupful and wandered back to the dancing.

As she finished drinking, a small boy came over to collect her cup. Ihva thanked him and stepped back toward the fire where a couple's dance was still underway. Another young male elf approached her.

"May I have this dance?" he asked. He took her hand inquiringly.

"Of course."

She smiled. His hair was the typical blond, the front half pulled back behind his head. The rest of his hair reached past his shoulders. His face was long and softly angular. He was certainly handsome. Ihva thought back to Malach's teasing. While the elf's appearance was attractive, she felt it clear no amorous sentiments were passing between them. It was just a dance.

The elf's voice interrupted Ihva's thoughts. "My name is Ellan. It is an honor to meet you, Lady Ihva."

The music began, and Ellan and Ihva circled each other, their hands meeting about shoulder level between them. Ihva looked at him shyly.

"I am pleased to make your acquaintance as well."

The young man was quiet as he and Ihva changed directions. The music sped up, and they turned to face each other. Ellan took both Ihva's hands in his own. They moved their feet in quick motions as they turned their bodies to match. Ihva became increasingly exhilarated as she concentrated on the steps. The dance intensified, and Ellan twirled Ihva in front of him, holding her hand above her head. He pulled her back toward himself and reached again for her other hand. She swung around his limber frame, then leaned her head back and laughed as Ellan let go of her left hand and sent her back into another twirl.

As she spun, she caught sight of the Prince looking at her. He had an expression she couldn't discern. He caught her eyes on him, frowned, and got up and walked out of view. She tried to smooth the frown that overtook her expression. What was that about? His looks the past couple weeks were nothing short of mystifying. Why had he left? How long had he been watching her? Her heart pounded anxiously as she tried to forget the whole thing.

But she couldn't forget. There was something magical about the fire tonight, something true and honest. Ihva remembered the night just a few weeks ago, when the blaze had been smaller but just as candid. Dancing in the light of flames and ardor, she found herself wishing the Prince would return and ask her for a dance. She wished she could see that rare, amused smile on his face and know it was meant for her. The pounding in her chest was familiar, yet something felt different tonight. Confused, Ihva found herself wanting to run away from it all-from the fireside dancing with the elves, from her traveling companions, from adventure, from being Oer's Blessing, and from the man whose presence was beginning to complicate everything.

———◆•◆———

The next morning, Ihva woke up to find the others gone and Linara waiting for her. She must have slept very late for even Kronk to have woken before her. Linara was looking forlorn, sitting cross-legged at the edge of Ihva's blankets. Ihva was still half asleep, so when the girl didn't speak, she didn't begin a conversation either.

She'd been dreaming just before she woke. Something about home. She'd been fleeing a suitor, doing all manner of un-ladylike things-jumping over barrels, climbing up buildings, and running on rooftops. Her mother had been yelling at her the pedigree and qualifications of the boy pursuing her, but she'd kept running.

Then Ihva remembered the previous evening. Her heart stuck in her throat. It was a beautiful celebration, to be sure, but she hadn't seen the Prince since the moment he'd walked off from the fireside and left her pining. Ihva tried to pull herself together. It meant nothing. The light of the fire, the events with the Shades, it had all confused her. Sure, she liked him, but that was all. There was nothing more to it. There could be nothing more to it. He was an engaged royal, and she was nothing more than a moneyed commoner, if her parents didn't disown her for the scare she'd given them when she returned. She was

Oer's Blessing, too, of course, but that was even greater reason she should stay away from any relationship that might develop.

She shook her head to rid herself of foolish thoughts and asked Linara in an overly joyful voice, "What's for breakfast?"

Linara looked at her and Ihva realized that the girl was crying. Ihva felt suddenly insensitive.

"Linara, I will return. I will find your mother and father and the others."

"I know you mean to do so. But Father meant to return with Mother as well."

Linara began to weep. Ihva understood Linara's fears and realized she had nothing with which to dissuade the girl from them. Instead, she decided to be honest.

"It's true. I can't guarantee I'll come back. Who can promise anything but the gods? Only they can aid me now. Pray for me, Linara. Pray for me."

Linara nodded, moisture gathered in her eyes, and Ihva stood up to give her a hug. The girl accepted Ihva's embrace and let her tears fall openly. The two were silent for a few moments while Ihva stroked Linara's hair. Linara needed her mother, and Ihva determined that, although she couldn't promise anything, she'd do everything in her power to come back and find the girl's parents.

She let go of Linara after a minute and let Linara's tears subside. "Why don't we go and enjoy a good meal together?" she asked when the girl had stopped crying.

Linara gave her a small smile and indicated the way down the ladder, then followed after Ihva as she descended. The girl still looked crestfallen as she reached the ground, so Ihva smiled a mischievous grin, took Linara's hand, and began to skip. Linara looked at Ihva hesitantly and followed in step. They danced in circles their way over to the platform where the rest of the party and the Elders were eating. By the time they had reached the breakfasting tree, Linara was giggling. Ihva beamed as well and they ascended the ladder, laughing.

As Ihva peeked her head over the top of the ladder, she caught Cor's gaze. He was smiling to himself and nodded when he spotted her. Suddenly she remembered the Prince, and her laughter waned into a few self-conscious snorts. She looked around for him but didn't see him. Relieved, she sat down next to Linara and began to eat.

The meal was full of gaiety, and many times Ihva caught herself laughing sincerely. The Elders and some other elves joined the party for this meal, and they seemed so different from the grim folk that their first impression had indicated them to be. Laithor was the most serious of the Elders, and even he was smiling, though only slightly. Ihva guessed his high spirits were tempered by the concern he held for his people. He looked northwest on repeated occasions throughout their breakfast.

When they'd finished, Laithor addressed them. "Before you take your leave, we of Rinhaven and of M'rawa desire to bestow upon you some gifts. Follow, and we will present them to you."

Darkslayer. Ihva was sure he was referring to Darkslayer. What kind of weapon was Darkslayer anyway? All she knew how to wield was the rapier. What if they gave her a weapon she couldn't even use? She held fearful anticipation as they climbed a ladder and crossed a bridge to another large platform. Laithor indicated for them to sit, and Ihva did so, nervous, wondering.

Chapter 31

JASPER SKIPPED BREAKFAST their last day in Rinhaven. He took a walk instead, a long one. He had a lot to think about, to figure out, and a lot to stamp out of his mind. It would take longer than his usual hour, he knew.

He thought about Jessica, about Oerid, about his father, about Cor, about Malach, about Eshad, about Ihva Marchand, about this new Yidda, about everything really. His walk led him far from the place where they'd slept, and by the time he turned around, he knew he'd have to rush to get back to the others before they finished eating. As it was, he slipped up the ladder to join them and caught the tail end of something Laithor had been saying.

"Follow, and we will present them to you."

At least he'd gotten to them before they left to follow Laithor and the Elders. Jasper slowed himself and fell to the back of the group. He was the last one up the ladder and across the bridge and settled behind the others when they were told to sit. He didn't feel like dealing with anyone right now, not unless he had to.

Laithor and the Elders sat as well, and Laithor began speaking. "Since Orla's disappearance, we have been awaiting a Champion. Instead of one, the Father brought us five. This morning, we honor each in turn."

"First, for our dear Kronk, we have a Ribbon of Light. We often gift these to our children to lend them the solace of moonlit nights when clouds hide the skies. We give this Ribbon to you, Kronk, to wear so that on the darkest day of Gant, the elves may remain a pure light to you."

He stopped, and a young female elf brought forward a translucent ribbon about as long as her arm. Jasper couldn't see Kronk's face, but her back straightened, and he heard her speaking thanks. Some of the female onlookers began to plait the ribbon into Kronk's braid. Laithor looked at the orc-blood woman with a pleased smile and moved his gaze to Cor.

"Cor Leviel Gidfolk, you are a dwarf with many loyalties, but each builds upon the other, and they intertwine to create great strength within you. Born an Eshadian, you became an Oeridian by choice, and now we offer you the friendship of M'rawa to recognize your willingness to make the utmost sacrifice to protect our people. We endow you with a Periapt of the Moon, something granted only to Friends of Rawa and only bestowed on three before you. May you carry our friendship ever in your heart."

Another young female elf brought forward a chain with a white, circular pendant. It was plain, but then, many things the elves made had a simple beauty that made Oeridian decor and clothing seem garish. Miss Marchand's dress last night had been plain, unadorned and unpretentious, yet she had been the most captivating woman of them all in it.

"Next, we have Malach Lav Shemayim, Prince and Heir to Eshad's Throne. Your courage to confide your station and plight has not gone unnoticed and is deeply appreciated. We commit to aid you in whatever way we might the day you choose to claim your inheritance, short of taking lives of the souled. We are a peaceful people, and violence does not become us, but whatever we can offer we will provide you. For now, accept this dagger, which we call the Returning Blade, as a pledge of our support. Rolim Miranan enchanted the Returning Blade to always find its way back into the hand of its wielder. I believe you will find it useful."

A young male elf handed the dwarf a dagger with a beautifully carved handle. Malach bowed his head and accepted the gift with quiet thanks.

Then Laithor looked at Jasper, and everyone else's eyes fell on him, too. "Prince Jasper Thesson Aurdor of Oerid, you are a man of many struggles, a man of conflict, though often not by choice. Your striving is not without fruit-remember it. Remember it most on the day everything is required of you and believe in the strength of virtue. You will always find friends in M'rawa.

"We offer this Cloak of Imperceptibility. Should the wearer keep to the shadows, any creature who might otherwise notice him will instead see only a faint silhouette, barely detectable. This garment has been worn by many an elvish scout to much success. It was woven from the hairs of the Black Monocero, a great evil that plagued the elves for many centuries before High Elf Orla hunted it down. Wear it well, Jasper Thesson Aurdor, friend of elves."

The next thing Jasper knew, a male elf brought him a cloak, dark and lusterless, and laid it in his outstretched hands. How did Laithor know all that about him?

"I am pleased to accept this gift." His voice didn't sound like it was coming from him, but he went on. "Your people are wise and discerning, and I am grateful to be counted a friend among you."

Diplomatic enough. How did Laithor know all that? Jasper knew the elves had been watching him, but he'd had no idea they were that perceptive. A man of many struggles. Surely, they didn't know. They couldn't know.

"Lastly, we come to the Lady Ihva Marie Marchand, for she is nobility among the elves. You already possess the elves' most treasured relic, the Horn of Orla. Wrought by the hand of Rawa herself, this was a gift to the elves for the time of their greatest need, and we bequeath it to you, as our salvation lies in your hands. We will keep it safe here in Rinhaven until your return, but it is yours. We would like to offer something more, though, something that is yours by right of having sounded the Horn. We would like to offer the blade called Darkslayer."

Darkslayer was a blade, then. That was a good sign. Laithor continued.

"You know the story of this blade, wrought from the Sidereal Stone. It will pierce the strongest metal and the deepest darkness. With this blade shall you impale the Shadow, and by its might shall you Heal the world."

Laithor made it sound like Miss Marchand would have a face-off with the Lady of Shadows. Jasper grew irritated. There was no reason to frighten her like that. She might be Oer's Blessing, but the Blessing had never come close to battling the Lady, and certainly not head-on. If anything, the Blessing had always done things that might have been considered the Lady's work, inciting mayhem, but Jasper knew Miss Marchand was far from a force of chaos and nowhere near allied with the Shadow.

"We present to you, Lady Ihva Marie Marchand, this blade, Darkslayer. May you wield it with boldness to accomplish the will of the Father."

Two elves, a male and a female, appeared carrying something between them. The scabbard at least indicated elvish make with its plain elegance. The elves stopped in front of Miss Marchand and knelt to present her the sword. This was Darkslayer, then. The elf nearest the hilt offered it to Miss Marchand, and she took it. Then she drew the blade from its scabbard. An awed silence settled over the crowd, and Jasper peered at the sword in her hand.

It was hard to describe Darkslayer. It was glowing with a soft blue-white light, and its shape reminded Jasper most of the arming sword he'd been given for practice when his lessons had begun all those years ago. Darkslayer's tip came to a narrow point, and both edges were sharpened along their length. It could be used for both thrusting or slashing. That was good, at least. He'd have to train Miss Marchand some different forms and swings, but she'd have a head start from their rapier lessons.

"Thank you," was all she told the elves at first.

Her voice was emotional, and Jasper hoped she wouldn't cry. Laithor just watched her, and everyone else kept silent as she went on.

"I accept this blade and the duty that you entrust me with it. I will do everything in my power to bring about what you have spoken."

Her words were striking. She knew she was assuming a burden much too heavy for her, yet it was her tone that Jasper hadn't been prepared for. She was solemn and dignified. Miss Ihva Marchand sounded resolved and somehow indomitable. Not that he'd ever considered her completely feeble or fearful, not exactly, though that first day when she'd met him and fainted, he'd found her a bit pitiful. Even so, he'd grown to understand her more over these past months, and he knew now she was far from helpless. Today, though, she seemed more exalted than a simple merchant's daughter.

Jasper realized Malach was speaking and refocused his attention on the conversation at hand.

"...will not have been given in vain. We treasure these symbols of our unity in the battle against Darkness. You will be ever on our minds and in our hearts. May Rawa shine upon you!"

Laithor stood, as did the Elders, then the rest of the onlookers. The High Elf bowed his head, then said, "May Rawa and the Father shine on you, night and day, the glory of their brightness."

There was a sudden bustle around Jasper and the others as the elves moved to disperse. Jasper and the party were caught up in the crowd and moved toward the ground. Once there, the crowd churned its way northwest, and Jasper had no choice but to head that direction as well. It was fine, though. He and Cor had decided to head toward Alm'adinat, as the elves had last seen Jessica in the northwest corner of the forest. The elves deposited the party just outside Rinhaven, where the last bridge ended, then dispersed and disappeared back into the city. Jasper and the others were left looking at each other. Apart from the hum of insects and chattering of birds, everything was silent. Someone had to take the lead, Jasper knew, so he gathered himself to inform the others of his and Cor's plan. Before he could speak, however, Yidda's voice chimed from his left.

"There is little time to waste. We must be going."

What did Yidda know? Then again, she might have listened in on his and Cor's conversations. Who knew what else the woman had overheard or witnessed? Where had she been? What had she seen? Jasper had no idea how old she was, as her voice was ageless. Who was she? What was she?

He realized the others had started moving while he was thinking, so he jogged to catch up. He felt agitated. Now he had something else to think about, to figure out. Not that he'd needed anything else, of course, but that didn't stop things from piling up. He sighed audibly, and Malach looked back. Jasper smoothed his face and gave the dwarf a curt nod. Having his own concerns and despondencies was no reason to bring anyone else down. He tried to maintain a neutral expression for anyone who might look back to check on him, but he didn't stop thinking until they laid down to sleep that night. Not even then, really. His dreams were anxious and filled with danger.

CHAPTER 32

"HOW MUCH FARTHER do we have?" Ihva asked.

It had been five days, and she and the others were trekking past what seemed like the ten-thousandth walking palm. She looked back at the tree as she passed it just to make sure the name didn't become a reality. Yidda had already informed the party that the walking palms did nothing their name suggested. The elves simple called them "walking palms" for their interesting, above-ground root structure, or so Yidda had said. Ihva maintained her suspicions and put her hand to Darkslayer.

"We have another week or so, at least, at this pace, Ihva," Yidda said.

Ihva felt a certain gratitude and affection rise in her at the woman's kind tone. Yidda was long-suffering. She'd put up with Kronk's complaining for the first few days until Ihva had quieted her, but this was only days later and Ihva was whining about their journey. It was just so hot and sticky and miserable in this forest. Rinhaven hadn't felt like this. Ihva wondered what the elves did to keep the city comfortable.

The trickling of water sounded ahead. That was a relief. Ihva had run out of water a couple of hours ago. A break for water meant a short rest. She'd been traveling long enough her feet weren't exactly throbbing, but they were sore, and a break sounded wonderful.

"There is a stream ahead. We ought to stop there for lunch," Cor said.

Cor always had wonderful ideas. The Prince sighed but said nothing. He'd been anxious to hurry along, but even he must have realized breaks were necessary. The Prince had been anxious in general of late. Ever since they'd left Rinhaven, he'd been acting on edge again. Laithor had called the Prince "a man of many struggles," and Ihva believed it, but she couldn't understand what those struggles might be. Sure, he was to rule a nation, the most powerful in Gant, and that came with its own set of problems. Yet even so, there had been peace in Oerid for a good while, and nothing indicated that would change just because the Prince took the throne. Then again, they'd just learned of Arusha's intentions to build a Raised army, which would pose a threat to Oerid's peace. That could be weighing on the Prince. Plus Lady Cibelle was still out there somewhere, in Jinad by now if Ihva had to guess, maybe on a ship back to Eshad.

Whatever it was concerning the Prince, he'd been acting aloof again. Not that he'd ever been quite amiable with Ihva, but now he didn't look at her except to teach her swordplay. He refused to speak to her and wouldn't acknowledge her unless she addressed him, which she'd done only once to ask how hunting had gone. The elves had provided the Prince a crossbow, which Ihva assumed made hunting a lot easier. When she'd asked, though, he'd just looked at her warily and answered something generic. She couldn't for the life of her understand what was going on.

It hurt, if she was honest. It had little to do with the fact she liked him, or not solely at least. What bothered her also was they'd seemed to be becoming friends of a sort. He'd helped her immensely with the rapier, and his assistance learning Darkslayer was proving very beneficial. Besides that, they'd been cordial. Never had the Prince been affable, but he'd spoken to her with pleasant sincerity. She remembered a conversation they'd had back in Eshad, before the whole thing with Aaron. The Prince had mentioned she'd have to learn her own style, and she'd asked what he'd meant by style. He'd explained in detail a few techniques he'd seen paired and demonstrated for her, losing his restrained demeanor for a moment. She'd been so afraid that whatever happened on the farm that night had ruined the budding friendship, but then he'd danced with her and that had seemed to break down whatever barrier the evening at the farm had erected. Ihva felt a little giddy remembering how he'd smiled that evening. It was a small smile-one definitely couldn't describe it as a grin-but it had been casual and untroubled. He'd looked happy, and she had this wonderful, miserable feeling she'd been a reason for that happiness. Not the reason, of course, but a reason.

Not that it mattered anymore, though. He'd decided to ignore her again. She'd never be more than a commoner girl to him, anyway, even if she was Oer's Blessing. He wouldn't have eyes for her, and really, he ought not mind her that way. Lady Cibelle held his affections and his hand, and that was all there was to it. Ihva had reminded herself of these things a few times over the past few days, but it had done little to curb her feelings. A longing, a tiny hope, resided in her, and she was finding that tiny hopes seemed the most resilient kind.

They arrived at the stream. Now was not the time to consider things like this. Better she contemplates what Oer intended for her to do after they'd found Lady Cibelle, as Ihva's plans ended there. After that, she'd have to figure out her journey on her own.

The rest of the day Ihva wondered who would accompany her in the rest of her travels. She concluded she'd have Yidda, at least, and Kronk, of course, but she wasn't sure whether the others would come along. In fact, she was worse than not sure-she was positive they'd go their separate ways. The thought was disheartening at best, so she spent the remainder of the afternoon and evening in low spirits, though she smiled at the others whenever she caught them looking at her. This was no reason to bring the others down when they were only fulfilling their duties, even if that meant they'd leave her to fend for herself.

Ihva had taken third watch that night to let the Prince get some rest. He often took third, maybe so he could wake her in time for practice, but he'd looked more worn out than usual today and she'd wanted to give him a break. She'd underestimated her own weariness, though. Her eyelids felt leaden, and she found herself fading in and out of consciousness. She got up and meandered around the clearing where they'd made camp, but soon she was too tired even to walk. She sat down at one end, cross-legged with her back against a tree.

The next thing she knew, Yidda's voice was crying out. "Night lions, from the west!"

Ihva shot up, drawing Darkslayer. The Prince and Cor were standing with their weapons readied by the time she saw them, and Malach and Kronk were shaking themselves awake. They had no fire because of the heat, so Cor had lit his orb, which left Ihva blinking blindly for a second.

When she could see again, a dark figure on all fours came sprinting from the treeline to the west. It leapt into the air and attempted to pounce on the Prince, but Cor struck it sideways with his hammer.

Another cat sped in from the northwest and pounced on Kronk, knocking the woman to the ground. It went to gash her with its claws, and Ihva cried out in panic. Not Kronk, anyone but Kronk! Ihva raced across the clearing to the woman's aid as another night lion appeared from the undergrowth and dashed toward Malach.

Ihva arrived at Kronk and tried a swing with Darkslayer the Prince had been teaching her. She connected with the night lion's side and drew a long cut along the animal's belly. The night lion roared its pain, then turned on Ihva and snarled. Its face was soot black, and the teeth it bared came to points much like her blade. Ihva jumped back just in time as the animal leapt for her, and it landed impaled on Darkslayer instead.

The weight of the creature dragged Ihva's arm to the ground, but there was no time to waste as another night lion landed between her and Kronk. Ihva wrested Darkslayer from the first animal's corpse and struck out at the second. She was relying on rapier jabs now. The creature was circling her, and she stabbed at it repeatedly. It dodged every blow. Finally, it stopped for a moment, squared itself, and bounded toward her.

Ihva only froze for a split second, but it was long enough that she knew she couldn't avoid the creature tackling her. She braced, ready to drop Darkslayer and unsheath her dagger. The creature bowled her down, and all she knew was the ground at her back and a dense, bulky feline with sharp teeth and even sharper claws pinning her to the ground. She still had her grip on Darkslayer, so she used the blade to ward off the animal's bites. The cat was strong, very strong. She couldn't hold it off long. Where was Kronk?

The night lion let up a moment, and Ihva looked around to see what had happened. Then something whizzed past, and there was liquid pouring down on her. The next thing she knew, the night lion was dead weight on top of her.

A moment later, she realized everything was quiet. She tried to roll the night lion's body off her, but it was massive, much bigger than she'd expected when the elves had mentioned the creatures. Then the weight lifted, and Cor was standing over her.

"Are you hurt?" he asked.

"No," she replied, then evaluated. Nothing felt broken, and she felt hardly anything that might become bruises, either. She'd twisted in a strange direction and pulled a muscle in her back, but that was all.

"No, I'm alright," she repeated.

Cor was still looking her over. He kept glancing at her face.

"You look frightful, lass, that's all," Malach told her.

Again with Malach, she wasn't sure whether to be offended, and her hesitation must have shown.

"The blood, I mean," Malach clarified. "You're really quite fetching without it. I mean, you're not my type or anything, just I notice these things. I'd never…"

The dwarf started rambling, and Ihva tried to contain her amusement. She felt the blood now, the night lion's blood, all down her face.

"I mean, she's very darling when she's not, you know, covered with gore. Wouldn't you say so, a lovely lass?"

Malach slapped the Prince on the back and gave him a pleading glance.

"Um, yes." The Prince seemed uncomfortable and broke Malach's gaze. "She's very lovely," the Prince added.

Now Ihva felt uncomfortable. He'd sounded almost like he'd meant it, his voice soft and strangely earnest. Ihva had been about to thank Malach but thanking the Prince didn't seem quite appropriate. She prayed for a distraction, and it came a second later.

"We ought to move forward. Other creatures will smell the kill and come to feast." It was Yidda who spoke.

"Indeed, it would be wise to move on from here before any more come to join us," Cor replied. "You should wash, Ihva, so as not to carry the scent with us. I will Heal Kronk"

Ihva nodded. Malach gave her a hand up, looking a bit flushed.

"You know I wouldn't do that to you, lass, right? We've got our own paths, and as endearing as you are, you're a sister to me," the dwarf told her.

He saw her as a sister? Ihva felt a surging affection for the dwarf as she replied simply, "I know."

He nodded his head. He understood. For some reason, he glanced over at the Prince, but the Prince had withdrawn and didn't meet his gaze.

"Here, take my water. We will find more soon enough, I pray," Cor said, holding out his water skin.

Ihva took it and slowly poured it over her face, scrubbing off the blood. She had to use her own water and Malach's as well before she was finished, and even then, it wouldn't come out of her hair. She really did hope they'd find a stream soon as they set off through the forest still an hour before dawn.

———◆◆◆———

It struck Ihva later, a couple hours before lunch that Yidda had been the one to warn them about the night lions, though the woman was not on watch rotation. No one had brought it up, and Ihva hadn't even thought about it, but now she wondered why Yidda had been awake to warn them of the attack. Ihva had wondered about Yidda a good deal the past week, really. Who was she? Why didn't she have a body? She clearly existed as much as any of them did. What kind of creature had a spirit but no substance?

The Prince had tried to ask Yidda about herself, but she'd deflected his questions, so Ihva knew she wouldn't get answers if she asked either. Still, the woman had been watching over them last night. Was that a regular thing?

"Yidda," Ihva started.

"Yes, Ihva," Yidda replied. She sounded like she was near the Prince at the front.

"When you woke us last night, how long had you been watching?" Ihva didn't think her question too threatening or accusatory, or she hoped as much. There was a pause, though, and she was afraid she'd offended the woman. Then Yidda replied.

"Since the beginning of first watch."

"All night?" Ihva asked, incredulous.

"Yes, every night."

The woman didn't sleep? Ihva was confused.

"Wait, now. You're telling me you stay up all night, every night, like a Shadow-cursed Shrouded?" Malach exclaimed, then gave an uneasy chuckle.

It was true, though. The Shrouded and certain Raised beings were the only creatures Ihva could recall that didn't need sleep.

"I'm no Shrouded, son." Yidda's voice was firm but suddenly commanding. Ihva believed her but still felt uneasy.

"We were told she is trustworthy. Let us not go questioning the words of Rawa," Cor said.

The Prince stopped, and Malach stumbled as he almost ran into him. "Then what are you?" the Prince asked, speaking to the air.

Everyone else stopped and was silent, then Yidda answered. "What I am should not concern you. I am for you, not against you. I live for Oer now. That is what matters."

More silence.

"How are we to know that?"

It was the Prince who asked again.

"It was Yidda who saved our lives last night, let us not forget," Cor replied before the woman could answer. "Rawa has proffered this woman to be our guide. Would you spurn the gift of Oer's daughter?"

The Prince glanced at Cor; his brow furrowed. The two stared at each other for a tense moment until the Prince looked away.

"If Yidda has no need for sleep, perhaps we ought to have her watch for us tonight. We could each use the extra rest," Cor proposed.

"Indeed, if I relieve you of that burden, we should be able to take fewer breaks, and we would make better time to Jinad," Yidda said.

Cor looked around at the others. Kronk was the first to nod, then Malach joined her despite the frown on his face. Sleep did sound nice, and Ihva was afraid her next watch might go like the last with her asleep for half of it. They needed someone to watch, and who better than the mysterious unsleeping woman no one could see? Ihva had to admit, it sounded like a ridiculous plan, but keeping watches with everyone so exhausted didn't sound like a great option either. They'd have to trust the woman eventually. Might as well let her earn that trust now.

Ihva looked at Cor and nodded. Everyone except the Prince had agreed. Ihva glanced at him.

"It seems I'm outnumbered," he said, his words dragging out. He gave Cor a circumspect look, his brow furrowed deep and his eyes sharp, then went on. "You win, Cor. She takes watches."

He turned and strode forward through the underbrush. Ihva looked at Malach, who just shrugged and started after the Prince. Cor shook his head before joining them, and Ihva pulled Kronk along at the back of the party. Ihva had her own doubts, but Cor was wiser than any of them, so she decided to trust him, even if that meant trusting Yidda, too.

Chapter 33

JASPER WAS HAVING A HARD TIME thinking straight. Again. The closer they got to Jinad, the more anxious he was that Jessica had fallen into the wrong hands. He'd concluded they needed to search the port of Alm'adinat but had a feeling they wouldn't find Jessica there. Perhaps no one would have seen her. She might have snuck onto a ship instead of seeking passage. It was what he would have done. Who knew which dwarves were privy to Arusha's plot and which were his agents?

In any case, he fretted that they'd have to find passage themselves. They had two dwarves with them. Cor and Malach could pass themselves off as traders well enough, but two humans and an orc-blood would attract attention, the wrong kind of attention. If Arusha had set a reward for their capture, Jasper and the others were in trouble. They'd have to stow away themselves to follow Jessica, and even then, they wouldn't know which port city she was headed to. For Oer's sake, why had she fled to Jinad?

Jasper gave an exasperated sigh and didn't look to see if anyone noticed. He was too discomposed to be concerned with what the others might see in him. There were too many thoughts in his head, too many questions distressing him. Who was Yidda? What was she, and what did she know? How would they make it through Jinad? How would they escape the dwarves and head back to Oerid once they reached Eshad? How would he explain the price on his head for the assassination of King Cherev-ad? His father would believe him, of course, but the Oeridian people might be harder to convince. Arusha was building an army of the Raised. What if they didn't get back in time to stop him?

So many concerns. So many dangers. It was all too much for one person to handle, but he had to. The only other person he could count on was Cor, and Cor had been caught up with Miss Marchand a lot lately with the whole Oer's Blessing business. Not that Jasper begrudged Miss Marchand time with Cor, but he really needed some moral support right now and it didn't seem like he'd get it. He was finally ready to accept some help, a little bit of it at least, and there was none to be found. Perfect. Anyway, he couldn't talk about it all with the others around, so even if Cor had been available, there was little chance for more than a brief conversation, not enough time to discuss what was on Jasper's mind.

He had to tell the others his plan at some point, though, the immediate aspects of it at the very least. They were two days from the border between M'rawa and Jinad. Better now than later.

"So, the death and the breaking, are they different? Whose breaking and whose death?" Miss Marchand was asking.

It was Cor who responded, of course. "That is highly debated. Some believe, since the breaking precedes the death, this line describes a process, in which case the one who breaks shall also die. Others believe the two events are simultaneous, making it two separate individuals. There also exists the third camp that sees the death and the breaking as belonging to a larger entity than an individual-a house or a nation, perhaps."

It sounded like Cor had finished, and Jasper opened his mouth to speak, but then the dwarf went on.

"If I remember correctly, your Reading might have shed some light on the matter. You translated that line, 'The breaking and his death' instead of 'The breaking and the death,'" which leads me to believe the two belong to two separate individuals. As far as to whom they belong, I cannot be certain."

Jasper cleared his throat as Cor stopped to take a breath. The dwarf could be rather long-winded when expounding on philosophical ideas, especially when it came to theological matters.

"I was just going to let you know my plan for when we reach Alm'adinat," Jasper said quietly, then paused.

Everyone else was silent, then Malach spoke. "Well, what is it?"

Jasper swallowed. "We'll need to search the port, the ships that is. We can't all go. That'll attract too many eyes and too many questions. Cor, Malach, will you try asking around? If anyone's seen Lady Cibelle, even glimpsed her? If she asked them anything? If she gave any indication of where she might have been headed?" He glanced back at the dwarves.

Cor nodded, and Malach was watching Jasper, grinning.

"The Prince of Oerid needs my help, huh?" Malach was gloating. Fine, let him gloat, as long as he helped.

"Yes, I do. The rest of us should remain far from the city so as not to be seen. I'm not sure the Jini would appreciate us near their city."

Malach laughed humorlessly. What Jasper had said was true. That the Jini wouldn't appreciate the party's presence was a gross understatement. They'd be captured, if not killed on sight, if the Jini found them outside the bounds of the docks. The Jini were a violent race-volatile, chaotic, and bloodthirsty. The only reason they made peace enough to trade with the dwarves on the docks of Alm'adinat was for the evadium the dwarves provided. Evadium, that precious pale metal so coveted among Oeridians for its use in crafting weapons and armor. The Jini used it for some ritual or another of which no one knew the details. Maybe their city was made of evadium, though all reports told of the city's clay walls, so that seemed unlikely. It was a mystery what the Jini used evadium for, but they had to consume it like a creature consumed water, as they never seemed to have enough of it.

"What will we do if we do not find her at the docks?" Cor asked, interrupting Jasper's thoughts. "There is the possibility none have seen her."

That was true, and the question stumped Jasper. Should they just return to Oerid in that case and hope she'd make it back somehow? He couldn't give her up for lost, not that easily. Perhaps another woman would love him as she did, but that wasn't the point. He had to rescue her. He was the reason she was in trouble in the first place.

"I know someone who can help." It was Yidda who spoke, her voice sounding just a few feet in front of Jasper.

"Who is it?" he asked warily.

"There is someone in Alm'adinat I know who keeps track of every visitor to the docks. He will have seen her if she indeed found her way there."

"Someone" was much too vague an answer for Jasper. Yidda was hiding this individual's identity for a reason, and Jasper meant to find out why.

"How do you know this 'someone'? Have you been to Alm'adinat, then? Do the Jini know you?" he replied to Yidda.

Yidda paused before answering, and even then, her words came out slowly. "I have known this individual for many years. I have indeed been to Alm'adinat, and the Jini do know me, but you would do well not to mention me there."

"Really?" Jasper replied. The word drew out as his hackles raised.

"The man's name it Ohebed. You should know he is a Jin."

Ohebed the Jin? Why in the world would they ever trust a Jin? The creatures were notorious for their sadism, greed, and treachery. What was to say Ohebed wouldn't tell them about Jessica but then take them captive to the Sultan and hold them for ransom, or worse?

It seemed everyone else was waiting for Jasper to respond, so he did. "Right. And why would we entrust something as precious as the knowledge of our presence and purpose with a Jin? Why should we trust such a dangerous, traitorous, abominable creature with our lives, Yidda? Even you must know that's utter foolishness."

There was another pause.

"Because you already have," was all Yidda said.

Jasper came to an immediate halt. They already had. That couldn't mean what Jasper thought it might, he hoped. Desperately he hoped, but Yidda's next words crumbled that reassurance within him.

"I am a Jin," she said, her voice quiet. "It is too much a tale to tell now. Let it suffice for the time being to tell you I am a Jin but I serve Oer."

Yidda was a Jin. Jasper felt suddenly dizzy. They were entrusting their lives, had entrusted their lives, to a Jin. This couldn't be happening.

"I have led you true this far, and I will lead you on with the same care. I side with you in this war," Yidda went on.

She was a Jin. It wasn't clear how the Lady of Shadows and the Jini were related, but it was plain enough they were. Some said the Lady created the Jini from the dust of Jinad. Others said she birthed them long ago. Whatever the case, the Jini were not a race to be trifled with, much less to place one's faith in. This couldn't be happening.

"You lied to us," was all Jasper could manage to say.

"I did not lie. I've given you no misinformation about my person or my history. I have only led you to where you must go and guarded you along the way."

Fine, she hadn't lied, but she'd kept information from them, vital information that would have changed Jasper's decisions about how to proceed from Rinhaven.

"She has protected us these past couple weeks," Malach said.

"Had you taken this journey alone, it would have taken you three weeks to arrive at this point. I cut off a week avoiding obstacles and taking watches," Yidda said.

According to the elves' calculations, it indeed should have taken longer than it had to reach this location, but that was beside the point. She was a Jin! He already had the Lady of Shadows in his head. Could he not at least escape having a party member commissioned by her?

Jasper turned and looked at the others. Malach appeared watchful, and Miss Marchand had her arms around her stomach and seemed guarded. Kronk was staring at the space where Yidda sounded to be. Unlike the others, though, Cor didn't look worried, just reflective. Jasper might have even detected curiosity in the dwarf's eyes. What did Cor know that he didn't?

"Care to share your thoughts, Cor?" he asked with just a touch of acerbity.

Cor looked at him with a slight smile. "I remembered her voice, son."

Remembered Yidda's voice? What was that supposed to mean?

Cor glanced to the space Yidda likely occupied and went on. "It was nearly eighteen years ago you spoke to me, was it not? I remember a woman's voice informed me of a birth, that a celebrated child had found her way into the world. You told me not to seek her then but that she had come, a child who bent Reality around her. That was how you described her. The Light in her, she was the daughter of the promise, you said, and we could not afford to lose her this time."

"You remember well, Cor Leviel Gidfolk," Yidda replied.

What in the name of Oer was going on? This woman, this Jin, had spoken to Cor eighteen years ago, blathered on about some "child of promise," and not only had Cor believed her, but it seemed now he hoped Jasper would do the same?

"Stop, Cor. Just stop," he said.

Cor's eyes turned to him, and his smile faltered.

"You can't tell me you believe a Jin would feed you the truth, or if so, not without ulterior motives. And besides that, why would you put stock in some voice you've never heard before speaking some lofty-sounding gibberish?"

Cor replied calmly. "I had not believed the full truth of her words until Ihva appeared." He gave Miss Marchand a kind look, at which she uncrossed her arms and gave a hesitant smile back. "It is clear to me now, Ihva is the child of Light I have been seeking. She is Oer's Blessing, and like Yidda said, we cannot afford to lose her this time."

This was crazy. Cor was crazy! The cursed Oer's Blessing talk again, believing a Jin's prophetic counsel, following a Jin into Alm'adinat. Where would it end?

"As much as I hate to say it, I think he's right," Malach interjected.

And thus, like dominos, the party fell again in favor of Yidda, with Miss Marchand nodding her head in agreement and Kronk following Miss Marchand. Why did Jasper always have to be the outnumbered voice of reason? But he needed the others. He'd never survive on his own, much less find Jessica. He had to abide by their decision by agreeing to it himself, or he'd find himself without any support at all.

"You say this Ohebed would know anything there is to know about Lady Cibelle's whereabouts?" he asked, still staring at Cor.

"Indeed, if there is any information to be found, it will lie with him," Yidda replied.

Jasper sighed, which did nothing to relieve his anxieties. If anything, they deepened as he conceded. "We will find your Ohebed then, Yidda."

"Very well." Her voice did not contain even a hint of satisfaction in the victory she'd just won, which irked Jasper more than if she'd held it over him. She just sounded patient and solemn.

"If anything happens to Lady Cibelle because of your misinformation or bad advice, I will make you wish you'd never spoken a word to us." There was nothing Jasper could do to hurt Yidda, and he knew it. "Anything at all, and you will pay for it, Yidda."

"Very well," she repeated, then instructed the group to follow her.

Jasper started forward; his steps heavy with reluctance. He headed up the party so no one could see the fear that was certainly showing on his face. Yidda might see it, he realized, but she already knew she had the upper hand.

It occurred to Jasper the next morning at the end of his lesson with Miss Marchand that Yidda might very well know about him and his situation if indeed she was aware of such Oeridian affairs as the birth of Oer's Blessing. He wasn't able to do anything with the realization, however, before Miss Marchand interrupted him with a request.

"Can you teach me to use that?" She was pointing at the crossbow in his hand. He'd been about to go hunting.

"Um," he stammered. "Yes, sure."

Wait, what? No. He couldn't take her with him. That was the last thing he needed. What he needed was to be alone, not with the girl who sent his head spinning by merely looking at him.

"Great!" she said brightly.

This wasn't going to go well.

"Follow me," he told her.

He looked at her for a second, and she smiled back. Oer, why did she have to be so beautiful? He turned and walked out of the clearing where they'd been practicing. Teach her the crossbow. There wasn't much to it, just aim and fire. If she picked it up as quickly as she was learning to wield Darkslayer, she'd be shooting flies out of the air from fifty paces away within a couple days. Maybe it wasn't going to be so bad, after all. Twenty paces outside the clearing, though, he realized he was wrong.

"Where did you learn the crossbow?" she asked.

He nearly stopped in his tracks. So, she wanted to chat. Her voice was so innocent.

"My father had me trained in it when I'd begun to master the blade," he replied.

"Oh," she said.

They walked for a little while longer, then she spoke again. "Is it hard to learn?"

"The crossbow? No."

"Oh, that's good."

Silence. What did she want him to say? He realized he'd stopped walking and was looking at her. She was staring back at him, her face childlike with fascination.

"You should be able to learn in a few days or so," he replied finally.

"I'd like that," she replied as soon as he finished.

Jasper started walking again. They were getting far enough from the others that game might start showing up, so he slowed his pace and crept along the ground. She followed. Finally, he found a fallen tree to crouch behind and motioned for her to hide behind it as well. He peeked up over the top, getting the crossbow in place, and watched for animals to pass by. Nothing happened for a few minutes.

"It's very noble of you, risking everything to find Lady Cibelle and all." Her voice was soft, almost imperceptible, and he wasn't sure he'd heard her right. His eyes darted to her. She was watching the space beyond the log like he had been, but then she glanced over and met his gaze.

"Not everyone would do that," she added.

What was she getting at? He felt confusion mark his face as he managed to reply weakly, "It's just what needs to be done."

She had no idea the real reason he was pursuing Lady Cibelle. He felt like a fool. He realized again just how self-serving his motives were, how self-preserving his purposes. He wished he could evaporate into the air. Her eyes on him were so guiltless, so pure, he couldn't stand it.

"What will you do when we part ways?" The words burst from his mouth before he'd thought about them. Anything to get her to stop looking at him.

It worked. She turned her eyes to the ground and murmured her response. "I don't know."

He nodded.

"I don't know at all," she whispered, her tone despondent.

He was supposed to say something comforting, to give some wise advice or speak something profound, but all he could think to say was, "I'll miss you."

She glanced up; her eyes wide with surprise. Great Oer in Heaven, where had that come from? He couldn't have actually said that out loud. Seeing her face, it was undeniable he had. He tried to recover himself.

"You've been keeping my rapier work up to par and all, you know? And your Kronk adds some levity that's sorely needed among us."

Great, now he sounded shallower than a puddle and cold besides.

"Oh," was all she replied, hurt in her voice.

"That's not what I meant." He tried again. "It's nice having a womanly presence around, that's all. Someone caring and kind and attentive. You remind me of Lydia, a little."

"Who's Lydia?"

She did remind him of Lydia. She fussed less over him than Lydia, and her words were not nearly as harsh as Lydia's, but her soft-hearted concern for those she cared about, for everyone really, echoed Lydia's motherly nature.

"A servant in the palace," he replied, unthinking.

Miss Marchand tilted her head at him slightly but didn't ask anything else. In fact, for a moment she didn't speak at all. Finally, her soft voice sounded just above the chatter of birds waking to the sun and wings of insects buzzing by.

"I'll miss you, too," she said.

It was Jasper's turn to look at her incredulously. What did she mean? She didn't explain, just looked at him, eyes genuine and solicitous. She was so near to him, less than an arm's length away. A sudden urge to kiss her came over him, but he fought it. How terrible it would be if he let himself.

He tore his eyes from her. "We should be getting back." His voice was thick. He didn't wait for her, just turned and strode back toward camp. They wouldn't have any meat this morning. He tore some fruit from the vines along the way, hoping that would suffice to explain why he'd gone off alone with Miss Marchand.

Chapter 34

IHVA TRAILED BEHIND THE PRINCE as they made their way back to camp. He was walking quickly, and she was confused. Her heart was fluttering inside her chest, and she couldn't breathe normally. He'd said he'd miss her, and she was sure he'd meant it, but why had she had to tell him the same? Now he must know she liked him. She'd never kissed a boy, and she realized she'd never wanted to, not like she'd wanted to just now. No wonder he was fleeing. How uncomfortable and awkward it must have been for him to realize the little merchant girl was falling for him. She'd run too in that situation.

She meandered back into camp, making a concerted effort not to cry. She was so embarrassed, humiliated. She couldn't look in the Prince's direction the rest of the morning, though she was acutely aware of his presence the entire time. By the time they set out, the incident had stopped replaying itself in her mind and she felt numb instead. She tried to think about something else, but everything that came to mind was depressing or frightening. Not that disgraceful was much better. She focused instead on watching the top of Malach's head bounce up and down as he strode along. He was in a jolly mood, which only seemed to aggravate her deflated feelings. Why had she been so foolish?

They stopped for lunch around noon, and Malach complained about having to eat fruit with their bread again. They'd run out of jerky a few days before. Their only option for meat would have been game from the forest, but obviously she and the Prince had failed to gather

242

any of that. She looked at the ground as she ate the apple-like fruit she liked best. Right now, it tasted flavorless.

They continued walking until an hour after dark when they reached the M'rawan border with Jinad. The forest was getting less dense, but before it ended, Yidda had the party stop to rest for the night. She said they needed to stay as concealed as they could, and Ihva didn't argue. She trusted Yidda, at least to some extent, though she knew the rest of the Jini were far from dependable, unless you were depending on them to cheat or kill you.

It was cooler that night than it had been since they entered M'rawa, but they didn't build a fire. Conversation was dull as everyone was trying to hide their nerves, and it ended early. They were all lying down under their blankets within half an hour of stopping for the night, and as much as Ihva had on her mind, she still fell asleep in just minutes.

Ihva awoke to the sound of voices, harsh but quiet, somewhere in the distance. She looked around. Kronk was snoring, and Cor and Malach were sleeping soundly.

"How much do you know?" came the Prince's voice.

"About what, Prince?" Yidda's voice answered.

"You know what I'm talking about," the Prince returned, his voice cool and stern.

"I am aware of greater forces than you know at play in this thing you think of as simple. I know your desperate need for Lady Jessica Cibelle and her need for you. I know she is in danger, a danger different and more calamitous than that of death. I know your shameful thoughts and your struggle. I know you, Jasper Thesson Aurdor, son of Theophilus and Theresa; I know your mother and your father, and I know you." Yidda's tone was calm but held authority.

Silence followed, then the Prince spoke in a small voice. "How?"

"I was there that night for your birth. I waited as anxiously as any to see if your mother would bear a son, and I was as overjoyed as the rest to see you born. Her first child, her only child, to be Oer's Chosen Son. I was there when..."

243

"Enough!" the Prince interrupted. "You will not tell them. You cannot."

"It is yours to tell, Prince. They will find out sooner or later, when you find Lady Cibelle, or when you do not."

"We will find her!" he said stonily. "We have to."

"Prince," the woman started in a comforting tone.

"I don't need your sympathy," he retorted.

"Prince, I too contend with forces too strong for me to fight alone."

The Prince said nothing.

"I will tell you the story, but I must ask you repeat it to no one. I will share it with the others when it is time. Now is the time for you to hear it, though."

Yidda's voice was quiet, and again the Prince said nothing, so she continued.

"It begins with Ohebed. We came into being at the same time and were naturally bonded that day. He is my Companion. He was a glassmaker, though now he is one of the Guard. I fell in love with him. It happens sometimes to Companions, though it is rare, and I tried to conceal it. To love and not be loved in return is an ache one can hardly bear at a distance, must less in such proximity as we were."

The Prince gave a joyless chuckle, and Yidda went on.

"We lived a pleasant life in Alm'adinat. We were thoroughly middle class, and we were happy. We were beneath the level of wealth that incurred the Sultan's constant surveillance but had enough that we did not worry about our provisions, namely evadium.

"I had a friend, Eliyah, who also appeared around the same time as I did. We grew up together, you could say. We struggled together against the forces within us that drove us to evil. We strove to do good, to free ourselves from the Sultan's rule and from the Voice.

"One day Eliyah began to talk to me about a rebellion. She was planning it with some others. I wanted to join but I knew Ohebed would discourage it, telling me it was too dangerous, that our struggle was inward, not against the Sultan but against the Voice. I hated the thought of his displeasure. I told Eliyah I would support her as I could, but I could not accompany her on her journey. It broke my heart to see her face, her disappointment. But that was only a small fissure in my heart. The real shattering would come later.

"I started to see her less often. Before, she would come over twice or three times a week after our long days of work, and we would talk of philosophy, politics, things of that nature. But she stopped coming. I was crushed. One day a compulsion came over me with a fright. I needed to reintegrate Eliyah into my life. I went over to her house the next day. I invited myself in and apologized for being distant, though in reality I knew she had been the one who was dissociating herself from me. I wasn't awaree then, but I was manipulating her. I needed to have her trust me again.

"You see, I didn't recognize the Voice at first. It sounded so much like my own, telling me I missed Eliyah, that I wanted to join her. When I started to suspect it was the Voice, I told myself it couldn't be. The Voice would not foment rebellion in me, nor would it encourage me to join such a thing. So, I carried on. I carried on without questioning.

"I joined the Rebellion without Ohebed's knowledge. I told him I was visiting with Eliyah, and I was, only there were more than just us two. Though guilt over my lies burdened me, I enjoyed my time with Eliyah and even lived for it. We plotted ways to take down the Sultan from inside the palace, ways to convert Alm'adinat officials to our cause, ways to steal evadium for our own use. I didn't hear the Voice then, or if I did, I was too caught up to recognize it.

"I had become entrenched, so entrenched that I knew nearly every detail of the Rebellion. That was when the Voice summoned me. It terrified me with images of the Rebellion being overtaken, overwhelmed by city forces. It horrified me with visions of death and destruction, the city aflame and disaster brought down upon us.

"I began to rethink. I felt constrained to action. Something inside me was obsessed with stopping the Rebellion. I was sure it would end badly if I interfered, and yet, fear drove me hurtling down that destructive path. I thought that day of ways to stop Eliyah and the others. I could go to the guards and tell them, but that was sure to end with jailing and execution of all involved. I could try to convince everyone to give up their intended cause, but that would take too long. The Rebellion was set to commence the next week.

"Instead I decided to convince Eliyah, for she was such a charismatic figure as could persuade the rest. I visited her that evening. I started indirectly, asking her the chance she thought we had of success. She was certain the Rebellion would see victory. I asked her if she was afraid of the repercussions. She was not. Sacrifices were necessary to instill change. She was steadfast and committed. I finally decided to face her.

"I told her that I believed we would fail and there would be a massacre. I told her I feared for the younger ones who'd hardly seen life in their couple hundred years. It wasn't fair to them. It was assisting suicide of such precious souls. I told her I could not participate, nor could I stand by and watch. I told her I needed her to convince the rest to halt the Rebellion.

"She refused outright. I pleaded with her, called upon the friendship we had, called on her devotion to bettering the lives of the rebels, called on everything I could think of, to no avail. Then the Voice. It had wormed its way into me over the previous years. It had taken hold of my mind and drove my actions so thoroughly that when I finally recognized it, it was too late. You see, it told me to strike down Eliyah.

"I tried to ignore the impulse. I tried to bury it deep down beneath my love for her, but it kept jumping to the forefront. My mind grew foggy with the effort of trying to escape it. I hardly noticed as I picked up one of the spears Eliyah had prepared for the nextweek's events. I was barely conscious of thrusting it toward her, but the jarring thud of the spearhead into her body awakened me. It was too late.

"The guards arrived quickly. They asked and all I could manage to say was 'Rebellion.' They hauled me away and tortured me until I divulged the names of the other participants. Their last form of sadism was the worst. They set me in the highest class of society and named me a State Hero. I had murdered the rebels, and they would never let me forget it.

"They put Ohebed in this 'place of honor' with me. He wouldn't let me forget it either. He is a pure soul, one of the very few I have met that can withstand the Voice almost entirely. He couldn't believe I had succumbed, and he treated me like an invalid. He monitored my every move, more so even than the palace guards. He wouldn't leave me, for that was not honorable, but he wouldn't let me live, either. His resentment broke me, and I could do nothing but heed him.

"I was worse than miserable, kept alive by the will of others but wishing only death for myself. I had another dream, but this voice was different. It was not a dark voice. It spoke not of fear, but of love, the love I had for Eliyah and for Ohebed and for the souls of Alm'adinat. It told me I must flee to a distant land where Light ruled and Darkness trembled, to the land of Oerid.

"I awoke from the dream and found myself alone. Ohebed had left the room. I took advantage of the opportunity and without second thought took flight. It was only hours before I would have to perform the Ritual, and I knew becoming immaterial would aid my flight, so I took nothing with me. I feared the Voice might compel me to return, but the new voice spoke comfort and encouragement. I left without looking back, no evadium in hand but somehow certain I wouldn't need it.

"You see, evadium is our remedy for the impulses and thoughts that the Voice instills in our minds, its incitements to evil and destruction. Using evadium we are able to take a material form made of sand and thus flee the Voice's influence more easily. No one would think to run from the city, the source of their antidote, so there are no guards on the inside of the gates. Evadium creates a forced dependence on the Sultan. We are either subject to the Voice or to him, and yet I was determined to be slave to neither. I could bow to them no more.

"To shorten a lengthy tale, I found what I sought in Oerid after some expeditions to various lands, gathering information. You are one answer, and Miss Marchand is another. Now I return with you to my city, my homeland, and seek my Companion. I seek to reconcile."

There was a long pause, and Ihva wondered at Yidda's story. The tragedy of it struck her deep within, and her heart clenched with sorrow over Yidda's anguish. She probably should have feared the woman, having learned about the Voice's forceful impulses and Eliyah's murdeer, but Ihva felt only compassion for Yidda, a profound and painful compassion. Before she could think further on the woman's words, though, the Prince spoke.

"You'll be killed, you know? If they catch you." His voice was flat.

"Perhaps, but I need to try. I think I have found the answer. A way to be subject to something greater than the Sultan or the Voice, a way to be subject to something true."

Another long pause. Ihva was wondering if the Prince would even respond when he finally spoke. "How did he do it? Ohebed, the Voice?"

"I don't know, Prince. I don't know." Yidda's voice carried the strain of sorrow and regret.

"We shall visit Ohebed, then," the Prince said quietly. "You make your peace, and I have some questions for him."

"Very well, Prince."

He said something inaudible, then Ihva heard him walking back to where the party lay sleeping, all except Ihva, but she pretended to be asleep as well. She tried to steady her breathing and slow her heartbeat but wasn't certain her acting convinced the Prince. Either way, he didn't speak to her.

She lay still but couldn't sleep for the next hour, thinking about Yidda, feeling a sea of empathy wash over her in the wake of the Jini woman's story. Unrequited love, betrayal of self and all that she loved, the loneliness of fleeing home without so much as a single companion, Yidda must have experienced a gamut of suffering emotions in her years. But there was hope to her story, too. A better voice, something true, a land where Light ruled. Ihva had never thought of Oerid in quite that way, for all the bandits and murders and theft and infidelities she heard of, but she supposed even Oerid must be a bright place by comparison to Jini lands. She lay in contemplation for some time.

After a while, her thoughts turned to the Prince. What secret was he keeping from them? Yidda knew about it, and from her memories of previous conversations, Ihva concluded Cor was aware as well. The Prince needed Lady Cibelle? For what? That he struggled, Ihva could believe, but she wasn't sure what Yidda meant about shameful thoughts and the supposedly simple situation being more complex than the Prince suspected. What was so complicated about a Prince pursuing his beloved to rescue her? There had to be more to it, apparently more than even the Prince knew.

Yidda had said she was fighting forces too strong for her to handle on her own and had implied the Prince was doing the same. He seemed determined to go it on his own still. There had to be some way Ihva could help. Her feelings for him aside, she cared about him, and she couldn't stand seeing him face whatever nemesis it was by himself. She couldn't stand to see him so lonely, so alone. The times he'd looked small started to make more sense. He was facing something much greater than himself, and whatever it was, Ihva was determined to find out what was going on. She was Oer's Blessing, after all. Surely something about her magic could help. There had to be a way she could help.

CHAPTER 35

IT WAS STILL VERY DARK when Jasper awoke. It had to be at least two hours before dawn, still too early to wake Miss Marchand for practice. He didn't feel like dealing with Miss Marchand right now anyway. His mind was on Yidda.

The woman knew everything. She might even have known about the voice. He couldn't be sure, but he didn't want to underestimate the Jin. The way she'd been talking about the Jini Voice, he gathered she at least suspected he experienced something similar.

He hadn't heard the voice in a while though, not since they'd encountered the Shades. That was a relief, though he knew that didn't mean it was gone. It was just dormant, waiting for a trigger. He just had to remain calm, that was all, and not use his Power. It shouldn't be that hard.

He tossed and turned for the next hour wondering what Yidda thought about it all. She knew-he'd resigned himself to that-but perhaps she had some wisdom she could impart. She might know even more than Cor, from what she'd been saying. The dwarf knew about that night, the night Jasper was born, like Yidda did, but only secondhand. Father had informed Cor a couple years later, when Jasper was almost two, when things had started going wrong. Yidda knew from the day it had begun, and that threatened to unhinge Jasper. All of a sudden, he had a sense like he was being watched, like he'd been being watched and had given something crucial away in his ignorance. He tried to ignore the feeling.

Anyway, what had Yidda meant about Jessica being in a worse danger than that of death? Perhaps someone would Raise her? Arusha had meant to, but Jasper knew about that. Yidda had seemed to be describing something he was not aware of.

He glanced around. From the position of the Dawning Star, he estimated they had an hour until the sun rose. Time to wake Miss Marchand. He cringed. He'd avoided speaking to her all of yesterday after the incident that morning. He wasn't quite recovered yet. Her eyes flashed in his mind and their emerald depths beckoned him, but he refused to think on them any longer. He would miss her, but he couldn't let anyone know how much, her least of all.

He walked over to where she lay and knelt. She was still asleep.

"Miss Marchand," he murmured.

She lay still.

"Miss Marchand," he said, his voice a little louder.

She didn't move. He sighed and reached out a hand toward her shoulder. Before he could reach it, her eyes fluttered open.

"Prince?" she asked airily.

She was still half asleep, her eyes coming into focus. As she looked at him, he detected something in them he couldn't quite place. A tenderness maybe, like she regarded him with some sort of fondness. It startled him, and he drew back.

She shook her head and looked surprised herself. "Sorry," she said.

"No, it's fine," he replied. "I mean, for what?"

Neither said anything for a moment, then Jasper came to himself.

"It's time for practice."

"Okay."

He stood, and she rose and followed him into an adjacent clearing. He held out a practice sword for her, and she took it. They turned to face each other.

"Counter me," he instructed as he thrust his blade toward her.

She lifted her sword and blocked him gracefully.

"Again," he said.

He swung at her left side, but she parried him again with ease. He didn't give her any warning the third time, but she knocked his sword away anyway. She was catching onto the new style she'd need for Darkslayer, and it wouldn't be long before she'd prove a challenge even for him.

For a few minutes, they danced around the clearing to the clacking of wood, jabbing and swinging and parrying, though neither landed a hit. Jasper felt at ease again. They were conversing but not with words. Their blades did the talking. He felt a small smile cross his face, and he didn't try to hide it. This was pleasant. This was how it was supposed to be between him and Miss Marchand. He wished everything could be this easy. He'd become so absorbed in the swordplay he jumped when she spoke.

"You know, if you'd say what's bothering you, we could find a way to help."

He defended against one of her swings, then stepped back. She was going to try to make conversation again. Seeing how well that went last time, he was reluctant to engage her, but he didn't want to be rude.

"Nothing's bothering me."

She gave him a disbelieving look, and he swung at her side to force her to parry, which she did. "We can help, Your Highness, if only you would let us."

The "Highness" struck Jasper. He realized he'd come to think of her much more familiarly, but that wouldn't do. Anyway, that was beside the point. She'd said she wanted to help, but he didn't need her help. In fact, he needed her not to help.

"There is no assistance you could offer me that I could use."

"Why couldn't you? What's stopping you?"

If only she knew.

"There are certain things only I can do. No one can do them for me."

He realized they'd lowered their swords, so he raised his to a readied position. She copied him and replied.

"You always want to do things alone. We care, you know? We want to be here for you."

Her "we" had the sound of "I." What could she want with him?

"I have what help I need. It's no use involving anyone else." His tone was more severe than he'd meant it. "Please, stay out of it." He added the second part in a quieter voice, trying to soften his words.

There was a silence as she peered at him. She seemed to be staring into his very soul with those eyes of hers, and he shifted, uncomfortable.

"Your Highness, there is something more than what you are telling us. I'm not asking to be privy to all your secrets, but Cor knows something, and Yidda knows, too. Why won't you tell the rest of us?" she asked, giving him a steady look.

She'd overheard! Jasper's muscles tensed. What had she heard? He frantically reviewed last night's conversation with Yidda. What could Miss Marchand have gotten out of what they'd said? What could she know that she shouldn't? She had to stay out of this, she had to!

Panicked, Jasper asked, "What did you hear?"

Something of his dismay must have shown in his face like anger, as she answered in a small voice, looking frightened.

"Nothing. I heard almost nothing. Only that finding Lady Cibelle is more crucial than you let on."

He could see Miss Marchand was trembling.

"Why? What is so important about one woman?"

Desperate, Jasper spoke before he could think. "Forget what you heard."

He heard himself. He sounded so forbidding. He knew his tone would hurt her, but he didn't know what else to do.

"These matters do not pertain to you, and I will not have you prying into them. Is that clear?" He could tell he'd upset her.

"Yes," was all she replied, the word choked.

He tried to make his face stern and his expression somber, but all he felt inside was trepidation and dismay. If Miss Marchand knew anything, she might try to get involved, and he could not let that happen. He loved her, and though he'd never have her, maybe because he'd never have her, he refused to put her in the danger he posed.

"You will not ask anything about this again. You will disregard what you heard and carry on with your task and your life. You have no part in mine."

His words pierced him deeply, and he had to keep himself from staggering. As for Miss Marchand, tears she must have been fighting sprang from her eyes. Her voice held hurt and anger as she responded.

"I'm sorry," she said. "I'm sorry I pried. I'm sorry I wanted to know. I'm sorry I wanted to help. I'm sorry I cared about you."

The last sentence stuck out and hit Jasper like a blow to the stomach, knocking the air out of him. She'd cared about him. The way she'd said it, with such sorrow and bitterness, it sounded like she more than just cared. How were things turning out this way? Did she care for him like that? It made no sense. She knew he was engaged. Yet his betrothal had not stopped him from falling in love with her. He cursed himself inwardly.

Smite her.

The command sent shockwaves through his mind. He was so confused for a moment he forgot Miss Marchand was standing right in front of him.

Strike her. Pierce her through the heart.

His view came back into focus. Miss Marchand was mere feet from him. His blade, his real blade, was at the edge of the clearing, and the voice urged him to use it.

Strike her down and bleed her.

He started to back away.

"What's wrong?" Miss Marchand asked, sounding bewildered.

Fell her. It shall be only one who stands in the end.

Her face grew confused, then frightened.

"I can't do this, Ihva."

She flinched, but he didn't pause his retreat. He backed ten paces farther toward the edge of the clearing, his eyes on her the whole time. He was afraid that if he didn't look at her, if he didn't hold her in his mind, the voice's compelling would be too strong.

"Can't do what?" she asked.

"This. Just this."

He turned and fled, away from the party, away from Ihva Marchand. She called out behind him, but he had to get away. He had to calm down. The Lady of Shadows was in his mind again, and he was terrified.

CHAPTER 36

IHVA LET HER TEARS FALL as she watched the Prince disappear among the trees. What had she done? Something was wrong, very wrong, and she'd only alienated him further by asking. She'd rattled him with her questions, and her desire to help had only pushed him further away.

She knew he'd never care for her as she was discovering she cared for him, but at least before this morning, he might have held some friendly affection for her. She had no part in his life, he'd said. All the amity that had been building between them, it had been ruined in one fell stroke, all because she'd had to push him for greater confidence.

Through her tears, she noticed the sun was beginning to illuminate the horizon. She looked to the west. A lone star hung there-one sun, hanging on as the deep blue ocean of a sky around it faded into morning's light. One sun in the disappearing darkness. All of a sudden, Ihva felt very alone.

ACKNOWLEDGMENTS

To Nathan, my husband, whose unfailing encouragement and reassurance have bolstered me through this whole process, thank you for abiding my endless requests for you to listen to scene after scene, chapter after chapter, and for providing astute observations and suggestions for improvement. Thank you for your patience and kindness in taking care of our boy while I head to coffee shops to think and write. More than that, thank you for leading me to the hope that inspires these books. I love you.

To Kimberly, whose unswerving support has carried me through the dry seasons of writing and whose suggestions have changed the entire scope of these novels, thank you for the endless late nights at the bookstore (by which I mean 9pm, of course), for the countless hours spent over tea and coffee listening to me read first draft scenes, for reading this book in its infancy, and for the many insights you have shared about just who these characters really are to me.

To those who read (or listened to) this manuscript in its unfinished drafts, I appreciate your kindness and faith in my ability to bring this story to life. Mr. Doyle, you might never read this, but thank you for indulging my curiosity in our conversations at the bookstore and for being the first to read any portion of this book. Richard, I have always admired your perceptiveness and acuity, which was why I asked you to help me root out inconsistencies and the like in this novel, but it was your confidence that this could become something that most deeply impacted me. Deniz, your interest and earnest excitement about this book encouraged me that others might find it interesting as well. Rebecca, thank you for participating in "story time" and for displaying the full gamut of reactions I had hoped for. Your enthusiasm has propelled me to work even harder to ensure this is the best work I can accomplish.

Finally, to my publishing team, thank you for all your hard work and belief that this could really turn into something. Mike, your suggestions were encouraging in just the right way and beneficial to my process. Jana, thank you for taking a chance on me. Your trust in my work and its potential has launched me into a process I never thought I would experience, and I am ever grateful for it.

There are plenty more I would love to mention who have shown kind support and interest in my work, but suffice it to say thank you to all of you who have cared for me in this process by asking about my progress, listening to me go on about my insights into my own work, following me in the journey, and of course, by reading this book.

ABOUT THE AUTHOR

Lauren Sergeant is a poet, a founding contributor for the Auburn-Opelika Moms Blog, a writer, and the author of *Light of Distant Suns*, the first book in the *Children of the Glaring Dawn* series. Her time studying to earn her bachelor's degree in International Studies, her fascination with world customs, the plethora of spellbinding stories she has read and watched, and her enthusiasm for the fantasy genre have led to her to write. Shaped by these influences, she creates compelling cultures and fascinating, relatable characters in lush imaginary realms.

In her spare time, when she is not writing, you can find her curled up on the couch with a good book, whether it be fantasy, history, physics, or calculus. She lives in Opelika, Alabama with her husband and son, though she grew up in Southern California and never imagined calling the American South home.

It seems the unanticipated things in life are sometimes the most delightful, though.

Continue reading for the exciting sequel in The Children of the
Glaring Dawn series by Lauren C. Sergeant:

A Rite of Hearts Undone

CHAPTER 1

A DAINTY, RED FAWN made timid steps into the wide clearing where Jasper had sunk down onto a rotting log. The fawn didn't see

him, and he didn't move, not because he was hunting, though. There was something so innocent and incorrupt about the animal, Jasper felt himself held motionless by its grace. He didn't want to scare it away.

She'd had the same look about her, Miss Marchand, that of bewitching purity and goodness. She'd wanted to help him. She *cared* for him. A painful lump formed in his throat, and he coughed. The fawn's head twisted toward him in an instant, and seeing him, it bolted and disappeared among the trees, leaving Jasper blinking.

Why was it he drove back everything worthy and beautiful in his life? What was it about him that repelled whatever he loved? He wanted nothing more than a life uncomplicated by the Shadow, something simple and straightforward in which resolve and effort could accomplish his pursuits. That was not what he'd gotten. No, he'd received an existence of secrets and snags in the most inconvenient places where a mistake could cost him his life, or worse, Oerid. This wasn't how it was supposed to be for Oer's Chosen Son, Oerid's sovereign.

Jasper exhaled an exasperated breath through his teeth. Anyway, it didn't matter that he'd destroyed Miss Marchand's affections, if they'd existed in the first place. It didn't matter because it could never be. He was betrothed.

The log beneath him gave way, and he swore, then stood and brushed himself off, muttering more curses under his breath. Besides his engagement, the Lady of Shadows seemed intent on tormenting him around Miss Marchand. She wanted the girl dead. Maybe Cor was right. Maybe Oer's Blessing *was* supposed to battle the Shadow, which would make Miss Marchand a threat to the Lady. But why did Jasper have to be the one the Lady was pressing to dispatch her? Why did it fall to him, of all people, to endure that agony? He knew the answer— because of his blasted connection to Hell's Mistress, because she knew her power over him. What was wrong with Oer to allow this? What in the name of the Light was Oer's problem that he let his *Chosen Son* suffer the harrowing compellings of Light's nemesis? Why wasn't Oer fighting? Was Jasper in this alone?

Jasper realized he was standing in the middle of the clearing and that dawn's brightness had replaced the starlight filtering through the trees. He shook his head. Futile wonderings, that was all these were. They were unimportant. No, what mattered was that he needed to find Lady Cibelle and make that blasted journey to the Shadowed Realm to retrieve what had been rightfully his all along. Then he would return to rule Oerid in peace. Maybe after it was all finished, he'd find his life the way he wanted it. He doubted it, though. Things never turned out right for Jasper Thesson Aurdor, never.